Winona's Web

A Novel of Discovery

This Large Print Book carries the
Seal of Approval of N.A.V.H.

Winona's Web

A Novel of Discovery

Priscilla Cogan

Thorndike Press • Thorndike, Maine

Grateful acknowledgement is made for use of the following material:

The poem "Desert Places" on p. 103, from *The Poetry of Robert Frost*, edited by Edward Connery Lathem; © 1936 by Robert Frost; © 1964 by Lesley Frost Ballantine; © 1969 by Henry Holt and Co., Inc., reprinted by permission of Henry Holt and Co., Inc.
The poem "The Descent of Winter" on p. 134, by William Carlos William, from *Collected Poems: 1909–1939, Vol. I*; © 1938 by New Directions Publishing Corp., reprinted by permission of New Directions Publishing Corp.
The poem "All But Blind" on p. 229, by Walter de la Mare, © The Literary Trustees of Walter de la Mare, and The Society of Authors as their representative, London, England, used with permission.
Lyrics from the song "Breaths" on p. 318, © 1980 Y.M. Barnwell; words by Birago Diop (adapted by Barnwell), music by Ysaye M. Barnwell, recorded by Sweet Honey in the Rock on the album *Good News*, 1981, Flying Fish Records.
Excerpt from "Sleeping Beauty" on p. 343, © 1991 by Lucille Clifton. Reprinted from *Quilting: Poems 1987–1990*, by Lucille Clifton, with the permission of BOA Editions, Ltd. 92 Park Ave., Brockport NY 14420.
All other material quoted in brief excepts for interpetive purposes is respectfully acknowledged.

This is a work of fiction. Some may recognize real places on the Leelanau Peninsula, however, all the characters and incidents depicted are meant to be fictitious. But, of course, all good stories are true.

Published in 1998 by arrangement with Face To Face Books.

Thorndike Large Print ® Senior Life Styles Series.

The tree indicium is a trademark of Thorndike Press.

The text of this Large Print edition is unabridged.
Other aspects of the book may vary from the original edition.

Set in 16 pt. Plantin by Juanita Macdonald.

Printed in the United States on permanent paper.

Library of Congress Catalog Card Number: 97-91274
ISBN: 0-7862-1322-1 (lg. print : hc)

For my parents,
Dr. Frances Capps Cogan
and
Dr. David Glendenning Cogan,
who gave me these gifts:
the curiosity of life,
the anchor of love,
the joy of labor,
and the pursuit of laughter.

Acknowledgments

For those who have crossed over, marking a trail for the others, I want to thank:

Larry Redshirt, whose manner of death forced me to reexamine my life;

Prof. Mary Bromage, who red-lined my manuscript and taught me to write in style; and

Dr. David G. Cogan, who extolled the discipline of the writing life.

For those who are still grappling with life's core meanings, I want to thank:

George Whitewolf for his tolerance of my naivete and for his authenticity;

Dr. Lesley Shore for her unflagging support and wise literary critique;

Dr. Jacob Goering, who encouraged me to follow my dreams;

The sweat-lodge communities that have shared their experiences with me; and

Jennifer Barker, Judy Noyes, Katie Rock, Beverly Harju, Janet Lindner, Polly Parson,

Food & Books Bookclub, Wendy Williams, Long Man, and numerous others who have been so generous in their response to this story.

Most of all, I want to thank my husband and best friend, Duncan Sings-Alone, who surprised me with my first computer and stated, "Now, it is time to write that book."

prologue

Chrysalis

★ ★ ★

It is the twilight zone between past and future that is the precarious world of transformation within the chrysalis. Part of us is looking back, yearning for the magic we have lost; part is glad to say good-bye to our chaotic past; part looks ahead with whatever courage we can muster; part is excited by the changing potential; part sits stone-still not daring to look either way.

— Marion Woodman,
The Pregnant Virgin

When and where the heart can celebrate each awakening day — that becomes home. When and where the spirit can mine for nourishment in the little moments — that becomes home. When and where the mind can distill meaning from the shadows as well as the light — that also becomes home. It took me

9

thirty-nine years to know this, to travel the circle, to return to where my ancestors lay rooted in the ground, and to retrieve what they already knew. Moving into my fortieth year, I thought my pupation was complete and that I had finally come Home.

In northern Michigan, the land and seasons are harsh and beautiful. Winter's visitation is long, lonely, and cold. Spring marches forth to the drumming sound of the wood grouse's breast, to the colors of white trillium, pink ladyslippers, and yellow Dutchman's breeches. Summer spills over with tourists, as the setting sun sprinkles golden paths over the dark surface of Lake Michigan. With Fall comes the renaissance of town life, after the tourists, known as "fudgies," have retreated to the gentler lands southward.

Until recently, I too was a fudgie. Since 1890, through four generations, my family had fled the summer heat of cities to the coolness of Suttons Bay in northern Michigan. Before the great Depression, my maternal grandmother purchased and built a house on Chrysalis, an estate of seventy-eight acres atop a large hill looking northward toward Suttons Bay. Across sensuous, rolling hills south and eastward, long ribbons of cherry and apple trees and rectangular

10

hay-fields seduce the eye. To the west edges one of the great northern woods.

I never knew my grandmother, but they say she was psychic. Soon after my grandmother died, Old Dora, the black maid, was serving my grandfather and mother their supper when she fell to her knees, eyes rolling, singing out, "Oh Lawdy, Missus Carolyn done be comin' up de walk dere." My mother said she peered hard into the dusk light but saw no ghostly reflection of her mother.

Still, I can swear to you this: my grandmother is here walking the land on Chrysalis. As a child, I'd sit in the crook of an apple tree she had planted, reading my summer adventure stories. Long before I knew of spirits, I knew of hers, in the way a branch would bend unnaturally or the wind would start whispering to me. She was walking the land, taking pride in her wildflowers, grapevine hedges, apple trees, and asparagus plants. I knew she was there watching me grow up in her likeness. Chrysalis and my dead grandmother — both were to teach me during long Michigan summers that the land was never owned by us, not even borrowed. We were simply the guardians of its grandeur.

My mother married a dark-haired Irish

fellow from Massachusetts, Kevin O'Connor, who, like her, had earned a medical degree. Chrysalis became their summer passion. My father would come when work permitted, but my mother would bring my sister and me up here for three months each summer and let us loose unto our own imaginings. It was soon instilled in us that if we wanted to keep Chrysalis in our future, we had to learn manual labor, forestry, and house maintenance to show our worthiness. That was no hardship. Already the land owned me, claimed me. The bonds were laid deep in the life's blood, far below the surface, forgotten over time while still nourishing the soul from deep, hidden streams.

And when I grew older and closer to the knowledge of my own death, when forty began to loom as a not-too-distant probability, so too Chrysalis reawakened me from the quagmire of conventional behavior and rational beliefs. For all my career work, I had forgotten to climb the apple tree. I had denied the knowledge of my grandmother's spirit.

Fifteen years of marriage had passed, and all I had to show for it was a divorce decree, an aching heart, and a profound distrust of the opposite sex. I quit my job as the chief psychologist at a New York hospital and, taking my dog with me, I fled to Chrysalis to heal. My friends warned me about the terrible intellectual isolation I would experience away from the big city. Leaving them was not easy. I treasured the security of my career position and the certainty of their friendships.

But there was no real choice. To say the land called me, pulled on me from deep within is to acknowledge that I, like the apple tree, was long ignored, untended, outgrowing my ability to nurture all my branches. For all my professional success, I was not blossoming as a human being.

I had to return home to see the land through all the seasons, to come to know its people in the dark nights of winter as well as the languid days of summer. It took a full year before the townspeople of Suttons Bay knew I was there to stay, that the long cold winter was not going to drive out romantic notions that "fudgies" are known to cultivate during the warm gin-and-tonic August afternoons. I, Meggie O'Connor, earned the right and privilege after that first year to call myself a "perma fudgie."

Like them, I could now look upon all the wandering tourists with disdain as they intruded into our paradise. They were the rootless ones, living in a state of suspended animation called *vacation*. They walked the land or rode over it in golf carts; they looked at the beauty but did not see the mysteries. Their migrations and momentary perchings left scats of money. With their Labor Day departures, Suttons Bay reassumed its quiet and rural nature. The community of townsfolk, farmers, Ojibway and Odawa Indians regrouped. Doors opened. The churches grew full again with the locals, and everyone talked of the relief that the summer crowd had vanished.

The oaks and maples draped themselves in celebratory fall colors. The talk of men drifted to deer hunting and its upcoming season. I cringed inside while listening to their discussions of guns, deer blinds, and the best way to set up the shot. I had disavowed the hunter in myself and wanted little to do with men.

I am no longer so ignorant. Now I know more about the hunt, the chase, the seduction, the yielding up of life that is true for all of us. Now I know that going into the forest is a man's way of hunting, whereas the little spider, she waits and takes her prey in her own net. I am learning these things, slowly, the way of natural time. I have come home to Chrysalis where my grandmother walks the land.

one

Cracks in the Wall

★ ★ ★

. . . We cannot live the afternoon of life
according to the programme of life's morning
— for what was great in the morning will
be little at evening, and what in the
morning was true will at evening have
become a lie.

— C.G. Jung

The fluid in the glass barometer held steady,
promising a day of no change. Yet the air
felt unsettled, the slight breeze shifty, as if it
couldn't decide upon its course. An afternoon and evening of psychotherapy appointments lay ahead. The morning, however, was
free to focus on the stone walls that terraced
the lawn around the house. Grapevine had
massed itself on the top and cascaded in
suspended falls over the walls, obscuring
deep winter cracks that insinuated themselves around large inset stones. The mortar

15

was old, and every year I would patch the gaping holes and slivers of empty space.

I found pleasure in working on the land. My parents had been worried about my life alone in the sprawling summer house. To reassure themselves of my safety, they had secured the services of a retired farmer, Olf Nielsen. On weekends, Olf would show up, unannounced, to have a chat and a cup of coffee and to see if there was anything that needed fixing. Of Norwegian background, he still spoke the broad "Ja" of his ancestry when giving assent. I welcomed his company, his willingness to offer practical tips on projects about the house, and his stories about his immigrant ancestors. His parents used to tap the maple trees for my grandparents, and so Olf and I go a long way back together.

Yet on this day Olf was working his own farm, and the cracked stone walls needed repair. The bag of Sacrete was too heavy to lift by myself, so I tore it open and, using a pan, gathered it up into the wheelbarrow. The hose wetted down the gritty mix to the right proportion, and, like a cook stirring up bread batter, I worked the hoe back and forth to the right consistency. Already my hands were feeling the drying effect of lime, as I scooped up overflowing cups of wet

16

cement and forced it into the gaping cracks of the wall. My fingers surpassed the trowel in persuading the unyielding stone emptiness to accept my offerings.

Whether the walls knew it or not, I was binding their wounds of time in the way of all good healers — through feeding, fixing, attaching, and smoothing over. Where there is a deep wound, there is always a scar. Yet I confess to finding the pattern of scars and gray mortar veins to be more interesting than an unsullied stone edifice, for in such intricacy is woven the history of a place.

Having repaired one section, I rooted under the dangling network of grapevine and uncovered yet two more areas with running open seams. The trowel slapped the mix on, edged it in with repetitive motion until all was flat on the surface. The large embedded stones, set in their concrete moorings, would hold now for another year.

Ja, in the same way, I have often experienced working with clients who, fearing their own futures, forget their inner strengths for survival. While their walls would be crumbling from the inevitable pressure of age and experience, I would be mixing my psychotherapeutic mortar, patching, strengthening, helping them to discover a vision for the future. It is not my ability to break down walls that makes me an effective therapist, but rather my appreciation for the endurance and the beauty of those walls, their containment of the person's history, and the way they give grounding to a soul in flight. My style is one of instilling hope and rebuilding, not bulldozing.

Cleaning up was done in haste. I ate a quick lunch, showered, and dressed. Gathering up an overstuffed briefcase, I kissed my wire-haired fox terrier, Fritzie, good-bye and left him at the end of a long chain. It would be late before I would return to set him free.

There was barely any traffic on M204 into Suttons Bay. Even an old car like mine seemed to feel the energizing onset of fall weather. The breeze grew stronger as the car zipped along the road; little specks of white could be seen topping the waves coming in the bay. The temperature of the air was gently embracing, seductive, no longer hot and humid. Lake Michigan encouraged this in-between time, of shifting seasons and uncertain weather, to linger along the coastline. Nothing could be taken for granted.

The early afternoon hours sped by quickly. I shared a private practice with Dr. Beverly Paterson, also a psychologist. Between our fifty-minute sessions, she reminded me that at six o'clock, I had scheduled a new client, a Mrs. Winona Pathfinder, whose daughter, Lucy Arbre, was a nurse at the Indian Health Center. Lucy knew Bev and had asked her to recommend a therapist for her mother. Beyond the comment that the elderly woman was probably suffering from depression, Bev couldn't tell me any more. Six o'clock came quickly. As I finished up my notes on the previous session, Bev entered my office with a strongly built, dark-haired woman in her late thirties.

"Lucy, this is Dr. Meggie O'Connor," Bev made the introductions. We shook hands; she had a forceful grip. Her face was that of a Plains Indian with high, flat cheekbones and dark eyes. Her shoes were as white as her professional dress.

"I've just come from work," she explained. "My mother is out in the waiting room, but I wanted to talk to you first."

I told her to sit down and make herself comfortable. As I shut my office door, I caught a brief glimpse of a short, stocky woman seated in the wooden chair in the waiting room, feet crossed and her head eclipsed behind a magazine. It was clear that Mrs. Winona Pathfinder did not want to be there.

Lucy briefly outlined the reasons for their

visit. Lucy's stepfather, Davis, had died of pneumonia six months ago. Like her mother, Davis Pathfinder had been a mixed breed, mostly Sioux, raised on the Pine Ridge reservation in South Dakota. Davis had been involved in medicine ways, as had Winona. Lucy had decided, however, early on that the old ways were not her ways. After graduating from the Indian high school, Lucy fled from the reservation as soon as she could to become a nurse.

"I wanted to work in Indian Health but not go back to reservation life. My husband, Larry, is Ojibway and a caller at the Bingo Hall in Peshawbestown. We've got two great kids, boy and girl, and life's been pretty good for us — until Davis died. I'm my mother's only child. What could I do? I had to ask her to come live with us. But it's not been a happy reunion." Lucy's face adopted a grim expression.

"What's the problem?" I asked.

"For one, we have had to double-bunk the kids to give her a bedroom of her own. Most of the time she stays out on the porch in the rocking chair, doing beadwork. She doesn't have to say anything for me to know what she's thinking. Always there has been this ability of hers to communicate in the silences." Sourness punctuated Lucy's voice.

"What does she say in the silence?" I was curious.

"She doesn't approve of the way I raise the kids. She says I'm too direct and blunt with them. When she thinks I'm not listening, she'll begin talking to the air. I know she is talking to the kids, telling them stories, teaching them in her round-about way. She tells them that the names I've given them are only their 'white' names, that they need to discover in ceremony their real Lakota names, strong names that they can then grow into. And they find their grandmother to be fascinating and mysterious."

"You resent that?" It was more of a statement than a question.

Lucy sighed. "Don't you see? When she talks that way, it just brings back reservation life to me. I want something different for my children. I want them to communicate like everybody else, to be able to get straight to the point of things. But you see, even now, I got off the point as to why we are here."

I waited for her to elaborate.

"This last weekend, Mom announced that she was going to die in two moons. I've never known her to make any pronouncement that she does not plan to keep. Nothing I say seems to change her mind. It doesn't make sense to me. She has diabetes but doesn't

have to take insulin. There's nothing terminally wrong with her health. But I know her,
and she means to die in two months." The
angry eyes softened into sadness.

Lucy opened up her hands in a gesture of
pleading, "Can you help me?" — the universal request to the therapist. I wasn't yet
sure who needed the help — Lucy or Winona. Little did I know that it was I.

"Of course, I can," I replied.

two

Carpets

★ ★ ★

*. . . The woven linen or carpet with its
designs is often used as a symbol for
the complex symbolic patterns of life and
the secret designs of fate. It represents
the greater pattern of our life, which we
do not know as long as we live it . . . it is
only in old age when one looks back that one
sees that the whole thing had a pattern.*

— Marie Louise Von Franz,
Interpretation of Fairy Tales

I suggested to Lucy that she ask her mother
to join us. Lucy was adamant about my seeing the old woman alone, as her mother
never confided in her. She thought that
maybe her mother might find it easier to talk
to me. I didn't realize that Lucy was praying
for a miracle. I swung open the office door,
let Lucy escape back into the waiting room,
and addressed myself to Winona. "Mrs.

Pathfinder, please, won't you come in?"

The large magazine didn't budge from in front of her face. It took me only two seconds of silence to reassess the determination of this old woman to avoid the whole business of therapy. In this awkward moment of non-encounter, Lucy took charge and snatched the publication from her mother's hands. Abruptly revealed was the weathered face of an elderly Sioux woman, no make-up and crow's-feet wrinkles around the eyes. The cheekbones were high and flat, the eyes dark and impenetrable, the edges of her mouth set in an expression of stubborn power. Winona's eyes intently stared at Winona's feet.

"Please, Mother!" Lucy said in a frustrated tone of voice.

Without a word or even a glance toward her daughter, Winona rose slowly to her feet, a squat woman with a body built low to the ground, used to heavy work. Without acknowledging my presence, she brushed past me into the office. Behind her mother's back, Lucy threw up her hands; she was turning the problem over to me. I closed the door and turned my attention to Mrs. Pathfinder. Winona headed for the overstuffed chair to sit down, wherein she resumed the studied focus on her feet.

She was dressed in a nondescript blue-black house duster. Beaded safety pins decorated her scuffed brown moccasins. Her hands, stained and deeply creased, looked as if they had been accustomed to picking berries in thorn bushes, the hands of a woman of the earth. Winona appeared to be in her late sixties. The eyes were black, indecipherable; the expression on her face was of a woman deep within herself, patient, waiting for people to go away and leave her alone.

"I gather you've never been to a psychologist before," I began. "There are certain ground rules to psychotherapy. First, what you tell me is confidential unless you report homicidal or suicidal intent, tell me about a child being abused, or subpoena me to testify on your behalf in court." I checked to see how she was receiving this piece of information.

The old woman didn't seem to be even breathing.

"It must be scary to come and see a therapist for the first time," I leaned toward her.

Immovable, one with the chair, she kept her eyes fixed on her feet.

I sat back. This client wasn't going to be easy. "Perhaps you didn't want to come and see a therapist," I ventured. Surely that was an understatement.

Still no reaction.

I plunged ahead anyway. "Your daughter is very concerned about you, especially after you announced you were planning to die in two months' time. She doesn't want you to go. How do you feel about it?" I left the "it" purposely vague.

Not even a stolen peek at me.

I was running out of things to say but was hesitant to move into more questions. Questions would be intrusive. Finally, that left just silence.

Sometimes silence can give both therapist and client time to think about what is happening. Other times silence creates anxiety for the client and forces the emergence of suppressed information. This silence, however, was disconcerting. I had the distinct impression that I was invisible to the old woman. Even if she was to look in my direction, she might look right through me. I began to stare at my feet, not so much in imitation, but more to reaffirm my own physical reality.

It was then that I noticed that my left stocking was beginning to develop a run.

Perhaps this would have gone on for a full hour, two adult human beings silently studying their own feet, when Winona finally took mercy and chose to speak. "Lucy," she pronounced, "is an apple."

It occurred to me that calling an Indian an "apple" was like calling a Black an "Oreo." Red on the outside, white on the inside.

I responded, "It must be hard for you to have to come and live with your daughter away from the reservation and your people."

Winona grunted an assent.

This small exchange had begun to warm up the gulf between us. I was assuming some visibility for her. It seemed important to follow up with eye-to-eye contact. But Winona seemed determined not to look me in the eye. While her short, stout body faced forwards toward me, hands clasped on her lap, she kept her head bent toward the floor, scrutinizing the design of the oriental office rug at her feet."

I didn't understand her body expression, so I mirrored it, trying to experience viscerally what her body was communicating. I too began to gaze at the rug, hands united in front of me, looking for a connection between us. A key, a metaphor presented itself, and I grabbed onto it.

"Our lives are like this rug here, Mrs. Pathfinder. . . ." Again I tried to make meaningful eye-to-eye contact, ". . . full of all kinds of intricate patterns; times from childhood, family connections, joys, and even the tragedies which add meaning to our existence. All of these are woven into the tapestry of life. Yet when we love someone deeply, and that person dies, it often feels as if someone came and slashed at the carpet of our lives with a ragged tool, scattering the intricate patterns into fibers reaching out to nowhere, disconnected and dangling into empty space. I also suspect that is how you experience living with your daughter in a strange land that is not of your people."

Winona peeked at me without letting her eyes make contact with mine. I had touched a part of her, whether it was the anger at Lucy, the loss of Davis, or the sense of alienation off the reservation — I didn't know. At least the seed of a relationship between us had planted itself in that brief insight. She shifted in her chair, a thought forming in the silence between us. I waited patiently, studying her face. Respect demanded that it was now her turn to respond. Her comment, however, caught me off guard. It was said with gentleness, as an explanation to my ignorance.

"To look an Indian in the eye is to steal the soul."

I turned my gaze aside. What to do next? Was she telling me I shouldn't look at her face at all? How was I to know what she was feeling?

She let her eyes slide past my eyes and resumed looking elsewhere.

"I know little about Native American customs," I confessed.

"I guessed as much," she replied, smiling, her teeth brown and tobacco-stained. She was establishing right off that honesty between us was the best policy.

By bringing her back to the point of our session, I also affirmed that I was in charge of the therapy. "Mrs. Pathfinder, your daughter is genuinely worried about you. About this dying in two months: she is afraid that you mean what you say and . . ."

"But, I do," she interrupted.

"Well, according to her, you're not ill. I wonder if you are thinking of doing yourself in?"

Winona tipped her head to the side in a questioning manner. "Do myself in?"

"What I am talking about is suicide. Are you planning to kill yourself?"

At that, Winona's face lit into a mirthful grin. The infectiousness of her expression made me smile in return. Somehow the joke was on me, and I didn't mind it in the least. What a relief to know that I didn't have a suicidal client.

"Well, then," I said, "if you aren't dying of any illness and you don't plan to kill yourself, what does it mean when you say to Lucy that you are going to die in two months' time?"

She looked up toward me over my right shoulder and replied, "Because, in two moons," she leaned forward to emphasize her statement, "it will be a good time to die."

It was at that moment I began to suspect that Lucy was right.

"I want you to come for psychotherapy twice a week, Mondays and Thursdays. You don't give me much time to know you or to get to the roots of your decision to die." Fifty minutes had fled by.

Winona shrugged her shoulders, as if indifferent to my feelings.

"Will you return on Thursday, Mrs. Pathfinder?" After all, it had not been her decision to see a therapist.

"What for?" It was a simple question that called for a simple response.

"So that you can teach me more about you," I answered. Truthfully.

"Then, call me Winona," she groused. Her body heaved off the chair. She opened the door, and without looking back, exited the office. She left it to the beleaguered Lucy to pay for the session.

three

Beginning Preparations

★ ★ ★

It is her child he is preparing for blessing
before her;
It is her child he is preparing for blessing
behind her;
It is her child he is preparing for blessing
below her;
It is her child he is preparing for blessing
above her;
It is her child he is preparing for blessing
around her;
For blessed speech from her,
For blessing in all her surroundings,
He is preparing her.

— Traditional Navaho Chant
For Initiation Into Womanhood,
Blessingway

The week was frenetic, full of emergency
consultations and psychodiagnostic evalu-
ations at Traverse City Hospital. Thursday

couldn't come soon enough to retreat back to the quieter setting of my private office in Suttons Bay. The first appointment of the day was Winona Pathfinder.

A red pick-up truck, at least ten years old and rusting on the under-edge, was sitting in the parking lot when I arrived. I parked alongside it. On the driver's seat of the truck sat Winona, smoking a long pipe — the bowl of speckled red pipestone, the stem of dark wood sixteen inches in length and decorated with beadwork and fringe. She caught my reflection in her side mirror as I opened my car door and hauled out my briefcase. Her eyes smiled. I had the distinct impression Winona was planning to have fun with me.

A bit defensively, I said, "Winona, you're twenty minutes early."

"*Wi,*" she pointed to the early morning sun with her right hand, "has been up a long time. Besides," she grinned, "I can smoke my pipe here without my daughter telling me all 'bout lung cancer. I'll be finished when the pipe's ready." Long trails of smoke rose from the smooth bowl which she cradled in her left hand, tamping the tobacco down with a curved sliver of deer antler.

I moved closer to the truck door to see the pipe. Her first question startled me. "Are you in your moon?"

"What do you mean?"

"Are you at that time of month when you are bleeding?" Winona looked at me as if I was retarded.

Curious question but simple to answer. "No," I replied.

Winona announced, "Then, I will teach you about this pipe when I know you better today, when I know that you will stop talking and be ready to listen. Whites," she looked at me meaningfully but without touching my eyes with her gaze, "act dumb. They spend so much of their time chit-chatting like the chickadees, asking this question and that — they don't learn nothing. Love their own talking. *But,* if they'd listen, be quiet and watch what's going on, they wouldn't need to ask so many questions!"

I didn't say a word.

She puffed some more. Her right hand caressed the stem of the pipe. She was thinking, lost in an old movement, one with the motion. I quietly picked up my briefcase and headed to the office door. Winona would come when she was ready.

A few minutes later, the door opened into the waiting room and Winona appeared, a long fringed bag clasped in her left hand. In her right hand she carried two sticks of gray leaves that she proceeded to strip and roll into a wad. Winona asked for an ashtray and placed the compacted leaves in it. She pulled a lighter from the pocket of her dress and lit the wad. It began to smoke. Walking all around me, Winona wafted the smoke onto my person.

"Now, you're clean," she declared.

I heard myself sounding both defensive and amused. "I didn't know I was dirty." Another voice in me told me to shut up, let her do the talking. Yet the dilemma was that I was the therapist, Winona was the client, and it was very clear that she was assuming control of our session. I reminded myself that only a novice therapist would get upset over that fact.

"Winona, tell me about this." I gestured toward the remains of the burning leaves. They smelled like marijuana.

"Man sage," she replied, "not horse sage. Not woman sage. Not your sage. Man sage. I looked it up in one of your fancy books. Said that it was Artemisia Silver *Queen*, and that woman sage is Artemisia Silver *King*. Whites," she threw up her hands in mock derision, "live in an upside-down world. Man is woman; woman is man. You can't tell them apart, and so you think there is no difference." Winona started chuckling. She sat down in the stuffed chair, laying the long beaded bag on the rug.

Ready to begin the psychotherapy session, I positioned myself opposite her, letting my eyes brush across her face, checking her reactions. "Winona, tell me of the differences in our worlds, how it is that the white man lives in an upside-down existence. If we lived in a righted world, what would that be like?"

"Balance, you'd walk in balance. Outside, on a car bumper in your parking lot, I saw a sticker. It says a woman needs a man like a fish needs a bicycle. No balance in that. Dumb."

I didn't tell her that the bumper sticker and car belonged to my colleague, Bev Paterson. Or that many feminists are proud of their independence from men. Winona would probably view that as a frivolous notion.

"Tell me about the pipe, if you are willing." I noticed the stem peeking out of the long fringed bag.

Winona pulled out the pipe stem, smoothed and pointed at one end; beadwork encircled a piece of leather midway down the stem. The multicolored beads depicted stylized lightning, jagging across a black sky. From the soft inner depths of the bag, Winona extracted next the salmon-colored bowl.

"This is all there is," she said, "Deer skin, sumac wood, catlinite stone. Or what you would call animal, vegetable, and mineral." With her left hand she picked up the bowl. It had a slight chip on the top surface.

"This bowl is woman." She lifted up the stem in her right hand.

"This stem is man." She then joined them together.

"Apart from each other, they are just bowl and stem. Joined together, they make up the whole universe. United, they are sacred." Winona looked at me, as if to make a personal statement. Holding the pipe, stem out, she inscribed a small circle in the air, then disassembled the pipe, placing it carefully back into the fringed bag.

"You are alone," she commented, "and that's okay, but you're not balanced. You don't have a man to balance you. And, inside, you don't yet know the power of woman."

Sadness suddenly flooded me; I turned my gaze to the floor, embarrassed. What was Winona touching, way down inside of me? Whose therapy was it anyway? I replied with a challenge, "Winona, how do you know that I am not in a relationship with a man?"

"The Spirits told me." She grinned. "After our first meeting, I needed to check you out.

From my medicine bundle, I took my other pipe, the sacred pipe, *Chanunpa Wakan*, and asked the Grandfathers about you. They told me you needed help, that you didn't walk in balance. They told me to teach you while I'm still here. They also say they like you, that you have a good heart."

Some endorsement, I thought. "These spirits, can you see them?"

"Sometimes."

"How do they talk to you? Inside of your head or outside of your head?" I had to check out whether Winona suffered from hallucinations. She hadn't appeared psychotic.

"Sometimes inside, sometimes outside. Don't matter." Her answer was clipped, to the point.

"Can you tell me about these spirits you sometimes see and you sometimes hear inside of your head and sometimes outside?"

Winona paused, took a deep breath, and said off into empty air, "Grandmother, she knows nothing." She waited, then emphatically said, *"Hau!"* as if in agreement.

Apologetically, she turned to me, "I'm not used to teaching someone I don't know. Grandmother says time is short for both of us. It is not important for you to know about Spirits now. Except that you, too, have a teacher somewhere waiting for you to wake up."

"When I wake up, what then happens?" I pursued this line to see where we would go.

Winona smiled, "Then you wouldn't ask so many questions!"

Back to square one. Who was helping whom?

"Why does time have to be so short, Winona? It takes time to trust someone, to talk to them. Why don't we have that time?"

"Because," she said, "I'm tired. I've worked hard for my people. I'm ready to go."

"Is Davis waiting for you, Winona?"

"That sonuvabitch!" she exclaimed, "to go on before me. Just like a man, to be in such a hurry. Next time I see him, I'm going to shoot him dead!"

Maybe I wasn't the only one with man troubles.

four

A Sacred Story

★ ★ ★

Friend, come do this!
Friend, come do this!
Friend, come do this!
If you do this, your Grandfather
will be watching you.

This sacred ceremony
when you sit down to begin,
remember me as you fill the Pipe!
If you do this, what you wish
will come true.

When you sit down and begin
the ceremony with the Pipe,
remember me as you fill it.
If you do this, what you wish
will come true.

Friend, come do this!
Friend, come do this!
Friend, come do this!
If you do this, your Grandfather
will be watching you.

39

— Traditional Lakota Song,
given to the people by
White Buffalo Calf Woman

To work with clients effectively, you have to go into their world, understand their meanings, touch into their language, and so the education of Meggie O'Connor by Winona Pathfinder resumed that Monday.

"It is good, this coming here. Lucy is happy too. She thinks you will bring me to my right senses," Winona grinned.

"But," Winona continued, "the sense is not on the right. The heart is on the left, and that is the hand that holds the bowl, and in that bowl is all of creation." Winona's left hand cupped the air, as if to cradle an invisible world. Her voice was quiet. In the stillness of my office, only a cricket sang. I could feel myself centering down into the heart.

"If you walk in balance," said Winona, "you will know the heartbeat of the Grandmother. You will draw your woman power from just knowing where you put your feet. Or as we say, 'walk in the Sun Dance way.' When you run from here to there and there," her hand flailed about, "everything becomes a blur, a bee buzzing! When you walk or stop, what's around you speaks."

Entering and moving into her world, I asked, "When it speaks, what does it say to you, Winona? When you stop and listen, what do you hear?"

Winona's eyes turned old, as if sinking deep inside, depleting the energy from the outward gaze. We sat in silence for a few minutes. I knew she would respect me with her honesty, but I didn't know then that her silence was also protective toward me, struggling with what to say and what I would be ready to hear. Finally, in the way of the storyteller, she decided to talk about her own life.

"Long time ago, when our people forgot the ways of respect, the buffalo and the deer — they came no more and the people got very hungry. Two brothers went out hunting, for their families were starving, and they saw this beautiful woman. Well, the first man, he says, 'I'm going to take that woman in my blanket. There is no man to protect her.' But the other brother says, 'No, that woman is *Wakan,* sacred. Better leave her be.' But the young man was already running fast toward the woman. She turned and with her hand signaled him to come closer. And when he got to her and started to put his hands on her, it is said that a cloud of dust swirled all around them. When it cleared, there was nothing left of him but a skeleton on the ground, with snakes crawling all over it.

"She signaled to the other young man to come that way. He was scared! But he knew she was Wakan and that he had to be respectful. She told him to go home and gather all the people and that she would come in three days to teach them. The people built a council tipi, and she came and taught them many things. She taught them the ways of respect, of walking in balance with their relations. She gave them the pipe and seven ceremonies we keep to this day. They say when she left, as she walked off in the prairie, a dust cloud enveloped her and when it cleared, there was a white buffalo calf rolling on the ground. She is known as White Buffalo Calf Woman. And so I have told you this story. Hau!"

A long silence ensued. From the leather bag, Winona pulled out the pipe stem and bowl, attached them together, and dropped pinches of tobacco in the bowl. Once the pipe had been lit, she sat back in thought, smoking. From the pipe, white puffs rose in the air like discrete thoughts. Winona spoke: "I will tell you things I do not tell another. Time is short, and you need to understand.

"I could say that Lucy's father was like that first young man and Davis like the second. I could tell the story of a young Indian woman raped by a half-drunk man whose only way of showing the white world his manhood was to pull his pants down and plow the tender earth. But I have since lost my anger. Then I lost my sadness for myself. Now I am an old woman with the gift of a daughter who doesn't know how she was made, how she was born, or even the field of her creation. The Grandfathers don't care how, so why should I?" She shrugged her shoulders in reply.

"Lucy is a product of that rape then?" I was guessing.

Winona ignored my question, as if irrelevant to her story. "For a long time, I drank cheap wine. I became the skeleton with the worms crawling through me. I wasn't much of a mother to Lucy, as you can guess. We survived, but she was a crying child and I . . . I was drying up on the inside. I got the wine when I had money, and I got the wine when I didn't. I didn't have much respect for myself, and I sure as hell didn't walk in any balance. In fact, most of the time, I could hardly walk at all. Yet, when my drinking buddies and I would get together, we'd sit on the ground and offer the Grandmother the first drop before passing around the bottle."

"Who took care of Lucy during that time?" The origins of their estrangement was becoming clearer.

"I did. And my brother's wife some. For seven years, I was just a two-legged, not a human being."

"And then what happened?"

Winona's face lit up. "Davis broke into my life. Just when I thought that bones and worms were all there was. And wine. I met Davis at the courthouse. I had just finished with a drunk-driving charge and was leaving the courtroom after being let go, when this good-looking man came over and took my hand. He said that I would never be happy in my heart, until I went back to the old ways of our people.

"What a handsome guy he was! Had a big silver watchband with an eagle carved on it. The eagle was landing on a piece of green turquoise. I thought this must be the first rich Indian I have ever met! He told me to come live with him and he would teach me, but only if I'd be willing to give up the booze. I told him I had a little girl, but that didn't matter to him. He said to meet him at the courthouse the next day if I wanted to do that. I said I'd give it some thought, because, of course, I thought he was just saying that, you know, to get something from me. And

44

then there was the other matter too. . . ."

"What was that, Winona?"

"Well, Davis was on trial for killing a child."

The story was getting increasingly complicated. I asked the next logical question. "Did he get convicted?"

"No." She paused. "The court found him not guilty the same day I got off the drunk-driving charge. So he was free and clear."

"So what was the other matter?"

Winona looked at me as if I was stupid and had missed the obvious truth of the situation, "Well, everyone knew. Davis had killed that child."

five

'Twas Wondrous Pitiful

★ ★ ★

My story being done,
She gave me for my pains a world of sighs:
She swore, in faith, 'twas strange,
'twas passing strange,
'Twas pitiful, 'twas wondrous pitiful:
She wished she had not heard it, yet she wished
That heaven had made her such a man; she
thanked me,
And bade me, if I had a friend that loved her,
I should but teach him how to tell my story,
And that would woo her.
Upon this hint I spake:
She loved me for the dangers I had passed,
And I loved her that she did pity them.
This only is the witchcraft I have used.

— William Shakespeare,
Othello

Winona obviously enjoyed ending the sessions with that little twist of information to keep me hooked, wanting to know more. Some clients will wait until the last few minutes in therapy and then unload a bombshell revelation because they are scared and conflicted about telling an awful secret. Others may be manipulative and save the juicy parts to the very end of the hour, to try and squeeze in a few precious minutes to prolong their therapy time. But Winona's end-of-the-hour presentations were the device of the storyteller. What I know now but didn't know then is how the experienced storyteller shapes the truth for the ear and the mind of the listener.

Tuesday and Wednesday passed like blurs in the site of my vision. Wednesday night, I went to bed early after a light supper, fatigued from a day of therapy. Fritzie settled down at the end of the bed. As my eyelids drooped, I gave up the effort of reading, turned out the light, and went to sleep. Generally I have a hard time remembering my dreams. The next morning, however, a dream lingered on in that curious half twilight of consciousness:

I am walking on a path and come to a fork. To the right, there is a straight, level road; in the distance soar tall, city structures. Clear signs point ahead; there is something sure and secure in that direction. To the left, the trail disappears into a hilly forest. There are no clear markers; the ground rises and falls; the footing is precarious. The forest is both dark and mysterious; I am drawn and frightened by its presence. I don't know which way to go and am momentarily frozen with indecision.

Then I hear a dreadful snort behind me. I turn and look. There is a fenced farm area, a place for the bulls and the cows. The fence is constructed of vertical red wooden slats that are shaking under a terrible pressure. Then I see it and am terrified. A large white buffalo is pawing at the ground and using his massive head to uproot the flimsy fence. His red eyes challenge me, and as soon as that fragile barrier falls, I know he will charge. I must choose my path now!

Deep in a puzzled quietness, I placed the pen on the kitchen table. Dreams have no real endings. They just pose the dilemma and say to the conscious self, "Wake up! You are at a crossroads in your life. And you must pay attention to the journey." My psyche was telling me I was going to have to choose to venture left or right — but my map was unclear, and I didn't know yet what I was risking. I pocketed the dream in hopes of future insight.

Taking one step at a time, Thursday proved to be a relatively easy day. My imagination effectively corralled the wild animals and placed them in a safe context. I was relaxed when Winona came in for her early appointment. This was our fourth session; we had reached a stage of some predictability for each other. I was glad to see her and greeted her with a smile.

"Winona, how are you feeling today?"

Winona settled down into her favorite spot, the overstuffed chair. She wiggled about, trying to find a position of comfort for a body that had lived a long time and had its own special contours. Her dress was another shapeless duster with a print pattern long since dulled by many washings. Nothing about her invited examination or second looks, except for the sparkle in her eyes when she chose to speak. Then she came alive and pulled in the listener. No wonder her grandchildren gathered around her when she talked to the air, for she had stories to tell.

"I am feeling my bones today. A hollow ache to them. *Mni,* the waters, are coming." She paused and added, "I am feeling old."

Winona said this with the same emphasis she used the other day to tell me that, in two moons, it will be a good time to die. I wondered if she was feeling depressed, although nothing was given away in her facial expression.

"Winona, is getting old painful for you?"

It was a set-up question, and Winona knew it. She allowed herself to indulge in bodily complaints. "My bones ache. The joining parts are stiff in the morning and sometimes at night. My teeth wiggle and feel like falling out, those that I still have that aren't fake. The thumbs get in the way. I have bad breath in the mornings, and my ankles keep swelling up. And do you want to know whether I had a number two this morning?" She smiled up at me. I knew she probably gave the nurses at the Indian Health Center a hard time. I started laughing and so did she. To be her therapist, it was evident that I was going to have to give up trying so hard to be a white psychologist. Better to follow my curiosity than my professional rituals.

"Tell me, Winona, about Davis and the child you said he killed."

Winona nodded her head in approval that we were now ready to resume the threads of her story.

"Others told me he had kidnaped a baby. Some say he was a witch and wanted to steal that baby's spirit. The baby's mother, she kept quiet and said nothing. All anyone really knew was that the baby was in the hospital and someone saw Davis coming in with a little baby blanket, and then the baby was gone. But, you see, I didn't know him that well . . . and I had Lucy and . . ." Winona held her hands out, palms up to show both the burden and the emptiness in that time of her life. "And I was a drunk, and he offered me a path." There was a slight hint of an apology in her explanation.

"So you made a choice to go with him, knowing that he had taken a baby and caused its death."

"It was a bargain between us. I struggled so hard those days to let go of the longing for the booze. He never shamed me, and so I never asked him about that baby. He let Lucy and me live with him. He fed us. I took care of his house, cooked the old foods he liked. Buffalo soup, fry bread, the berry stew — *wojape*. We didn't talk much then. It was a knowing time. I cleaned his house until everything sparkled and smelled fresh. It felt so good to finally get clean inside, and I just loved that lemony smell in those cans of furniture polish. I'd put my nose right down on the wood and take long whiffs. And when he'd come into his freshly cleaned house, he'd sniff the air and wrinkle his nose. He never shamed me, but when he thought I wasn't looking, he'd smudge those rooms with cedar smoke. For you see, that was what smelled like home to him. . . ." Winona drifted off her sentence into a memory. She was falling in love with him all over again.

But Winona had been the one to cast the bait, and so I pursued the unasked question.

"Did he ever tell you about the baby and what had happened?"

"He told me when it no longer mattered to me. Like I knew the truth of it, before the words." Winona looked up and past me. "You can know the basket, the feel of it, the shape and the wood frame, before you have created it with the reeds and worked the design. He waited to tell me and, for a while there, I had a sense of sharing the shame with him — the booze and the baby. But it was the silence we were sharing, coming to know each other in that place of no words. Davis told me when I was ready to listen. Because if he had told me before I was ready, I'd have no place to put his words. Words can be like water spiders, skating on the top of the pond, reaching out, but never in."

I waited. The story was going to emerge in Indian time.

Winona reached into a small leather bag made of deerskin and pulled out a toothpick. She placed it in her mouth, slid it from tooth gap to tooth gap and began making tooth-sucking sounds.

"The baby's mother had come to Davis as

soon as she could leave the hospital after her baby was born. It was a little girl child. The mother was aware that Davis knew the old medicine ways, and so she came to him for help. The baby girl was born without a full brain and could only be kept alive through tubes. Her hospital baby bed was a glass prison, surrounded by all these big, fancy machines pumping food into her veins.

"The mother begged Davis to ask the Grandfathers to heal the child, and he did pipe ceremonies. It was made clear to him that she was one of those special beings who makes the earth-walk for only a short time, just long enough to do what she needs to do here. He told the mother what he learned through the pipe. Then she knew the truth of it and so made ready to let the child die. She asked to take the baby home, off the machines. Even the white doctors knew the little girl would die in time and seemed to be willing to let her do this.

"But there was a white social worker in the hospital who said that this Indian woman didn't love her baby enough to try and keep it alive. She tried to get others to take the baby. The hospital got scared and wouldn't let the baby go home to die. So, the machines pumped the life for the baby day after day. They would not let the spirit of the baby cross over but trapped it between machine and flesh. The mother's crying could find no ending. It is not the way of the Grandfathers!" Winona's jaw tightened in anger. She paused for a moment.

"It was not respectful of life. It was not respectful of death. The whites, they are so afraid of dying." Perhaps that was the truth Winona had to wait to learn. Perhaps that was the truth I was now having to learn.

She continued, "Davis entered that hospital during the night shift. He unhooked that poor baby girl, wrapped her in a blanket, and walked out of the hospital with her. He took her to the hilltop, put her down on the Grandmother with the blanket underneath her. He took his sacred pipe and offered tobacco to all the directions. He sang every song he knew, prayers for her little spirit. And as the night began to fade, so too, the baby's movements grew slower. She was a quiet infant, that one — barely a sound from her during the night. But as the sun began to peek up over the eastern rim, chasing away the darkness, the tiny girl gave up one last cry, and her spirit crossed over. Davis told me he wept, for the beauty of the sun, for the farewell song of the baby. He buried the body in the way of respect, and only he knows where."

"Why did they charge him with killing her, Winona, when she was already doomed to die at some point?"

"The white social worker. She was angry. Everyone knew he had just walked in and unhooked that baby with nobody's permission. Nobody, though, saw him walk out of the hospital. Ain't that something? Nobody, but Davis and me — and now you — knew what he really did with that baby. They couldn't prove nothing."

Winona asked, "How do you think he got out of that hospital with the baby without anyone seeing him?"

I shook my head, wondering if I would ever get Winona back to the topic of her own death.

She answered her own question: "I'll tell you how. He was invisible."

"I don't understand, Winona."

"He couldn't be seen. The Spirits told him to get that baby and to give that baby respect. He was able to walk right by the hospital security, that baby in his arms because nobody could see them. They do that, you know. If you take the ways of respect seriously, They'll help you. It's like prayer. They may not give you what you want, but They'll give you what you need."

Winona folded her hands down into her

lap, a gesture of closure. Our hour was over. For once, Indian time and white time flowed together.

Bev nodded to Winona, as they passed by each other in the waiting room. Winona did not acknowledge the greeting but flung on a ratty coat and headed out the door.

"She's a tough cookie, isn't she?" Bev commented upon entering my office.

"That's an understatement. She's not clinically depressed, terminally ill, or suicidal, yet she plans to die in two months — no, make that one and one half months." I had to subtract the time and client money I had already wasted tracking Winona's thoughts.

"She has you on a time-line even." Bev was grinning at my predicament. "Are you preaching to her about the joys of life?"

"Hardly. She does all the talking. I'm no longer sure who's in control of the therapy."

"Meggie, I've yet to see a client who can withstand your powers of persuasion." Bev had great faith in my professional skills.

My eyes swept over the session notes in the open file titled: PATHFINDER, W.

Again I shook my head, puzzled. "I've never met anyone like Winona. She asks nothing from me except to understand what she is saying."

"So?"

"But what she says is not for her benefit, Bev. Her words are meant to teach me. She is working on me, as if I'm the wounded one and she's the healer."

"Interesting," Bev reflected, arching her eyebrows. "And the more she works on you, the more incompetent you feel."

six

At A Pitch That Is Near Madness

★ ★ ★

If I could only live at the pitch
that is near madness
When everything is as it was in my childhood
Violent, vivid, and of infinite possibility . . .

— Richard Eberhart,
If I Could Only Live at the Pitch
That Is Near Madness

Friday, the Canadian jet stream perked the air with the chill of oncoming winter. Colors edged the maple and oak leaves. An introverted brown mood settled upon me, like a warm familiar blanket. Fritzie was delighted that I wasn't going to the office. He bounced about with a sense of glee, chasing chipmunks outside. After coffee, I too went outdoors — to cut the grass and clip back the grapevine hanging over the stone walls. If I had my druthers, I would never prune, for I like the way Nature grows wild and woolly.

The weight of my parents and all of civilization keeps me etching some small mark on my surroundings, as if to say: We were here, we existed once.

As I pushed the whirring mower over the tall grass, an old memory from childhood sprung up before me. At thirteen years of age, I was walking home from the bus stop and arrived at a shortcut through the woods behind a church. The shortcut took only about five minutes' traverse time. As I stepped off the sidewalk into the woods, I shucked my human mask. In a place where no one could see me, a miracle occurred.

My chunky thighs and calves transformed into the long legs of a sleek and swift black horse. My fingers metamorphosized into the experienced hands of a rider with fine control over the enormous energy of the beast within. My hooves pawed the ground. In the excitement of anticipation, the horse danced me sideways. My hands gentled, directed, and reassured the animal. The wild mane of hair flung about in exuberance; nickers and whinnies displaced the human voice. And for the initial moment all was potential — the gathering rush to gallop in abandonment, the fine thread of control — a magical, about to be spent, moment. Then, like a force of energy breaching the wall, we plunged ahead.

Rider and horse as one catapulted forth in sheer motion, tearing past the trees, hooves pounding on the pine needles. Five minutes in the woods and then, the street reappeared. The animal tucked back into the human form and the adolescent face resumed its human complexion.

Thirty-nine years old — and, inside, that black horse still nickered, as I pushed the old mower. No longer sleek and with a mane flecked with gray. I have learned how to harness her, at times make her a plow horse, steady, strong, and incredibly enduring. The workout with the mower felt good.

After lunch, I took one of my professional journals and stepped down in the living room to share the solitude and the shining sun with my sleeping dog. An old stuffed chair accepted my tired but refreshed body. I began to scan through a series of tedious abstracts, looking for that one relevant piece of information that would illuminate my work with therapy clients. Fritzie started to snore.

Thup.

A sound of something hitting the glass on the old French doors. I looked up from my reading but couldn't see anything. I bent my head down and returned to the journal.

Thup.

Fritzie looked up, ears shifting back and

forth, head cocked to catch any additional sounds. Nothing. He put his head back down on the floor, resting his chin on his outstretched legs.

Thup, thup.

This time, both of us jerked up our heads. We decided to investigate. Fritzie started sniffing over by the glass doors. I stood up, moved closer to the doors, eyes alert, watching, waiting. Then I saw it — a flash of red.

Thup, thup.

A bright red cardinal came winging in, off the stone wall, slamming into its own reflection in the glass doors. Beak out and ready to bash his handsome opponent, the bird took aim and flew straight at the enemy. What anger he must have felt to see that upstart of his reflection coming toward him, beak out in a reciprocated hostile manner. This was war!

Thup, thup.

The cardinal backed off to his perch on the stone wall. As did his nemesis, staring at him through the glass. The reflection mocked him. Head to one side, the cardinal watched his territorial competitor imitate him. But his alter ego did not answer any of the challenging bird calls. A silent enemy. Again, he hoisted himself off the wall, wings out in ferocious display. Zooming in, the red bomber attacked the glass image.

Thup, thup, thup.

Realizing that the bird had no way of invading his territory, Fritzie returned to a warm spot on the rug and proceeded to fall asleep. I was worried about my feathered friend's narcissistic woundings. His beak would soon be dulled by the battering against the glass. He needed a strong beak to break the seed pods for the fall feasting. It was obvious that repetitive experience was not about to teach anything to this bird-brained fellow, swollen up in his own instincts. Luckily I knew just where I could lay my hands on a rubber snake I had used that summer in the vegetable garden. I retrieved the snake, went outside, and carefully placed it right in front of the French doors. The cardinal warily stayed his distance on the stone wall. I returned inside and resumed my post, studying the situation.

Thup, thup.

The cardinal paid no heed to the unmoving piece of rubber. So much for painted, textured images and mobile reflections! I didn't know what else to do. If it weren't for the knowledge that soon the cardinal's beak would be permanently damaged by the glass, I would have laughed at the bird's dilemma.

Fritzie was in another world, sound asleep.

I sat down in my chair, surrounded by the silence of a fall country afternoon and the interruptions of a bird beating his head to death, because he couldn't tolerate his own self image.

seven

Convolutions

★ ★ ★

*. . . Neither straight nor crooked, neither
here nor there
but shadows folded on deeper shadows
and deeper . . .
. . . Oh lovely last, last lapse of death, into
pure
oblivion at the end of the longest journey
peace, complete peace!
But can it be that also it is procreation?*

— D.H. Lawrence,
Ship of Death

Bev called late Friday to try and set up a double date on Saturday. I declined. I wanted to be alone.

"It's been over a year and a half since the divorce, Meggie. It would be good for you to get out and meet some available men."

"I'm not ready." It sounded like a hollow excuse. She was about to protest, when I

64

added, "I've got work to do. Maybe another time."

"That's a promise, Meggie. I'll hold you to that," Bev replied before hanging up.

I wasn't ready to date. There were forces working through me that I didn't understand. Standing in the Suttons Bay Bookstore on Saturday morning, I became convinced that my knees would not be able to hold me up much longer, but there was no physical reality to that fear. I was trapped in the realm of metaphor. Saturday afternoon, I was about to descend from the second floor of the house, when the image of myself tripping and tumbling head over heels down the stairs burst into consciousness. I held onto the rail.

Saturday night the images grew more intense. In the dark, I climbed the stairs to go to bed. Fritzie bounded up before me. I heard him jump into the comfort of his own bed on the floor. As I stepped into the unlit room, a voice asked, "What kind of darkness are you stepping into?" The light revealed no one but myself.

It was a relief to go back to work on Monday.

Bev was already there and dying to tell me of her weekend date. She chided me for not coming along with them. The new man in her life had declared himself a feminist and didn't seem threatened by Bev's political stance. She really wanted me to meet him. He had a very good friend who was unattached. There were not many forty-year-old unattached men, Bev reminded me. She had also checked out whether the friend's friend was 1) just separated, 2) in love with his mother, or 3) had some terribly disfiguring deformity. Bested by the thoroughness of her investigation, I finally agreed to go out as a foursome the following weekend.

I knew I would regret it later.

Despite the impending storm inside of me, I found myself able to remain sensitive to the half-spoken truths of my clients and to delve deeply into the pain and turmoil of their lives — in a way that was both respectful and healing. The day began to close with a renewed sense of productivity.

My last appointment was Winona. I noted that she preferred to stay in her pick-up until the previous client had left. Looking out my window, I could see her watching the client, but in such a way as not to let the woman know she was being studied. I wondered what interested Winona in my other client.

Winona opened the truck door and spilled out in a lumpy fashion. She ambled to the office door, eyes to the ground. I pulled away from my window to get ready to greet her. In she came, heading straight for her favorite chair, lowered herself into it gingerly, and then set down her bag. She nodded in my direction, and I, too, sat down.

We began the session in silence. With Winona, I knew she was going to lead anyway and so let her take charge of the silence. She arranged her house dress and settled her bones into a comfortable position. Then she looked up toward me, smiled, and asked, "Well, what did you learn this weekend?"

It was not a facetious question. With my day-long self confidence restored by productivity, I didn't want to open myself up to any more vulnerability. Whose therapy was it, anyway? I parried, "And you, Winona, what did the weekend teach you?"

She ignored my question and proceeded to talk about the weather. "The leaves know their time is coming. They're holding on, getting bright and full of the sun's color. The winds soon will be blowing out of the North, shake 'em good, and if you watch 'em real careful, they stay up there by just the thinnest tie, until one day, in a group they come floating down, letting go. They move in circles coming down, round and round, drawing medicine circles in the air. They know when to let go, after all that holding on."

A poignant shaft touched my heart. Her words gave me an opening. "And are you about to let go, Winona, after holding on?"

She became silent. Had I moved too fast to the central focus of the therapy? Quietness settled on the room, and the shadows of night deepened. Then, as if there had been no interruption, she resumed her teaching:

"From the West comes the vision. From the North comes the purification. From the East comes the insight. From the South comes the knowledge of the children and of the path taken when we have finished here. All around you, Meggie, is the sacred wheel. The Grandfather above, the Grandmother on whom you walk. All around you is the turning. Nothing stays the same. You are still fearing my death. Look again, Meggie." Winona cupped her hands, palms up, as if holding something very precious.

"The wholeness of life is round, don't you see?"

I didn't see, but I was paying close attention.

Winona tried again. "Even the seasons move in a circle. You can't have the beauty of Spring without the death in Fall. Or did you not know that death comes before life? But . . ." she looked at me meaningfully, "the leaf doesn't just easily jump off the tree.

No, there is a sap in life that runs its course with all of us. We hold on tightly, Meggie, without really looking at what holds onto us. Until . . . we can know the fullness of the circle. And then we can come swirling down in the dance of wind, telling and retelling about the sacred roundness of our lives."

"Is that what you are trying to do with me, Winona? Tell me the roundness of your life?" Only by sticking close to her words, could I begin to understand what she was saying. Yet there was nothing I could really grasp and relate to the work we were doing. Which was, of course, to persuade her not to die.

Frustrated, Winona barked at me, "Now listen, Meggie. The white people want to cut away, get to the point, tell the truth, nothing but. The whites go in lines, A to B and only A and only B count, and all that's in-between is a passing of pretty scenery. The sun sets and isn't that lovely?" Winona assumed a mocking voice of a fudgie.

"The whites," she continued, "live in squares and rectangles. They add on. They subtract. Don't you see, Meggie? Don't you see, that in your own life, it isn't the big moments that count? It's the journey, the movement, and the centering in that circle which is the medicine circle for you. It is the morning when Wi rises, and you sing a welcoming song, and you say, 'Thank you for my life,' and you say, 'Today is a good day to die.' And when the Grandfather heads West, and there is that moment between light and dark, and the two worlds touch . . ." She sat back, waiting for my reaction to her lecture.

I was lost. Winona didn't seem to understand that I had a job to do, to persuade her to stay alive, and that I was failing miserably at the task. I also knew she was trying to break through years of angular thought in me. Her appraisal of me was accurate: I was dense, confused, and exposed. The image of the darkness, the voice saying, "And what kind of darkness are you entering?" reverberated within me.

Winona's voice grew gentle. "All life is a transparency. You've seen those gray tablets on which children write with a pointed piece of wood? You know, Meggie, the kind of gray paper you can lift up and watch the words just fade away? It's like that, Meggie. The words are still there, but then they're gone for what's underneath. Point A and Point B disappear. They had seemed to be important, but . . ." Winona paused. "We get caught in our own reflections."

From the periphery, Winona studied me

to see how I put this all together. Damn it, this woman somehow knew more about my storms than I did! She deserved my honesty. And what did I have to lose? Like a blind woman, I stumbled forth, "And if I get caught in my own self reflection, Winona, you are saying that I will lose my life in the process? Like my friend . . ."

"The red bird," Winona finished the sentence. She broke into a smile. Maybe this white woman really was going to be able to learn after all!

eight

The Nature of Truth

★ ★ ★

Once upon a time, there was a master craftsman with a fine job, a loving wife, and four beautiful daughters — in short everything which should make a man happy. But the man was restless and discontent. His wife asked him, what was the matter? "I want to find Truth," he confessed.

"Go then," she said, but being a very smart woman, she added, "Leave everything in my name."

Off he went in search of Truth. Up mountains, down into valleys, along the coastlines, deep into mysterious forests — he searched for days and weeks and months, until he was about to give up. Then one cold day, on top of a mountain peak, he discovered a cave in which dwelled a wizened old woman — whose skin was so old, it was the color of leather, whose hair was scraggly and greasy, whose hands were gnarled with arthritis, and whose mouth sported but a single tooth.

But when she beckoned to him, she spoke in tones so pure and lyrical, he knew, at last, he had discovered Truth.

He stayed with her for a whole year and a day, learning everything she could teach him in that time. The time came when he knew he had to return to the outside world and his loving family.

At the cave's entrance, he turned around to say farewell. "Truth," he said, "you have been so kind to me this past year. Is there anything I can do for you?"

She thought a moment and then raised an ancient finger. "Yes," she replied, "when you speak to them out there, tell them that I am young and beautiful."

— Traditional Folktale

My colleague, Bev, called me on Tuesday to say that she was going to open up the office on Wednesday evening for an emergency appointment. She had been seeing a couple in which there had been a history of spouse abuse; violence had apparently flared up again.

"I'd rather not be alone in the office area with them. Who knows what might happen?"

"Okay, I'll be there. Would you like me to bring the fearsome Fritzie?"

"You've got to be kidding," Bev snorted.

"All you would need is a tennis ball to throw in the middle of the feuding couple; Fritzie would take care of the rest!" Bev never owned a terrier, so she didn't understand my humor. "Okay," I reassured her, "I'll come and do paperwork in the next room. What's the pay scale for female bouncers?"

Bev, however, hoped to make my extra trip to the office a profitable one. "I met Lucy Arbre in Bay View Hardware yesterday. She wants to come in and talk with you about her mother and asked me if that was appropriate, being that her mother is your client. I told her all about confidentiality, and that you couldn't tell what had been said in the sessions with Winona. She said that she understood that. Why don't you see her while I am seeing the couple?"

A good idea. My only reluctance was that Lucy might ask me how the therapy was progressing. It would be hard, indeed, to describe what kind of headway Winona and I had been making.

I needn't have worried. Lucy was pleased when I called her to set up the appointment. On Wednesday evening, when she arrived at the office, she was attractively made-up and smartly attired in a warm burgundy suit and short heels. She gave me a grateful smile and sat down on the couch.

"I want to thank you, Dr. O'Connor, for what you have done for my mother. It has made all the difference in the world in terms of the home atmosphere."

What could I say? I waited to hear more. At least I wasn't going to have to explain that it was going to take some time to get into Winona's world before I might actually have some therapeutic impact.

Lucy continued, "My mother seems more alive these days. It kind of reminds me of the old days on the reservation, when she was so busy doing for other folk. She'd have an energy about her."

"What kind of doing for other folk was that?" I was curious.

"Well, I don't know too much about it." Lucy shifted her position on the sofa, as if uncomfortable. "You see, after I left home for school, my stepfather, Davis, began to teach her about the old ways." Lucy crossed her legs and folded her arms in front. Something about this topic made her uneasy. I gently pointed out to her that she seemed to be feeling unsettled.

"Dr. O'Connor, my mother is a very respected woman out there on the reservation, because of what she has learned in the traditional forms of healing. But I am a nurse trained in the medical science. The two systems don't go together, and frankly, I think much of what the traditional healers do is hocus-pocus. I am sure you know a lot about the 'placebo effect.' People get well because they *think* the treatment is going to make them well. They hear the rattles and the old songs and they have faith and the condition clears up anyway, and then they say, 'See, it works.' Only I don't believe it. They would have gotten well anyway, with or without treatment. The body has its own recovery system."

Lucy added, "But Mom genuinely believes in what she does."

"And does this cause problems between you two, that you are both healers in different traditions?"

"Oh, we don't discuss her work. To be honest," Lucy smiled, "she won't talk to me about it. A lot of that shamanic stuff never gets talked about, except, I guess, between two medicine people. She certainly doesn't let me into that world. And that's okay with me. She's my mother and the grandmother to my kids. I don't have anything to do with that world of magic." Her hands fluttered in a gesture of dismissal.

Lucy continued, "Before she would agree

to come live with me, after Davis died, she insisted that I had to set aside a closet or little room in which she could put her medicine bundle with the sacred pipe and other medicine articles. So, I gave her the closet in the bedroom. When she got here, she bought a key lock and had my husband install it on the closet door! I asked her why she had to have that door locked. She told me that the kids might try to get in and play with her medicine articles. But you know what I think?" Lucy looked straight into my eyes.

"What?" I asked, turning my eyes away.

"I think she's afraid I'd go snooping around in that closet when she wasn't there. Not that she's worried I'd take anything, but that I might somehow hurt those objects. She doesn't even like me touching her social pipe, the one she uses for smoking and teaching."

I wondered if Winona was a bit paranoid. I asked, "How might you hurt those medicine objects in the closet?"

"Oh, by handling them when I'm in my moon. You see, she doesn't really trust me. She thinks the white world has uneducated me, taught me not to see. Now I may not agree with her world-view, but I know enough of the old ways that I wouldn't go into the closet during my menstruation. Not that I think it would do any real harm, but just because we live in two different worlds, doesn't mean that we can't have respect for each other. Does it?"

This last question of Lucy's was a loaded question, asked in plaintive tones. Even though she had chosen to live the modern life, she still hungered for her mother's old-fashioned respect. It occurred to me that I could facilitate a reconciliation between mother and daughter. That would be, at least, one significant accomplishment in the thorny progress of therapy with Winona.

I needed to know more about Lucy's childhood experience of her mother. "Tell me about your growing up on the reservation. What was that like for you?" Lucy didn't seem to notice that I hadn't answered her question.

"Well, you probably already know about Mother having had a drinking problem. I don't remember too much about that time."

I took note of this fact, as it is not unusual for adults with traumatic or neglected childhoods to block out such painful memories.

Lucy continued, "I do remember the change in my life when we went to live at Davis' house. I was really proud to have a daddy all of my own. You know how kids are. Davis was good to me. He'd take me out into the woods and show me the different animal tracks. He'd get both Mom and me to search for plants that he used in his medicine work. I remember how, before he'd take a plant, he would offer tobacco and make a prayer of thanksgiving for the life of the plant. He'd tell me that the plant was 'giving away' its life so that we could live. Often he would use that expression about the 'give-away.' That made a big impression on me, only . . ." Lucy began to chuckle, "when he told me that on my birthday, I had to give away a gift to my best friend, as opposed to getting gifts — well, I didn't much like that!"

"It sounds as if you really wanted a father."

Lucy nodded. "I never knew my biological father. I never knew anything about him. When I'd ask my mother, she'd just shake her head, get an angry expression 'cross her face, and tightly seal her lips. It would be like a storm cloud had suddenly come into the room. I learned quick enough not to ask. But you know what? Since she has started coming here to see you, she's begun to open up and talk more."

My ears perked up at this. I was interested to know just what therapy was doing for Winona and what she was beginning to say to her daughter. Maybe, being able to talk to a therapist was stimulating an initial movement toward rapprochement between mother and daughter.

"What has your mother told you?"

"Well, she said that my father, my biological father, was a very intelligent man, good-looking, and someone with a promising future. I liked hearing that he was really bright. She said that, unfortunately, he got killed in the Korean War, that he hadn't known that she was pregnant with me, and that they had a one-night affair.

"I asked her why she hadn't told me this before, because then I could meet my father's family. She told me that the man had been married or something like that, and that it would have been too much of a scandal. She said that my father really was a fine person, a loving person who, if he had known about me, would have wanted to become part of my life. She said he won a lot of medals in the war, because he was really brave. He had thrown himself on a grenade that had been tossed into the foxhole near his buddies. You know, a real hero. That's how he got killed."

Lucy looked wistful, "I really would have liked to have known him."

It was hard to keep my expression clear of

astonishment. Hadn't Winona just told me that Lucy was a product of a violent rape? I couldn't believe that she would have strung together such a series of lies about Lucy's father; yet my lips were sealed in confidentiality. Winona had traded the truth to make a truce.

Lucy had more to say. "But I can't complain. Davis was real good to me. Yet, he scared me. At times he could get real angry and storm out of the house. Kids at school told me he once killed a baby, and so, I was frightened of his anger. It was a contradiction, you know? He was a very gentle man, and yet there was something unpredictable about him. Finally, the mother of one of my school friends helped me understand that. She told me he was a *heyoka*."

"What's that?"

"Well, the heyoka medicine people are the most powerful of the healers, but the people are scared of them. I don't know much about all this. I don't care to know much about it — but the heyoka people are the people of the lightning. They are seen as powerful, capricious, dangerous, quick, and unpredictable. It helped me understand that while I loved Davis as a father, I also kept a protective distance from him. I think he was really sad to see me go away to school though

. . ." Lucy trailed her sentence.

I remembered the design of lightning on Winona's pipe. "Is your mother also heyoka?" I asked.

"I don't know. She didn't become a healer until after I left. It takes a long time. You don't really get much respect until you're in your fifties, because in the old ways, the learning is slow and deliberate."

One last question. "What kind of healing does your mother do?"

"That I do know," Lucy answered. "Some medicine people specialize, just like in the white world. You have the bone setters or those that work with cancer, or you have the generalists like the internist. There are those who work with herbs and those who work with spirits in the sweat-lodge or the more extreme *yuwipi* ceremonies, in which the medicine man is bundled up in a star quilt and tied with seven knots. Davis would do both herbs and spirit-healing. But my mother has a specialty."

"What is that?" I asked.

Lucy replied, "My mother works with those people who have never found, or are in danger of losing, what whites would call their souls. It is on the sickness of the spirit, not of the body, that she was known to work her healing. I guess you could say," and Lucy smiled at this insight of hers, "that my mother is kind of a therapist, like you, but in the traditional ways of the people."

Lucy looked up at the clock and saw that the session was over. She reached out to me with her hand to shake mine, saying, "Again, I want you to know how much my mother enjoys working with you."

In more ways than one, I thought.

nine

Story Telling

★ ★ ★

*Small wonder that spell means both
a story told, and a formula of
power over living men.*

— J.R.R. Tolkien,
Tree and Leaf

Thursday, Winona entered into the therapy room, grinning. "Lucy is real pleased at how you are helping me." She found her chair and sat down. "She hasn't heard me talk about dying now for some time. She tells me that I seem to be feeling better."

"And are you, Winona?" I knew her well enough now not to trust her.

"Am I what?" She was looking in my direction, amused.

I acted dumb to her maneuvering, "Are you feeling better?"

"Oh much, much better! You don't know, Meggie, how wonderful it feels to become regular in one's old age! Not to have to hold it all in." She began laughing at her own joke.

Despite her resistance to the therapy process, I liked her playful spirit. Truly, therapy is often about letting go, body and emotion. We both relaxed and laughed. But I was not to be deterred for long from the hard questions. I ventured forth.

"Lucy told me pretty much the same thing. She also talked at some length about the heroism of her biological father and the brief 'affair' you had with him, Winona. From her telling, he sounded like a really nice guy. But quite different from what you told me. Don't you think that Lucy deserves the respect of truth?"

She evaded my question skillfully. "It was a good story, don't you think? I had to spend some time on that story. I didn't want just any old story about him. Lucy needed a good story, a powerful story, to make her strong for the rest of her life. Something to tell the kids, to help them find the warrior spirit when they needed it. It was a good story, Meggie."

"But what about the truth, the rape?" I was stunned by her obvious pleasure in the ornamentation of the lie.

A look of mild exasperation crossed her

face, as if she were talking to someone who was slightly retarded. She gathered her thoughts together, and I sensed a teaching was about to come my way. I settled back into my chair, wondering why the therapy had to be such a struggle between the two of us.

Winona crossed her feet and chose her words slowly. "Lucy just don't want to know about the old ways of healing. She's got what she calls 'science' as her truth. When somebody's sick, they come to her and them doctors, and they got all kinds of fancy medications and injections. They got machines that look into your head, and machines that can read the pumping of the heart.

"But what can they tell, Meggie, about that heart and why it breaks? What can they tell about the soul that is sick and carries the body into its darkness? They got pills to put your brain into a empty space, but, hell, I found that wine does it even cheaper! And that's where you stay — in that gray space of nowhere. That's a truth." She paused a moment in her telling of it.

"Once I tried to tell Lucy about these things. About the nature of things, how you can't take the brain and say it's alone without the heart. You can't take the beating heart without knowing the spirit's web that holds it all together. And she talks proof, and something she calls double-blind experiments, and tells me that none of what is right in front of her exists, unless science says it is there. I told her to just look, and she closes her eyes. And that's a truth, Meggie." Anger edged her voice.

"You ask about respect, Meggie. What about that man who raped me? He had no buffalo to hunt, although his father and grandfather spoke often of the buffalo. He lived in a square shack, when he knew of the roundness of life. The reservation was a prison for his spirit, because it offered him a vision of what life is about, but no way of living that vision. And in the white world, he couldn't be a man, because there was no job for him on the reservation. If he left his people to get a job, then he had to give up being of the people. So he chose the prison over death and drank the wine.

"I didn't know him, Meggie, and he probably didn't know himself. Perhaps, he could have been a great warrior. Perhaps, if he had chosen that path, as many of our young people do, he would have gone off to whatever war was happening and chosen to die with honor for the people. Perhaps it was the wine which confused him into thinking Woman was his enemy. We all have that hero, that warrior spirit within us. And that's a truth too."

She sat back from her intensity, smiled at me, and finished, "So the truth is that it was a good story, Meggie. A spirit-nourishing story with healing in it. I told it well. And Lucy's scientific spirit took it in and said yes to it. It was for her, her children, her children's children, I told that story."

"What about you, Winona? Was it a healing story for you too?" I asked.

"Oh, when I cross over to the other side, I am going to look that man up. I got an old score to settle with him. After I finish with him, he'll wish he could have been a ghost trapped between the worlds!"

They were fighting words. Winona's approach to men who opposed her was to do battle, not let them belittle her. Mine was to hide and avoid, to camouflage the fragile heart behind the mask of a psychologist.

ten

Inner Fires And Empty Walls

★ ★ ★

Sex — The pleasure is momentary, the position ridiculous, and the expense damnable.

— Lord Chesterfield

Friday, the weather began seriously to hint of winter. The chill in the air required the woodstove at night. Fritzie bounced around me, as I cracked apart large sections of wood with a mechanical nineteen-ton log-splitter. The stack of cut wood for the stove grew higher and higher.

In the afternoon, Olf came by to give me a hand for the two-person jobs. Together we strung snow fences near the house entrance to keep the coming drifts at a distance. As usual, Olf didn't talk much while working, except to comment on what we needed to do next. He welcomed my suggestion, after a couple of hours' work, that we take a break for a hot cup of coffee and some homemade bread.

Coffee mug in hand, Olf talked farmer talk. The conversation always seemed to be the same, comforting in its predictability. The harvest of corn or soybeans or wheat was never as good as it could have been — due to drought or flooding or early frost. The market prices were discouraging, and the government just didn't seem to give a darn for the small farmer.

"But what can you do?" He shrugged his shoulders. "All the price supports go for those big California farms. I'm not getting any younger, but I don't know if any of my boys will keep up the farm. It's a hard life. Ja. But then again, I'd probably chose to do it all over again, if given a second chance." He laughed and shook his head — the paradox between passion and conventional wisdom.

What could I say? Except to fill his coffee cup and nod my head in assent.

"Well, I better get back to what needs to be done. Complaining never solved any problem." That was as close to philosophy as Olf would ever get.

I asked him to check the caulking on the dormers way up on the highest part of the roof. I wanted the house shielded against the wind and rain. Olf promised me he would take care of it.

Saturday morning, I awoke early, feeling anxious. Something was not right with my world. Then I remembered. I had agreed to go on a double date that evening with Bev, her new man, and Mr. Wonderful. I groaned, rolled over in my bed, and tried to recover the sanctuary of sleep. No such luck. For just one cowardly moment, it occurred to me that I could feign a twenty-four hour virus. But I knew Bev, and she'd be able to spot the lie. A mocking voice within me muttered, "And doesn't she deserve the respect of truth?"

Damn! Hoisted on my own petard and as ever, susceptible to the well-meaning intentions of my friend. Well, I figured I could endure this one evening and then, maybe, Bev would leave me in peace. Not only had I exiled men, but also sexual desire, from my existence. Three months after I had left my husband, Tom Lockheed, I even ceased masturbation. I didn't need a man in my life.

Dread stretched the minutes into hours. The day inched along, as I tried to hide in the compulsivity of little chores. I got a lot accomplished but was unable to take pleasure in that fact. The target hour of six o'clock slouched closer. I became aware that absolutely nothing in my wardrobe was suitable for a dinner date. I decided to dress professionally, to demonstrate that I was not a frivolous person. The brown skirt and blouse was aptly conservative and dull. It would help insure that no more double dates would have to happen.

The three of them arrived while I was putting on the last pretenses of make-up. Bev knocked, opened the front door, and entered, dates in tow. Her date was handsome, of medium height, and with a lovely smile. I liked him instantly. She introduced him as "Coulter"; he extended his hand warmly toward me.

The second man, my escort, hung back. After briefly looking me over, his eyes scanned the foyer. Bev, assuming the role of matchmaker, formally introduced him, "Jackson Jalenko, this is Meggie O'Connor." She looked askance at my bland outfit.

Jackson Jalenko was tall, good-looking, with dark brown hair and an athletic build, attired with a red tie perfectly matched against a deep-blue shirt, scrimshaw cuff-links, carefully pleated and pressed pants, and polished shoes. He smiled and said, "You can call me Jack. Everyone does."

Bev began to explain where we were going to eat. While she was talking, Jack discovered the mirror in the foyer and subtly tried to rearrange his hair with his left hand. I should have noticed the cues right then and there, but I didn't.

Off we went in Coulter's automobile, a car that had seen better days and was now testing the manufacturer's promise of rustproof undercoating. Bev sat in front with Coulter; Jackson and I occupied the back.

"The deer hunting must be wonderful on this place," he commented, looking out the window. Perhaps it was too dark for him to notice the myriad DO NOT HUNT signs I had posted all over the driveway and by the main road. He turned to me, adding:

"I love to bow hunt, to stalk the deer and wait for that precise moment to release the arrow, to see it knock the animal right off its feet. I hate it when I miss and only wound the animal. Then it runs for miles, and I have to spend a long time tracking the blood trail, until it collapses. Often I have to walk miles dragging the carcass back to the truck. But it makes for great eating!" He patted his taut stomach.

It was definitely a bad start. I cautioned myself to give Jack another chance to redeem himself. I redirected the conversation. "Have you ever read William Faulkner's story, *The Bear*?"

He shook his head.

"It's the story about the spirit of a bear and the spirit of a boy, and the archetypal dance between them."

Jackson looked at me, puzzled, and then turned to study the lighted houses we were passing. Perhaps he didn't know the meaning of the word "archetypal."

Silence fell between us like a damp blanket. We listened to the animated conversation on football between Coulter and Bev.

Dinner at The Windows restaurant, however, chased away the group awkwardness, and soon we were all having a good time, talking and eating smoked whitefish and cherry pie. Jack had an M.B.A. and was currently managing a store in a chain of hardware stores in Traverse City.

"But I have my eyes set on bigger fish to fry," he revealed. "I'm hoping soon to leap over to managing a department store. Not only is the salary larger, but one gets to meet the important business people. My goal is to move to Chicago where the real action is." He leaned toward me as if confiding a secret.

It was obvious that Jack suffered no crisis in self-confidence. I envied him for that.

"I'm pretty good at what I do," he admitted. "I don't avoid the hard decisions. When the budget is tough, I cut staff. As manager, you can't be concerned whether you are liked or not by the employees. What is good for the store, ultimately, is good for them."

While Jack was being serious and intense, Coulter and Bev were making bedroom eyes at each other, laughing at private little jokes. I bent my ear in their direction.

Seeing that my attention was wandering, Jack began to tell risqué stories to all of us. "Do you know the story of the man who caught his wife in bed with his best friend? Well, he shot his wife. Another friend asked him why he shot his wife and not the man? The man replied, 'Well, he *is* my best friend!' "

Jackson broke out into a real chuckle, Coulter smiled in warning, Bev's face grew dark in offense, and I changed the topic.

"Have you ever been in therapy?"

"Never needed to," he replied. "By keeping my body in good shape with exercise, I manage to keep myself in good mental health." He smiled flirtatiously and whispered, "Are you interested in doing some therapy on me?"

Truthfully, I wasn't quite sure what he meant.

He reached out and touched my hand. For all his chauvinistic humor, I couldn't deny that Jack was one handsome man. I found myself leaning toward him. It had been a long time since anyone had touched me, except for Fritzie's cuddling, Olf's slaps on the back, and Bev's morning hugs. I didn't realize how much I had missed that. I thought of my ex-husband, Tom, and our early courting days.

"Have you ever been married?" I asked him. It was time to find out more details.

"No, but I would like to. It seems like most of the women I've dated wanted to play the field. Or things would be going along fine, and suddenly the woman decided to leave. So, being hurt like that, I've grown cautious. You can understand that." He again smiled, and his left hand dropped off the table and reached over and just briefly touched my thigh. As he talked on about his former love relationships, there really was no excuse for my missing this last clue about Jack. However, my libido was attending mainly to the anticipation of the next touch.

By the time we had coffee and snifters of brandy, I was feeling warm indeed. Jack had a gorgeous body and a handsome face; his smile dazzled me — or was it the brandy?

Jack spoke to Bev and Coulter, "Why don't you just drop Meggie and me off at my place? I'll drive her home."

Bev waited for me to give her a signal

whether that was all right with me. I could see she was not impressed with Jack. On the other hand, I knew she would welcome the drive home alone with Coulter. I nodded to her that the plan was just fine with me. Jack squeezed my hand under the table.

His townhouse sat within the city limits, in a new development fronted by billboards boasting of hot tubs, tennis courts, jogging trails, indoor gym. Except for exterior color, all of the houses looked alike. Once inside his house, having said good-bye to our dinner companions, he gave me a tour of the rooms and antique furniture — the mahogany dining-room table, the cherry wood desk, the wing-tip chairs. He said he had a collection of antique guns in his basement, which he promised he would show me someday. He helped me off with my coat, but what I kept noticing, as he took me from room to room, was that there was nothing hanging on his walls. No photographs, paintings, posters. Nothing. Except for an occasional mirror.

Still, I missed the clues.

Finally, we came to the bedroom. The headboard was massive and of a high-glossed, grainy wood. A handmade quilt covered the king-sized bed. Everything in the bedroom was incredibly neat. No dirty socks dangling off the bedspread, no magazines cluttering the bedside tables, no coins or batteries or safety pins heaped on top of his bureau. I realized at that moment that I could never allow this man to enter into my disorganized bedroom.

Standing by his bed, he put his hand upon my arm. I felt uncomfortable. "Shall we go downstairs?" I suggested.

His hand pulled away. Downstairs in the living room, he pointed out the liquor cabinet and asked me to pour us each a small glass of Irish Cream, while he built a fire in the fireplace. Soon, the warmth and the liqueur had us both relaxing together on the couch.

Jack's compact-disc player and high-priced stereo speakers were set to a lulling, soft pitch of ocean music. The gentle sound of surf and gulls, embedded in keyboard chords of repetitive phrases, created a dreamy atmosphere. Jack turned down the overhead lights in the living room, so the fire drew us in with its dancing flames. His arm encircled my shoulders while his hand played with my hair.

"Your skin is so soft to the touch." His finger traced a line down my cheek, down the side of my neck, to my shoulder.

I was at a loss for conversation, aware of

a flush arising in my face.

"It was hard to sit there at the table with Coulter and Bev," he continued, "when all I wanted was to be here alone with you, in my house, by the fire." His voice was smooth, hypnotic.

He removed his hand from my shoulder, flexed his fingers as if to limber them up, caught one last glimpse of us (himself?) in the ornate glass doors of the fireplace, and then, like a maestro, cupped my face between his hands. I no longer felt very steady and so placed my glass of liqueur down on the adjoining side table. He picked up his glass, moistened his lips, and then brought the glass to my lips so that I might join him in the sacred communion of our spirits.

I unabashedly sipped to the very last drop.

He then put down his empty glass, and while the flames licked around the logs in the fireplace, he skillfully unbuttoned the top two buttons of my dull blouse, wrapped his arms around me, and begun to nibble on my neck. My breathing began to catch. I just sort of let things happen.

Jack seemed to know exactly what he was doing. Button by button in slow and deliberate time, he unfastened my blouse. His mouth came down on mine, and his tongue began to probe, circling my tongue. It had been a long time since a man had kissed me! Independent of what his mouth was doing, which was setting me on fire, his hands next unhooked my bra. My admiration for his dexterity grew in leaps and bounds.

For just a brief moment, I asked myself if this was what I really wanted to do on a first date? My body resounded with yes, yes, and again yes. While the mind was saying no, no, and again no. Caught in the imbalance, the glass tumbled off the table onto the carpet, as Jack and I shifted our bodies in unison.

He got up off the couch to pick up the glass, rub the carpet with his handkerchief, and remove his gold tie-pin, tie, cufflinks, shirt and pants. He did it quickly. The time to stop slithered by.

Just when the flesh was about to succumb to the explosion of long dormant lust, my funny-bone began to twitch on the edges of consciousness. Jack stood before me be-decked in purple bikini undershorts, deco-rated and encircled by a herd of pink piglets. It had to be a gift from a former girlfriend. No man in his right mind would ever have bought himself pink-and-purple piglet pants. I grinned, hoping Jack would mistake it for sheer lust.

He was not fooled. "Why are you laughing at me?" His voice was defensive, wounded.

"I'm not," I lied. A giggle gurgled in the back of my throat.

And then the phone rang.

Jack turned around, piglet tails and piglet snouts pointing the way, and headed for the phone. It was a business call. For a full five minutes he talked, his voice reconditioning itself in the sounds of power.

Now, at last, I had time to think. What was I doing? Jack turned back twice toward me with a grin and a wave, as if to say, don't go away.

Which is exactly what I did.

With his back to me, I silently and quickly retrieved my dignity, got my blouse buttoned, and then sat waiting for him to finish talking.

After hanging up the phone, he turned, surprised to see me fully dressed, sitting upright on the couch. "Hey, what's going on here?" he asked, his voice registering sincere disappointment.

"I'm going home," I announced.

"But, we haven't, ah, finished our business." For once, Jackson seemed to be at a loss for words.

I looked at him, and in that moment, understood that Jackson Jalenko was a true narcissist — interested in high-priced items, business success, mirrors, and sexual performance — but the inner walls were empty. So, I spoke to him in terms I thought he might understand. "Jackson, you've got more important business to attend to right now." I walked out of his house, heading toward the nearest convenience store to call a taxi.

By the time he got his pants and shirt back on, I was already halfway there. He had to sprint to catch up to me. He grabbed hold of my arm and forced me to turn and look him in the face.

"Who do you think you are, anyway?" Jack was breathing hard from the run — hard, and angry. "What gives you the right to act like a know-it-all bitch? It's not like you're a great catch for a man." He clamped down hard on my arm with his fingers.

"Take your hands off me," I replied in a threatening voice.

My expression backed him off. He dropped his hand, stepped away, and glowered, "Queen of ice, aren't you? It doesn't get better than me. You're dumpy, frumpy, and frankly, not worth the effort. Go home and get a life, Meggie. There are lots of real women out there for me to hunt." He spun away and headed back down the street.

But not without his arrow having gored its target.

eleven

Moon Spaces

★ ★ ★

Snow falling and night falling fast, oh, fast
In a field I looked into going past,
And the ground almost covered smooth in snow,
But a few weeds and stubble showing last.

The woods around it have it — it is theirs.
All animals are smothered in their lairs.
I am too absent-spirited to count:
The loneliness includes me unawares.

And lonely as it is, that loneliness
Will be more lonely ere it will be less,
A blanker whiteness of benighted snow,
With no expression — nothing to express.

They cannot scare me with their empty spaces
Between stars — on stars void of human races.
I have it in me so much nearer home
To scare myself with my own desert places.

— Robert Frost,
Desert Places

A dark and brooding self-doubt, laced generously with self-pity, left me feeling restless, empty. Even Fritzie kept his distance from me on Sunday, as if I exuded an odor of distaste for anything living.

Snow was forecast for Monday afternoon. I wanted the whole world to bed down in white obliteration, a cleansing through frost, ice, and whirling snow. A quieting of all that was outside might help settle the internal storms.

Monday morning, Bev arrived at the office before me. "Now I want to hear all about your date with Jack," she eagerly pressed.

I shot her a malevolent look.

"What happened, Meggie? Did he try to rape you?" Bev was always ready to assume the worst when it came to men.

I shook my head. I was embarrassed. Bit by bit, Bev teased out the details of my pathetic first post-divorce date.

" 'Frumpy, dumpy, and hardly worth the effort'? God, Meggie, what a creep! I should have insisted we drive you home. He's not even a close friend to Coulter. It's just that it has taken you so long to start dating again, and then I go and fix you up with a bastard. *Mea culpa,* Meggie, *mea maxima culpa.*" Bev pounded her chest with exaggerated penitence.

It worked; I broke out laughing. "Bev, cut that out. You aren't even Catholic, and your Latin pronunciation is atrocious!"

She grinned. "Yes, but some of my best clients are Catholic! They've taught me more about guilt than I ever wanted to know. Friends again?" We hugged each other.

Despite the day's affectionate beginning, I was still too preoccupied to be as effective a listener to my clients as they deserved. I talked too much in session, a sure sign that I was avoiding the silence of internal thought. My timing was off. My clients were too much into their own issues to notice.

By mid-afternoon, the outside temperature dropped, the wind picked up, and the snow started to fall in earnest. Bev's evening clients called and canceled, as did all of mine — except Winona. I called her residence and Lucy answered the phone. She told me that her mother was outside right then, offering tobacco in thanks for the first snowfall of the year. She promised to pass the message on to her mother that she could come in early for her appointment. I was hoping that Lucy would suggest that it was too snowy to drive and that we should cancel the session, but she didn't.

I finished up my session notes for the day, said goodnight to the departing Bev, opened up the office curtains, and watched the snowflakes dance to the ground. After forty-five minutes, Winona's truck came into metallic focus against a background of a soft and moving wall of white. The truck door opened. Winona had on a pair of old-fashioned rubber boots, snapped together with metal bands and hooks. Her red ski parka looked new and warm. Winona clumped through the freshly fallen snow to the office door, pipe bag and handbag held in her mittened hand. I opened the door and gave her a hearty smile, two prisoners of the storm.

"Whew," she exclaimed, shaking off the snow and hanging her jacket on a wooden chair in the waiting room. "This is going to be one helluva storm! *Wazi*, the Grandfather of the North, wants us to pay attention. It is the time for the purification of the land and the people. Here, I want you to have this." From her snow-dusted pipe bag, Winona pulled out a smudge stick of sage and cedar, wrapped round and round with a fine red twine.

"You need it, Meggie, for the work you do." Without waiting for me to comment, Winona handed it to me, "You need a way to clean yourself up before you do healing work, just like Wazi out there is cleaning up the Grandmother." Winona nodded her head toward the window and the blizzard.

"You need it, Meggie, to clean up what's inside as well." She bent her head toward me. "Light the stick each morning, smudge yourself in the circle of smoke, and then smudge this room here to get rid of all those leftover shadows. Smudge this room at night before you leave. That way, you clean this place of anything bad that might want to linger here." She plopped herself down with a relaxing sigh.

She could not know how truly dirty I felt; the slimy impression of Jackson's hands on my body haunted me. "Thank you, Winona," was all I said.

A storm-enclosed silence fell down around us. The falling snow blanketed all external sound. Only the faint whirring of my wall clock intruded into the no-sound. You could sense day deepening into the corners of night. It was a long silence.

Finally, Winona spoke up, "It's good to go down into the dark of oneself. It took me a long time to learn that."

Her statement jarred me from my internal self-condemnations. I resumed my therapeutic role with her, "Is that something that Davis taught you about?"

Winona looked up at me for just a second

and exclaimed, "Hell no! My moon cycle taught me that."

I was puzzled.

She said, "A woman is always either going into the full of her moon or else she is going down into the dark of herself. See here . . ." Winona scrounged around in the flotsam and jetsam of her handbag, retrieving a short pencil with a dull point and the backside piece of an envelope. She drew a ring of circles on the envelope, then shaded them in gradations. It was the waxing and waning of the moon cycle. She laughed and said, "You can see that I am no artist. Still this will do."

Pointing to the two half moons at opposite sides of the circle, Winona stated, "Most of the time, we women are here, betwixt and between, coming and going — except when you get to my age. Then you become of the Grandmother Lodge. But listen carefully, Meggie, this is for you."

I leaned over in her direction, concentrating on her drawing. I didn't know where Winona was heading in the session.

With the lead point of the pencil, Winona tapped the apex of the circle, where she had drawn the full moon. "At the full of her moon, Woman is at the most giving of herself to those around her. She shines for them. She is at service to them. Her reflection is a full light to her family, her friends, her circle. Her life is lived within that full circle." Winona's hands moved outward in circular expression, to emphasize how a woman is to give-away of herself.

"You whites like to call it the fertile time, and perhaps that too is a good name. For our fertility is in the reception and the reflection. We shed light on those around us. But . . ." here Winona paused for the right expression, "there comes a time each month that Woman goes down into the dark of her moon." Winona pointed to the nadir of the circle, where the time of no moon was depicted as a black circle.

"It is during this time," Winona continued, "that Woman needs to draw inward to the silence, away from her circle of friends and family. The old ones knew this well and used to have a place she could go to be in the quiet. It was called the moon lodge. It is the time of self, alone. For only in the aloneness can a new moon be born within her."

"And if she doesn't withdraw?" I asked. "If she continues to be in the middle of everything, what then, Winona?" Winona could not have known I was a workaholic.

"Then, Meggie, she is always in the half-moon, never fully there for others, never fully there for herself. There is no new life. There is no death. The seasons don't exist. All is sameness."

"A friend of mine, David Grove, once said about psychological problems, 'Pathology is the *same* damn thing day after day. Life is a *new* damn thing day after day.' "

She smiled, "He's right, you know. One damn new thing after another."

I returned us to the topic. "I thought that women had to be apart from the men when menstruating, because they were seen as dirty. You told me that a woman couldn't smoke or touch the pipe when she is in her moon. That your medicine articles had to be locked up for that reason."

Winona started laughing. "Dirty? Where did you hear that?" She shook her head in amused disbelief. "Powerful is more like it. When her body lets go of all that it has been holding onto, and the bleeding starts, it is the time of fall. It is the time when the woman's body says, 'No baby this month,' and there is the giving way of the bed for that baby. It is a time of sadness for many women, an emptying time. There is death there, and in that death there is real power. The witches know of this power. They know how to use it, and the men are afraid. And well they should be afraid, because the woman in the dark of her moon can call upon all those energies of death. But dirty — no, never dirty."

"Have you ever called upon those energies of death, Winona?"

Winona appeared startled by the audacity of the question. "I'm not saying no. I'm not saying yes. There are some things I won't talk to you about." She paused and then said, "But I am saying that if you call upon those energies, they have a way of coming back on you — maybe not hurting you, but maybe someone in your family. Better to leave those Beings alone!"

I pressed her. "And did Davis' death have anything to do with those energies?"

Again, Winona seemed startled. She grew quiet, reached down in her pipe bag, pulled out her stem and bowl, tamper and lighter, and started filling the assembled pipe with her blend of tobacco and herbs. With her right hand, she wafted some of the smoke back over onto herself. It was obvious that she wasn't planning to answer any more impertinent questions. I had pushed her too far.

Or, as I later reflected, it may have been that Winona had decided that she had pushed me far enough into a world I was slowly beginning to perceive without much comprehension.

Before quitting the session, she warned, "There is danger in the rushing to knowledge. There is danger in finding the answer before the questions. There is danger, Meggie, in giving oneself over to a faith of allegiance, rather than to one built on experience."

Not only did I feel I was making no headway in the therapy with her, but now the old woman was rebuking me. "Hardly worth the effort" as a woman (according to Jalenko), ineffective as a therapist, and now incompetent as a student; my self-esteem drooped under the heavy load. What had happened to the self-assured Meggie who came to Michigan to prove her independence?

That evening, winter arrived. Intensified by its journey across Lake Michigan, a blizzard sailed inland and wrapped itself around the house at Chrysalis, driving flakes of crystalline snow against the windows. I watched in fascination, as the snow obliterated the familiar landscape and suppressed the night sounds outside. I felt restless, wound up like a tight coil about to be sprung.

Inside the house, a warm fire and a sleeping dog rebutted the tempest. Deep into the silence, except for an occasional crackling of the burning logs, I forced myself to read. A dull ache nudged into the small of my back and wrapped around to the front. I shifted position in the chair, but that didn't stop the hurting. Fatigue washed over me, as a wetness begin to seep down between my legs.

"Oh shit, I'm bleeding!" I lunged from the chair, startling Fritzie from his nap. I jumped into the shower, swallowed an Anaprox for the cramps, and retrieved the heating pad. Outside, the snow swirled, resolving, absolving nature's imperfections in white; inside, my body yielded, purifying itself in the crimson blood of the dark moon. I took my smudge stick, lit it, and wafted the smoke all around the bedroom. It was the right thing to do. Then I crawled into the warmth of my bed. It felt good to be alone.

twelve

Animal Nature

✦ ✦ ✦

Then suddenly my heart is wrung
By her distracted air
And I remember wildness lost
And after, swept from there,
Am set down standing in the wood
At the death of the hare.

— W.B. Yeats,
The Death of the Hare

All night and all day, the snow kept falling.
The storm afforded me a day off from work,
as traveling on the roads was treacherous.
Fritzie responded to the changed terrain of
snow by going outside and marking the territorial boundaries. Proudly, he held his leg
aloft, announcing to any wildlife visitor,
"Here is my place!" — the line between do-
mestication and the fauna of the forest.
Stubby of leg, Fritzie occasionally lost his
balance in the snow and momentarily disap-

114

peared into a drift. Despite their dignified appearance, terriers remain the slapstick comedians of the dog world.

His yellow mark on the bushes soon obscured by the snow, Fritzie clawed at the door to be let back into his den of warmth. I scratched the back of his ears in recognition of a job well done, wondering how it was that man and dog ever first agreed to their mutual covenant.

Winona came to mind. "There are the four-leggeds and the two-leggeds, the tree nation and stone nation, the winged ones and the crawling things," she had said. "They are all your relations, Meggie."

Already we had used up seven sessions. I figured that, by Winona's calculations, we had about nine more at the outside. Whether I wanted to or not, Winona was determined that I should be her student, albeit her last one. Despite Lucy's newly found optimism, I no longer doubted that Winona meant what Winona said. As a therapist, I didn't know what else to do but be Winona's student and hope that somewhere in her teachings I could find the key to keeping her alive.

Outside the window, a rabbit hopped into view, foraging for greenery amongst the hedge of snow-shrouded grapevine over the stone walls. Fritzie's head jerked up with interest. Hop, hop, stop, stop, journeyed the rabbit with the ritualistic steps of a cautious animal. Perhaps he was sniffing the scant remains of Fritzie's circle. He ducked under the grapevine, until only his cottontail and hind legs were visible, as the shadow of a bird fluttered by. Fritzie bounced in frenzy at the living-room door, yapping at me to let him out. The rabbit was large and would give Fritzie some needed exercise in the snow. I swung open the door, and Fritzie burst out in a dead run.

Into the snow-encrusted hedge, the rabbit burrowed, but the terrier dove in after him. There was nowhere for the rabbit to go, except over the edge of the stone wall. With a mighty leap, the rabbit catapulted himself high into the air and out into the white space. Likewise, Fritzie jumped in fearless abandon, jaws flashing open. I flung open the door and rushed out after them.

Before I had reached the stone wall, I heard the rabbit scream wildly, sharply — a piercing scream, soon muffled as Fritzie broke its neck. Then silence, the scream reverberating only in my head. Fritzie stood over the limp body of his prey, proud of his deed.

"No, Fritzie! No!" I yelled. He backed away from me, away from the rabbit. Enraged, I raised my hand to hit him, but stopped mid-air. Reason took over. Fritzie had only done what a terrier is supposed to do. My hand fell to my side.

I picked up the limp creature, four red puncture wounds on its side, the neck at a peculiar slant, two long rabbit ears dangling, and eyes that were open, but unseeing. Fritzie feigned disinterest, keeping a wary distance from me. With all my strength, I heaved the rabbit's body into the woods. My stomach felt sick, and tears stung my cheeks, growing chapped in the cold.

Together, the four-legged warrior and I retreated back to the house. Fritzie promptly found a place near the fire to warm himself, letting the hunt sink into memory and dreams. I sat there a long time, wondering about my revulsion. Was the hunter also a part of me?

thirteen

Web Strands

★ ★ ★

Look towards the West!
Your Grandfather is sitting there
looking this way.
Pray to Him! Pray to Him!
He is sitting there looking this way.

Look towards the North!
Your Grandfather is sitting there
looking this way.
Pray to Him! Pray to Him!
He is sitting there looking this way.

Look towards the East!
Your Grandfather is sitting there
looking this way.
Pray to Him! Pray to Him!
He is sitting there looking this way.

Look towards the South!
Your Grandfather is sitting there
looking this way.
Pray to Him! Pray to Him!

He is sitting there looking this way.

Look up to the Sky!
The Great Spirit, He is sitting over us.
Pray to Him! Pray to Him!
He is sitting there looking this way.

Look down at the Ground!
Your Grandmother is lying underneath you.
Pray to Her! Pray to Her!
She is lying there listening to you.

— Traditional Lakota
Inipi Ceremonial Song

After the snowstorm, the roads reopened and nature retreated before the world of work. Winona was grinning when she came into the office the next Thursday. She looked a bit more disheveled than usual, but her eyes reflected delight.

"My cousin's boy, Hawk, has come!" she announced. "He's a fine man. Used to ride the rodeo circuit, until he injured his leg. Good-looking Indian boy. Women always making eyes at him. He does odd jobs, can do just about anything. All the way from South Dakota he comes to spend time with me," Winona couldn't refrain from boasting.

Perhaps Hawk could give Winona reason to stay alive. I needed to know more about their relationship. "You seem really happy with his arrival. He probably has a lot of family gossip to share with you."

Winona shook her head, "No, he doesn't talk much about those things." She put on a face of mock disappointment. "Men, they just don't know what's important, do they?"

I couldn't help laughing. As a way to prime the pump and pick up the thread of continuity, I brought us back to her opening statement. "And so, he came a long way to spend time with you."

Winona's face was gleeful. "Hawk is here, because he wants to know things, and Davis can't teach him, because he's on the Other Side. So, I guess I'll just have to do it."

"Do what, Winona?"

"Teach him. My cousin raised her boy in the old ways. Hawk is an *inipi* man." She looked up at me and saw my puzzled expression. "Oh!" Winona realized that I didn't have the slightest idea what an inipi was.

"The sweat-lodge or inipi, Meggie, is our church. It is the oldest church on this turtle continent. Long before we had the pipe, we had sweat-lodges. All the tribes have them."

"Why is it called a sweat-lodge?" I was curious.

"Because in the dark of the sweat-lodge, there are hot rocks, which have been heated in the fire for a couple of hours. And when you close down the door, water is ladled on the rocks, and the steam makes you sweat buckets! It grows very hot in there, and the prayers get going really good then."

"So, it's like a sauna?"

"I don't know about saunas. Never been in one. I do know that when a couple of Danes came to the reservation and sweated with us, they said it wasn't much like their saunas. They sent us back a postcard though, saying that when they got home, they found that in the countryside, some of the old ones knew of sacred songs that used to be sung in such places. So maybe, their sauna used to be a sweat-lodge, I don't know. I do know they had quite a time in our inipi!"

Winona elaborated. "Davis was pouring the waters for the men's sweat. He put the two Danes in the back of the sweat. Now, Meggie, an inipi is made of saplings bent over with lots and lots of blankets and tarpaulins over the saplings. The inipi is about this high in the center . . ." Winona indicated a height of about four feet with her hands, "and about as wide as the distance from my chair to that wall." The distance was about six feet.

"So, you see, when you enter into the sweat-lodge, we say you are coming into the womb of the Grandmother. You have to crawl in, and you sit on the ground around the pit for the stones. Everything is in a circle. The door is made of blankets, topped with a star quilt. When the door comes down, it gets really black inside, except for the wonderful red glow of the stone people. You can't see the two-leggeds in there, but your ears grow real alert, and your nose searches for the familiar smells of sweet-grass and sage and cedar and tobacco.

"You don't have any of those fancy prayer books, like in the Christian churches. You don't sit with your back to anyone. And as for your fine church clothes, all you got on is a towel. We say you are truly naked, like the day you were born. And when the waters touch the stone people, steam swirls up and comes rolling down your back. Sometimes you can't tell what is steam and what is just your body purifying itself. It is a purification ceremony, and when it gets really hot — I mean *really* hot — then you get down to praying hard!

"So the Danes came in, and Davis put them in the back. The door came down. Davis sang his spirit-calling song and began to pour the waters. I was on the outside with

122

the rest of the women, keeping door for the men's sweat that day. We could hear those two young blond-headed men go 'Ahh . . .' as the heat first began to wrap 'round them. Then their 'ahs' grew into moans, 'oh . . .' and finally sighs, 'uh,' as if the heat were about to kill them. What they didn't know was that the first round is like childhood, quick and fast. It wasn't long before we pulled up the door to let the steam roll out. Davis had told the young men to go down on the Grandmother if they were too hot and that She would cool them off.

"I think when we opened the door, the young Danes were trying to dig their way out of the sweat-lodge! It was a really hot sweat, but do you think that the five other Indian men in that sweat would admit to it? No, they talked about what a gentle round that was! Of course, the poor young men were sure that they would not last another round, not knowing that the second round would be cooler. Yet they hung in there. Got to give them credit for that. It wasn't at all like their sauna." Winona gave a hearty laugh.

"So it was the intensity of the heat then that was so different from their sauna?" I interjected.

"No." Winona gave me a look — the same

kind of look my high school Latin teacher used to give me when I would slip on a translation.

"It's what happens in the sweat-lodge. It's the Spirits coming in. It's the praying and the singing of the sacred songs. It's the dancing lights all over the sweat-lodge. It is a sacred ceremony, Meggie."

Winona resumed her interrupted story. "So, after cooling off and resting a few minutes, the door came down and the second round began. One of the young men had a wrist that was bothering him. In the middle of the round, he felt an eagle wing tap him on the wrist, and then that eagle wing began to tap him up one arm and down the other, all over his body. Later, he told me, that he knew Davis had an eagle wing, so he was sure that Davis was doing some kind of healing on him. But you know, when you first sweat, you're more curious than you are respectful. So, the young man lifted his right hand up into the air to sweep the air. He wanted to make contact with the arm and hand that was directing that eagle wing. As his arm searched the dark space in front of him, that old wing tapped him up and down good. It finally dawned on this blond young man that there wasn't nobody holding onto that eagle wing."

"So what did that young man do, Winona?"

"He yelled 'Oh shit!' and then began to say something rapidly in his own language. Of course, it wasn't really respectful to say that in the sweat, but I think the others realized that the Spirits were having fun with this young man. The young man started praying really hard! In response, Davis began pouring on the waters, to help the young man who was praying. The faster the Dane prayed, the more water Davis put on the rocks, and the steam whomped up the heat higher and higher.

"The only way we women knew to open that door was for someone in that sweat to shout, *'Mitakuye oyas'in,'* which means 'All My Relations' in Sioux. Nobody was going to interrupt the powerful prayers of this young man. He got to praying faster and faster, louder and louder. Of course, we couldn't understand his language, but we knew he meant what he was saying. Finally, the young man yelled out in English, 'Open the goddam door!' What we didn't realize was that he had forgotten how to say 'Mitakuye oyas'in,' and he was trying out all kinds of statements in his own language to get that door opened. Nope, I don't think his sauna was much like what we do."

Winona sat back, grinning. This obviously was one of her favorite stories. I could imagine her sitting around the kitchen table with other Sioux women laughing at the folly of young, foreign, blond men.

Frankly, I didn't have time for all her stories and digressions. I wanted to turn away from the subject of foolish Caucasians to Hawk. His arrival might buy the time necessary to have the psychotherapy process take hold. Trying to bring Winona back on track, I said, "So, Hawk is a sweat-lodge man."

"Yup."

I asked, "What does he want to learn from you that he doesn't already know?" I wanted to know how long the Indian boy, her cousin's son, was planning to stay. Hopefully, a long time.

Derailing my train of thought, Winona digressed, "Are you smudging with the cedar and sage like I told you?" She looked past me and could see the smudge stick sitting in the ashtray, partially burnt. I nodded.

"Good, you are learning, Meggie. When things happen to you, don't sit there and analyze why and how and what. Just accept it for the moment. Be receptive. You can always do your thinking later. But your head gets too important sometimes, and you for-

126

get your eyes and ears and nose. Or you say, 'Why, that can't be!' and then you look but you don't see. Now, Meggie, I want to tell you something really important." Winona leaned forward as if to whisper a secret. I, too, leaned forward; I didn't want to miss out on what she was going to confide.

"Meggie," she said softly, "Hawk is only about two years older than you and real good-looking." She sat back mischievously, leaving me huddled forward to catch her great statement of truth. That was it?

I suspect that the insect who suddenly flies into the spider's sticky web has a moment of stillness before the struggle, caught in its own bewilderment — a moment of transition when the past begins to flow toward future. I could see Winona's direction quite clearly. Stuck, not knowing which way to turn in my life (or in the therapy), I could feel the web bend to the force of the spider, moving closer to her prey.

fourteen

The Handyman

★ ★ ★

The Spider holds a Silver Ball
In unperceived Hands —
And dancing softly to himself
His Yarn of Pearl — unwinds —

He plies from nought to nought —
In unsubstantial Trade —
Supplants our Tapestries with His . . .

— Emily Dickinson,
The Spider Holds a Silver Ball

Early next morning, Hedda, Olf's wife, called
to tell me that "The old fool was chainsawing
trees like he was just a youngster and pulled
a back muscle. He's supposed to do nothing
for a couple of weeks but take it easy. Fat
chance of that! Still, he asked our neighbor,
Jacob Hassler, if he knew of anyone to come
work on your roof. Jacob has a man who'd
be willing." I told Hedda I needed someone.

I was afraid that the roof would leak soon if I didn't get some work done on it.

I made Olf oatmeal cookies. The house soon filled with the sweet smells of baking in the oven. I had just retrieved the last batch, set them down to cool on the stovetop, when I heard a rapping on the glass window in the kitchen door. Fritzie barked in alarm. I told him to hush, wiped my doughy hands on my jeans, and opened the door. Standing before me was a man in his early forties wearing a beat-up black hat, the kind one used to see in the old television westerns. His face looked weathered but not hard; there were smile crinkles at the edge of his eyes. About six feet tall, more or less, his body was compact, strong and muscular.

He looked shy and uncomfortable standing there. He stammered, "Mister Hassler says you're looking for someone to help you, ma'am." He took off his hat and held it in front of him, almost like a shield.

I invited him in and shut the kitchen door behind him. "Would you like a cup of coffee and some oatmeal cookies? Sit right there." I pointed to the kitchen table and chairs. He remained standing, awkwardly. I extended my hand in greeting, "My name is Meggie O'Connor, and yours?"

"Slade, ma'am." He shifted his weight

from one foot to the other. With his hat, he pointed across the kitchen room to the chairs and table, saying, "My boots are wet, so I best get on out and do the work." During this whole interchange, Slade never really looked at me once. I summed him up as yet another man put ill at ease by me.

His eyes scanned the whole room, stopping only at the pan of cookies.

"Have one," I insisted and peeled one off the baking tray, so fresh that it singed my fingers.

"I like them when they're piping hot." The cookie disappeared rapidly into his mouth.

I told him what needed to be done on the roof, where to find the ladder and the tools in the old garage, and how much I would pay him. He listened to what I had to say and made no comment, except to shake his head up and down that he understood. Then he turned and was out the door, striding through the snow to the old garage.

I brewed up a fresh pot of coffee, poured it into a carafe, donned old clothes — patched work jeans, turtleneck shirt, sweatshirt, winter jacket, insulated gloves, and snow boots — and went outside to join him. He was already up on the roof, checking the dormers.

"Do you need any help?" I inquired.

He shook his head and bent to his work. I shoveled pathways around the house, put out birdseed into the feeders, filled the suet holder for the woodpeckers, threw Fritzie into snow drifts, and ran out of things to do outside. After two hours, I yelled up to the roof, "Slade, it's time to take a break. Coffee is on." He nodded an affirmative and clambered down off the roof. I told him he could leave his boots on while in the kitchen. I would mop the floor later.

Slade sat down at the table, as bidden. I put a steaming cup of coffee and a plate of Olf's cookies before him. Mug in hand, I joined him at the table. Fritzie sniffed around his pant legs to get a scent of the man, to know of his origins and intentions. I, too, was making my own observations.

His rugged features and dark complexion reflected Indian, Spanish, or Mexican heritage, or some mix thereof. Of medium build, his arms appeared muscular and capable of lifting heavy objects. His hands were large, yet his movements were slow and graceful. A man at ease with his body.

"Where are you from?" I asked.

"The West." That answer I could have surmised for myself from the slight twang in his speech. He seemed to be enjoying the cookies.

"What do you think of Suttons Bay?" I was going to have to work hard to make conversation with the laconic Slade.

He shrugged his shoulders. "It's okay."

I got up to fetch the carafe and more cookies. His eyes trailed me, studying me — when he thought I wouldn't notice. One got the sense that Slade didn't miss much in his scanning.

"What do you usually do for a living?" I knew my questions were intrusive, but I wasn't about to let Slade best me into silence.

"This, that. 'Bout everything. 'Bout anything that pays, to feed the belly and keep a place to sleep. Don't need much more than that." He was eating his eighth cookie, obviously a hungry man. I could see that Olf was going to have to settle for a smaller batch of cookies.

I persisted, "What brought you here at this time of year?"

"Family," he replied and then pushed himself away from the table. "Well, best be back up the roof to finish the work. Does anything else need to be done? Mister Hassler needs me a couple of days a week, so I've got some free time." Fritzie got up too and stretched his whole body, letting out a contented yawn and a small belch.

I thought quickly. "I have wood to be split and a couple of dead trees to be brought down. I'll work with you. It's a two-man job. How about tomorrow?"

"Do you know how to use a chainsaw?"

"Sure I do." What a ridiculous question!

Slade looked surprised. "Okay, tomorrow." He nodded his head, shook hands with me, and stepped out the door. He quickly finished up the work on the roof, put the tools away, and was off before I could pay him.

Fritzie came over near the woodstove to settle in for his Friday afternoon nap. I scratched his ears, "Well, what do you think, old man? Our new handyman doesn't talk much, but you seemed to like him well enough." Fritzie looked up at me and thumped his tail on the floor.

Months later, I discovered that while Slade had appeared to be eating an enormous number of oatmeal cookies, fully half of them made their clandestine way under the table into Fritzie's devouring mouth. No wonder they had become instant friends.

fifteen

Wood Cuttings

★ ★ ★

in this strong light
the leafless beechtree
shines like a cloud

it seems to glow
of itself
with a soft stript light
of love
over the brittle
grass

But there are
on second look
a few yellow leaves
still shaking

far apart

just one here one there
trembling vividly

— William Carlos Williams,
The Descent of Winter: 10/28

By Saturday, Winter had temporarily erased itself. The ground was soggy from the melted snow; the temperature was cool but not cold. Around ten o'clock, the sound of Slade's pick-up could be heard coming up the sand and gravel driveway. I donned a sweatshirt and heavy work gloves. By the time I got outside, Slade was already in the garage, looking for the power tools. I located the old, red, heavy chainsaw, "That's the one my father uses." I pointed to another corner where there was a shiny, small, yellow model, "That's the one I use."

Slade gave me a thoughtful look, but he didn't say anything. He examined the red chainsaw, testing out the sharpness of the blades and how much tightening needed to be done. I retrieved the oil/gasoline mix and the bar oil to fill the saws.

Unhappy to be tied up, Fritzie complained vociferously, yapping. I wasn't about to have him playing underfoot when we brought down the two large trees.

Slade hoisted the two chainsaws and saw-horses into the back of his open pick-up. It was an old truck, dented and used to hauling loads. I climbed up into the front cab, making room for myself in the bench seat, cluttered with old paper coffee cups, candy wrappers, a grimy blanket, a smudged map of Michigan and Wisconsin, and three pens on the dashboard. A hawk feather on a rawhide string dangled from the center mirror. Sitting in the truck felt like an intrusion into his private world, an act of intimacy when I didn't yet know much about him.

Slade swung himself into the driver's seat, smiling. "Like that dog of yours. Noisy, but he's got spirit." The engine reluctantly turned over.

I grinned and nodded in agreement. Anyone who liked my dog was all right by me. Still, with Slade, it was obvious that one should maintain one's distance. I directed him down the driveway, past the first two bends to an area dominated by sumac wood. The stand of sumac was trying to usurp my grandmother's apple orchard. The crusty apple trees, while still bearing fruit in the summer and early fall, were losing the battle with the upstart sumac. Deer prints circled round and round under the trees in search of apples, long since fallen and rotted on the ground.

The sumac trees were anything but stately; they extended their long, scraggly arms heavenward, as if at a revival meeting. Carrying the chainsaws and the sawhorses, we finally emerged into a clearing on top of a small hill, bowing our heads as we made our way through the density of sumac. There stood

136

a large dead pine and an old dead maple.

From the vantage point of the clearing, Slade could see all seventy-eight acres of Chrysalis in the morning light. Right below us, the green pines bowed respectfully in a soft breeze. Down past the driveway, the brown field of harvested corn shimmered with its bent stalks, while to the right, a black copse of cedar excluded the sun from its dense interior. Beyond, the steel-blue waters of Lake Michigan sparkled in the bay. Slade whistled under his breath at the stunning vista. "Is all this yours?"

"I don't own the land. I think it owns me." Again the trees bowed, as if in total agreement.

"Yes." He understood. We stood there, surveying the view for several minutes before turning to the work at hand.

He took the larger maple; I took the pine. We both revved up the engines of the chainsaws, after yanking on the starter cords, a task that always seems to threaten to pull my shoulder out of its socket. The woods reverberated with the whining sounds of the saws as they bit into the wood. Mine was the easier task, as the pine was softer and smaller in diameter than the maple. Several times, I caught Slade glancing over toward me, as if worried. As I edged the blade closer into the core, the pine tree began to shudder, presaging its fall from grace. The trembling converted to a large swaying motion; I stepped back, switched off the saw, signaled to Slade, and then gave the tree a shove with my foot. It yawed and tried to stay upright; for all of its life it had been addressing the heavens. It swayed a bit more earthward, then back again, reluctant to give up its stance. One more yaw toward the ground, and a great cracking sound erupted out of the cut. The pine plunged in one committed motion. The trunk slammed into the ground with a large thud, shaking the earth. With the chainsaws turned off, all became quiet.

Slade gave me a thumbs-up sign, pulled the starter cord on his chainsaw and went back to work on the maple. He sliced a wedge to the downward side of the tree and then cut in from the back. His arms held steady as the saw bit in deeper and deeper to the core. With his head, he motioned me to step out of the way. He yanked back the saw, cut the engine, and yelled, "Timber!" as the old maple lifted off its base and sailed effortlessly downward. Boom, it landed, and the ground shuddered and shook.

"Good work!" I shouted. A triumphant grin spread across his face.

My arms ached from the hard work. Slade placed the chainsaw on the ground, covered the blade with its plastic sheath, and then went to survey the damage. He sat down on the fallen maple, pulled out a crumpled pack of cigarettes, and offered me one. Perhaps it was curiosity, perhaps it was a gesture of camaraderie, but I accepted. He didn't know that I was a non-smoker. He found a book of matches in his denim jacket and lit one for me. I caught him watching me as I puffed without breathing in the smoke.

"I've tried to quit the damn things several times, but . . ." He shrugged his shoulders and inhaled deeply. It was the first time he had used the word "I" in his statements.

The rest of the morning we worked closely. After cutting up large pieces, he stacked the logs onto the sawhorses; I sectioned them into shorter lengths for the woodstove. We worked up a sweat but didn't stop until the task was completed. Then we hauled the cut logs down to his truck on the driveway. By the time we were finished, it was well past noon. After driving back up the hill, we stacked the wood in the woodshed. Unleashed, Fritzie ran wildly about our heels, bringing us old tennis balls smeared with mud.

"Lunch?" I offered.

"Got to go," Slade answered. "Sometime soon, we need to eyeball that old birch tree hanging over the driveway. Some of the top branches look mighty dead to me and could fall anytime."

I asked him how much he expected for his morning's work, and he grinned, "Whatever you're paying these days."

I paid him the equivalent of what I would have paid Olf, although Slade had done about twice as much work.

While Slade returned the chainsaws to the garage, I gathered the paper cups from the bench seat of his truck and threw them in the trash. He came up from behind and startled me. I felt embarrassed. "I hope you don't mind my cleaning. It would just give more room for your passengers."

He grinned in response to my discomfort. That made me mad. I yanked out the ratty blanket, folded it neatly, returned it to the seat, and declared, "There, that's better."

Only then did he speak. "Gets to be quite a mess sometimes, but then I don't have many passengers." He climbed up into the driver's seat. His hand rumpled up the blanket to spread it over the seat. He muttered, "Now, that's more like it."

I shut the passenger door and was about to turn away, when Slade laughed (at me?) and nodded, "Be seeing you before long."

It sounded like a promise.

sixteen

The Voices of Stones

★ ★ ★

And tezi means "stomach" or "womb." So this lodge is tezi. That's where the stone-people live. They contain all the elements that form the human structure. So there's a fire. There's also a fire that lives in you. There's a spark in there. We call it soul or spirit.

— Wallace Black Elk,
Black Elk, The Sacred Ways of a Lakota

Winona's truck rounded the corner, moseyed up the street, and parked in the usual spot before the office building. Winona perched on the passenger side. Driving the truck was a man with long hair and a black felt hat with a feather attached to the brim. He looked from that distance to be in his late thirties. As he emerged from the truck, he moved stiffly. I figured that must be Hawk, her cousin's son. He stopped and talked briefly with Winona, pointing his hand toward the hardware store. She nodded in acquiescence. For a moment there, I had begun to wonder if Winona was planning to bring him to her session. I wouldn't put it past her. But Hawk headed toward town. Winona was right in one thing; even from a distance, his body and facial features were striking.

Winona entered into the waiting room, wearing a house dress and brightly-colored beaded earrings — a pattern of earth browns, reds, bright orange, and soft yellow. She touched her ear lobe. "Hawk brought me these earrings from the reservation. They are the sunset pattern."

"They're beautiful, Winona."

Whereupon, Winona unhooked the earrings from the ear lobes and handed them to me, saying, "Now they are yours."

I protested, "I can't accept those earrings."

"Meggie," she scolded, "they were meant to be given to the person who would value them the most. It is in the Giving Way that all things can be shared by all people, that we can truly become human beings. Just as the four-legged gives away of his life so that you may eat and live, so too we must learn to give away what is important to us; we are all part of the same circle of life. Keep those earrings, until someone comes along and says, 'I wish I could have earrings like that,' and you will know that it is time to let someone else enjoy them."

Winona sat herself down, arranged her dress modestly around her knees, reached into her ever-present pipe bag, and pulled out a gray stone. It was a Petoskey stone, found only on the beaches of northwestern Michigan. Winona spat upon its water-worn surface. An intricate pattern of cells materialized out of the stone grayness — life frozen, hard and ancient, from the time when Lake Michigan was a large inland ocean, before the winds and sand and glaciers sealed it off from the Atlantic Ocean.

Winona spoke, "These are the most ancient voices on this turtle continent. People would do well to listen to the stone nation. They have things to tell us." She spat again upon the stone, and the cellular structure glistened.

"All around you is life, Meggie. My grandson and I watched the television last night. In New York City, everything is breaking down — the water pipes, the bridges, the roadways. People were moaning and groaning about how could this happen, but they forget that under all those tall buildings, underneath their cars, underneath their streets and bridges, there is the Grandmother. Have they ever asked Her how She feels about so much weight being placed upon Her? Do they ever stop and give thanks to Her for letting them dig underground veins in Her or scarring Her body with their highways? She'll only take so much and . . ." Winona began shaking her head back and forth.

"And what?" I asked.

Winona smiled, "Well, She'll shift." As if to make the point clearer, Winona moved around in her chair for a moment, seeking a more comfortable position.

I waited. Winona spat on the stone again.

"My people have always known, Meggie, that the stones speak; it's just us two-leggeds have trouble listening. As the old ones say, their breath may take a thousand years, but they are alive. In the sweat-lodge, if you know how to listen, they can teach you a song that will help you survive whatever life has to offer. They know about endurance."

My ears perked to the words "survive" and "endurance," words to offset a death wish. An opening presented itself. "Winona, I want to tell you about my mother."

Although I had interrupted her teaching, Winona leaned back in her chair, ready for a story.

"As my mother, a physician, has grown older, she has become more and more detached from the daily lives of all those around her. Not withdrawn or uninvolved. But her attention seems to be directed to other things. Stones, for instance." I nodded my head toward the Petoskey stone, cradled in Winona's palm.

I continued, "She collects rocks on the beach in Suttons Bay during the summer. She searches for the agates, reads about rock formations and the glacial history of Michigan. Every day, she hauls bags of stones up from the beach and tumbles them, slices them, peers inside of them as if researching the anatomy of time. Our family teases her about all her piles of rocks ready for autopsy. In light of what you've just said, I wonder if . . ."

Winona interrupted, "You wonder if maybe she isn't trying to understand more about life than she is about death."

"Yes," I replied. "But I also wonder if, as she holds those rocks in her hand and cherishes their beauty, if she doesn't somehow think more and more about the time when she, too, will return to earth."

Winona chimed right in, "And is that not truly the meaning of the giveaway, Meggie?"

The circuit of life. The insight about my mother brought me back to the issue of Winona's life, Winona's death. I put it to her,

"And is this the truth then for you as well? You plan to return back to the Grandmother?"

Winona's smile told me she was pleased at the progress I had made this hour. "Today, Hawk will accompany me to the lawyer, so that I can make out my will. It will be my last giveaway — on this side, at least."

"What about endurance? What about survival? These are the qualities of the stone nation. Why are you so obsessed with death, Winona?" I challenged her.

She didn't seem surprised at my outburst. "Those are the very qualities you need to learn from Them. But when you get older, Meggie, like your mother and like me, it is natural for your thoughts to be about returning home. Take this," she handed me the Petoskey stone. "You have so much to learn, Meggie, and there is so little time."

seventeen

Questions: No Answer

★ ★ ★

*Be patient toward all that is unsolved
in your heart and . . . try to love the
questions themselves like locked rooms
and like books that are written in a very
foreign tongue. Do not now seek the
answers, which cannot be given you
because you would not be able to live
them. And the point is, to live
everything. Live the questions now.
Perhaps you will then gradually, without
noticing it, live along some distant day
into the answer.*

— Rainer Maria Rilke,
Letters to a Young Poet

Winona's mention of writing her will galva-
nized me into action. The next day I caught
Bev in between clients and told her that we
had to discuss the case. As the day began to
shimmer down toward dark, we met in her

office. Before settling into the peer supervision, Bev grinned and asked, "Do you want me to fix you up on any more dates?"

"No way," I said. "That last date just about soured me on all of mankind! If it weren't for Coulter, I'd lose hope that a good man could be found." We both laughed; she acknowledged that all was going well between them. I was happy for her.

"What I don't understand," Bev said, "you have no problem with male clients, even if they try to verbally bully you or manipulate you. Yet when it comes to dating, you don't want to have anything to do with them. What happened to you?"

Perhaps Bev was expecting that I would reveal some dark secret from my past such as rape or incest. But it was much simpler than that.

"I thought when I married Tom, love would solve all problems."

Bev waited for me to elaborate, despite my reluctance to rehash history. I felt embarrassed but she was not about to back off.

I began, "You always hear stories about new husbands pestering their wives nightly for sex. It was just the opposite with us. I think he was both disgusted and frightened by the female body."

"Oh my God," Bev exclaimed, "you married a homosexual!"

I shook my head. "No. I married a deeply neurotic man. He resented my self-confidence, my sense of power, my love of work — all the things he wanted to feel in his life. And when neither my love nor his career success gave him that, then he grew angry." I didn't want to say anymore. Already this was proving much too painful. I looked away.

Bev prodded, "What happened when he got angry?"

I sighed, "Then he'd hit me."

Feminist fire flashed in her eyes. "Did you hit him back?"

"I'd try to get away from him, but he'd plant himself by the door yelling at me."

"What then happened?"

"I'd stand there with my body shaking."

Bev couldn't believe her ears. Meggie as victim? "You were shaking with fear?"

"Heck no! I shook, because I wanted to kill him, and I don't believe in violence. I wrenched my body into contorted spasms to keep myself from hurting him back."

"How long did this go on, Meggie?"

I shrugged my shoulders. This was too painful. I wanted to go on with my life, to obliterate the past, forget Tom — and Bev

149

was insisting that I dredge it up all over again.

"Years."

"Years?" Bev was incredulous.

"I told you earlier — I thought if I could just love him strongly enough, that would work miracles. But it finally became clear to me that the violence would only escalate over time. So I left. But in the meantime, the violence had entered into me. It sits there, like a foreign body in my psyche."

"A rage, undigested," commented my colleague.

"Satisfied?" Anger tinged my voice. "Can we now talk about Winona?"

Bev wisely nodded and ceased pushing me for any more personal detail.

"Winona told me that she came into town to have her will drawn up so she could have her last 'giveaway.' "

Bev sat upright in her chair, "My God, Meggie, she's really serious about this dying, isn't she?"

"Yes, she is," I replied, "and the crazy thing about it is that she doesn't seem the least bit depressed to me. As far as I can tell she isn't suicidal, she isn't mortally ill, and nobody is planning to do her in."

"Well, then," Bev relaxed, "what is there to worry about? You've got a patient preoc-

150

cupied with death but with no means to bring that about. Perhaps this is all just a manipulative bid for attention."

"No, I don't think so." I shook my head.

"What's her diagnosis?"

Bev's question was basically irrelevant, but professional classification offers a buoy of apparent certainty to psychotherapists, when awash in the uncertainty of life currents.

"Winona has no health insurance, so I haven't had to come up with an official diagnosis. 'Adjustment Disorder with Mixed Emotional Features' would be the closest. Yet it no more tells the truth of her decision to die. Or of her capacity in our sessions to take an old world in her hand and turn it, so that it scintillates with new meaning."

Bev tried another tack, "Look Meggie, you have this elderly client who says she's going to die in a few more weeks, but she doesn't have the means to do it. Yet, you've accepted her proposition that, indeed, she is going to die. And now, you don't know what to do, because everything in your profession says that your job is to keep her alive, until she regains a sense of hope."

I interrupted Bev, saying, "Only Winona doesn't show any sign of despair. So giving her hope isn't the answer. And that's where I am stuck."

Bev again puzzled. "But if she doesn't have the means to die, then where is the real problem for you in the therapy? Isn't it like the end-of-the-world people who say that on such and such a day the Apocalypse will arrive, and when that day comes and goes, well then they have to go about rearranging their lives?"

"But what if, Bev, what if in the Indian world you know enough that you can choose to die, without any act of suicide?"

Bev shook her head in disbelief, "I don't know what you mean. Like bring on your own heart attack?"

I nodded in affirmation. "I truly believe Winona knows what she is doing. And, damn it all, I really like this woman! There is something solid, rooted about her. I sometimes feel like a second grader around her, because she is constantly showing me new slants of light on an old world. She is one of those clients who forces the mutual growth of both of us. Although she can be pretty hard on me, I look forward to our meetings." My throat begin to tighten up against sad feelings. "I don't want her to die."

Bev could hear a long sigh emerge out of my intense feelings. A dark rain began to pelt the windows of the office. In a soft voice, she responded, "You're really coming to love this woman, Meggie. And you are afraid that your caring for her may blind you to your task as a therapist."

I nodded and kept silent, fighting the tears.

Bev adopted a therapeutic tone of voice. "I don't believe she's going to die, Meggie, because I've always been skeptical about these claims of people who can will their own deaths. I just don't believe it's possible. But I do believe that you think it may occur. And that you can't see a way to prevent it from happening, as she isn't depressed or in despair. It really taps into all your feelings about death and loss and what that means to you."

Bev knew she had struck home. Her voice became gentle, soothing, comforting again. "So, if she is going to die, then you are going to have to find a way to deal with that."

I nodded, miserable in the knowledge that she was right. I had nothing to say.

Bev continued, "All I can do for you, my friend, is to tell you I love you and am here for you, if Winona does die. You can come cry in my office — in between clients, that is!" Bev was bringing me up from my own sense of despair. She knew exactly what she was doing.

"Meggie," she asked in a tone of curiosity, "I've known you too long as a friend and as a colleague, and I know that despite how puzzling or how difficult a case is, you never just roll over and give up. So what have you been doing with Winona to try and keep her alive?"

I struggled with my answer. "In her later years, Winona has found meaning in her life from being a teacher to others, in a way that is healing to the sickness of their souls and psyches. She has decided that I am to be her last student, and so . . ." I was embarrassed by the implied narcissism of my answer but it was the truthful one. "I am trying to be a good enough student." Even as I said it, I knew of the inevitable downfall of anybody who tries to be "good enough" to keep the other person around. It never works.

There was a softening in Bev's eyes as she understood the trap I was in with Winona. She leaned forward and touched my hand, "I'm here, Meggie, when you need me."

eighteen

Heroic Action

★ ★ ★

The labyrinth is thoroughly known. We have only to follow the thread of the hero path, and where we had thought to find an abomination, we shall find a god. And where we had thought to slay another, we shall slay ourselves. Where we had thought to travel outward, we will come to the center of our own existence. And where we had thought to be alone, we will be with all the world.

— Joseph Campbell,
The Power of Myth

On my way into town the next morning, I saw the black-haired man, Winona's visitor, Hawk. He wore a red bandanna, wrapped tightly around his head, to keep his long hair from flying into his face. As I parked my car by the Post Office, I watched him enter into the Suttons Bay-kery for some morning cof-

155

fee. I deposited my letters of loneliness to East Coast friends and then debated what next to do. Of course, I knew what I wanted, but was it the smart thing to do? A cup of coffee on a chilly Michigan morning could do wonders for an indecisive spirit. The stomach won out over caution.

The baker had just put out some warm bran muffins, and there was a pot of decaffeinated Columbian coffee. Hawk had seated himself over in the far corner, reading a newspaper with the headline logo of *The Eagle.* He wore a checked red shirt, like a Canadian lumberjack, and old blue jeans with a few sparse white threads at the end of the pant legs. The tooled leather of his cowboy boots looked recently buffed.

The bran muffin was cooked to perfection, breaking open easily and melting the inserted pat of butter. I nibbled in between my covert observations and sips. Hawk turned the pages of his newspaper and didn't look up. From where I sat at my table, I could study his face. It was an intense face, an intelligent and handsome face, dominated by high cheekbones, dark eyebrows, and long black hair down his back. An austerity, a sternness in expression suggested hidden strength, a man not about to be pushed around by anyone. His left earlobe was studded with two silver earrings. When he rose and walked to the counter to refill his coffee cup, I noted a large beaded belt buckle with the End-of-the-Trail design on it cinched in a waist that was neither thin nor thick. His legs were long, but he didn't seem to move with the gawkiness of most tall people. He looked to be comfortable with his body and with himself. The thought went through my mind, that whereas the new hired help, Slade, was strong and compact, this fellow seemed built more for speed and fluid motion. Again, I had to admit to Winona's accuracy of description.

Unfortunately, a bran muffin, whether nibbled or crumbled into tiny brown dough balls and savored, soon disappears. I had no more excuses to sit and study Winona's prodigy. I gathered up my winter jacket and headed out the door, knowing that Hawk hadn't even noticed that I had been there. Or so I thought.

Brushing past me in the doorway was the town drunk, Clyde Bassett — unshaven, cigarette half-burnt and dangling from his lips, in a jacket that had seen too many winters. With his left hand, he gripped the arm of one of his teenage daughters. Her expression was sullen and resistant. He was, in effect, pulling her into the bakery, and she

157

was doing her best not to cooperate. Everyone in Suttons Bay knew the Bassett family, full of unhappy kids and a mother too worn out to give a damn anymore. Everyone knew that there was physical abuse of the children, but Clyde was too smart to hit them in a way that left bruises. Instead, he managed to belittle them, deprive them of necessities in the name of punishment, and threaten them. There was a suspicion that, as his daughters reached puberty, he abused them sexually while his wife turned her back and left the house.

Whether by fear or mistaken loyalty, none of the children divulged any sexual abuse; the Department of Social Services found itself unable to intervene. The sheriff's department treated the domestic violence in the Bassett home with indifference, masking their helplessness by occasionally cooling Clyde off with an overnight stay in the lockup and letting him go after breakfast. For everyone also knew that Mrs. Bassett would not press charges the next morning.

The Bassett daughter looked to be about fifteen years of age; already her face had hardened into set lines of anger. Pretty in a tough sort of way, her face this morning had turned ugly with the hatred. Clyde yanked her past me through the doorway. He smelled of alcohol gone foul in his system. He hadn't shaved for a couple of days and probably desperately needed a cup of coffee to orient himself to the new day. Something in his passing made me feel unclean, as if I was suddenly immersed in a contaminated space. I hurried on out the door.

I stopped at the Bay Theater marquee to see what was coming up for the weekend movie. Loud noises, shouts began coming out of the bakery, as some more patrons opened the door and left. I heard the girl yelling and knew that her anger had finally burst through into profanity. The door swung shut and the sounds of the argument were muffled. I lingered for the outcome, knowing that something was about to happen. Sure enough, the door flung open and out stumbled Clyde Bassett, head first and bent over, his arm twisted up behind his back and held securely there by Hawk. Clyde's face was contorted with frustration, rage, the wish for retaliation, but Hawk's grip was too strong. With one last shove, Hawk pushed him out of the bakery. Clyde lurched off-balance and stared back at Hawk menacingly, then thought better of it, and clumsily fished around in his pocket for his truck keys.

Hawk stood there, ready to accept the challenge. The daughter brushed by Hawk and ran to her father, the female comforter. She turned around and faced her rescuer, the doer of good, looked him straight in the eye with the bravado that her father now lacked, and said, "I never asked for your help in there, you mother-fucker. I can take care of myself!"

Hawk smiled and responded, "I'm sure you can."

Seemingly tired of this exchange, he surveyed the sidewalk and the street, letting his eyes fall upon me. He tipped his head at me in acknowledgment.

Clyde, meanwhile, tried to recover his dignity by getting in his truck, his daughter climbing in on the other side. They had, at last, achieved a negative kind of peace, united against the interloper in the family quarrel. Their truck pulled out and headed home.

Now that calm had returned, bakery patrons left the front window and returned to their coffee and muffins. Hawk pulled out a cigarette, lit it, and started to smoke. I was about to cross the street to my car when he said, turning toward me, "It wasn't the girl. It's just that hatred like that curdles the sweetness of a morning."

Glad to be noticed, I answered, "Yes."

nineteen

Male/Female:
The Dance of Wholeness

★ ★ ★

. . . But firm at the center
My heart was found;
Her own to my perfect
Heart-beat bound,
Like a magnet's keeper
Closing the round.

— D.H. Lawrence,
Kisses in the Train

"What do you think of him?" Winona's eyes were mischievous.

"Think of whom?" I played dumb.

"My cousin's son, Hawk. Fine-looking man, isn't he?" She beamed a grin, full of teeth, at me and decided not to wait for my answer. "Now, if I were young and going to be living awhile, that's the kind of man I would want. Strong yet gentle. Quiet and deep. He knows what's important. He's not looking for any woman to carve him into strength. He's his own person. He remembers the place of the old ones; he respects the children for what they can see, and he cannot. He's a good man, Meggie."

"I'm glad he came to be with you, Winona." A feeble response. A self-protective response. Still the image of him standing there, calmly smoking his cigarette after throwing out Clyde Bassett, flashed clearly into my memory with an electric charge.

Winona warned, "It will take a special kind of woman to snare him. He's been married twice before he was ready. His first wife ran off with another man after six months; it was the only way she could think of getting off the reservation. That's when he grew quiet, careful. His second wife rode the rodeo circuit with him. She even convinced the doctors it was okay for her to ride in the ring until she was six months pregnant. He admired her determination. One day, she wasn't paying attention, and the horse spooked and dropped her. She lost the baby. Maybe she felt bad about riding. She got to drinking, and she tried to get him to join her. He did for awhile, but their love got washed away in all that booze. I know myself how that can happen. He just upped and left. If it weren't for the sweat-lodge, he might be a dried-up, bitter chokecherry of a man." Winona laughed at the metaphor.

"But you can see that didn't happen. Lots of women are drawn to him; lots of women around him, making eyes, putting love potions near him, sitting next to him. He's looking for what he hasn't found yet. It's like he's got the scent; he just hasn't found the footprints."

I was curious. "While he's here, what does he do during the day?"

"I'm teaching him about herbs and healing. I'm teaching him some of the old songs he doesn't know. He's built a small inipi by Lucy's woods where it's real private. Mainly, we're doing a lot of talking while there is still time. He helps Lucy's husband chopping wood and picks up odd jobs here and there to give Lucy food money. We all like having him around. And he's got the one thing all women need most in a man."

"What's that, Winona?" I knew she wanted me to ask that question.

"A sense of humor. He makes us all laugh till our sides hurt from the shaking."

I started to say, "A man without humor is . . ."

Winona completed, "A man without vision."

She was right. That thought started Winona off on another tangent. "Lucy thinks that a man is someone who should come straight home from work, hand the paycheck over to her, do the chores, listen to what she has to say, and make her world his world. She gets angry at Larry for wandering off, taking time away from her and the kids. She tells him that home is where he needs to be. Larry works hard at that bingo hall, doesn't drink, and brings her the money, but a man, Meggie, needs his time alone. And women are always to the gelding of them."

I shook my head, puzzled. "I don't understand, Winona."

"Meggie, listen. You are a woman. Who are you stepping upon, when you put your feet on the ground?" A rhetorical question. Winona didn't wait for an answer. "You are walking upon your Grandmother. You draw strength from Her. You are her granddaughter, and in your body, you have the knowledge of Her the man does not. You won't understand this now, but you may later. You carry the sacred space in your womb. The man has to build his inipi, his sweat-lodge. You have it within your body, and each month your body purifies itself. The man has to enter into the womb of his Grandmother for purification, to get back into touch with the creation. When the woman enters into the inipi, she is entering into that sacred space already within her."

I understood and still was confused. It was as if two parts of my brain were competing for attention. What I knew, I discounted. And yet, I even discounted my knowing that.

Winona continued, "It's like this, Meggie. In your world, the mother is all. In our world, it was the grandparents who did the raising of the children, so it was the grandmother we turned to. The young boy, he looks at his grandmother or at his mother. He knows deep down, he is different from her. The young girl looks too and sees that she is of the same matter. And the boy, he grows up with the knowing of this difference. He learns to be alone, and he searches for a woman to make his world round again, whole. The girl, she is never truly alone. She is part of that togetherness of woman. She is joined to the Grandmother. She is frightened to be alone, for that is strange to her."

Winona shifted her position in the chair, gathering her thoughts. "Listen, Meggie. The man is searching his whole life. He looks to what binds him to the circle. He reaches out to Wakan Tanka. He goes to the hill, all alone, and cries out for a vision. He asks, 'What is my life about?' And he waits for the

Great Mystery to speak and give him a path. And then, for the rest of his life, he is moving on that path, always reaching out, always restless."

"And the woman?" I was curious about her path.

"The woman, Meggie, knows where her feet stand. From the ground up, it is within. She knows the rootedness of things. She says to her man, 'You don't have to fly off to meet the sacred in some other space. It is right here, alongside everything else. And sacred time, it is right here, behind the fog of everyday time.' "

"Yet, you think Lucy is gelding her husband?" I was trying to understand the implications of what Winona was saying.

She was growing impatient with my questions. It was so obvious to her. "Don't you see, Meggie, the world is made up of both parts? The man, he has the vision. He wakes up the woman from her sleep. She lives always below the clouds, and he pulls her to fly with him. He says, 'This is not all there is to life.' And when the man becomes so much of a bird, flying from one nest to another, one exploration after another, and all is a restless moving, she tells him that home is where the heart is. She lets him know about the spider who spins the design from within and the web between our relations. She taps her foot upon the ground to let him know what is solid.

"Don't you see, Meggie? A man needs a woman and a woman needs a man. The bird was born to fly in the air but needs that strong tree tethered to the earth. The woman was born with sacred space, but needs to go exploring out there before she can find it within herself."

A quirky thought occurred to me. "Winona, I know of a type of swallow that sleeps, eats, mates in the air and rarely lands on any branch to rest."

Winona looked up, grinning at me, "And isn't that just like some men nowadays?" We both laughed.

Winona still wanted the last word. "But . . ." she added with emphasis, "Hawk is different."

twenty

A Worthy Enemy

★ ★ ★

*The more I see of the representatives of
the people, the more I admire my dogs.*

— Alphonse de Lamartine,
Letter to John Foster

Lucy Arbre called the next day. She had
discovered that her mother had gone and
written a will. Her voice was upset, exasperated, scared. She wanted to come to the
Monday session with her mother. I agreed
to the family meeting. Winona was getting
her affairs into order.

Another call came from my parents, announcing they were going to brave the cold
weather and would arrive Tuesday night in
order to celebrate Thanksgiving at Chrysalis.
I reassured them that the earlier snow had
retreated.

"Is everything all right?" My father's voice
was anxious. My independence worried him.

"Of course," I lied.

Mother interrupted the phone conversation, "How's your social life?"

"I've yet to be invited to the local bingo games," I answered. "But I've got my eye on a Spanish fellow by the name of Manual."

She took the bait. "Manual who?"

"Manual Labor," I chuckled. It was an old joke in the family and still worked.

"Meggie," Mother chided, "you spend too much time alone." Without a man, she meant.

I gave her my most eloquent "yes, but . . ." response: "The colors of fall, the crispness of the air, the wild geese heading south from Canada, the beauty of an early winter storm, the darkness of the Bay — there are some compensations to loneliness."

After talking with them, I called Hedda to find out about Olf.

"He's out of commission for the winter, Meggie. Can you use the new man? Olf says he'd love to get out of the house and come help you, but I'm not letting that foolish old man injure his back again. By the way, he loved your oatmeal cookies."

"Slade will work out just fine," I reassured her.

My only problem was that I didn't know

how to get a hold of Slade. No need. At ten the next morning, his truck came roaring up the driveway. Fritzie greeted him with the joy usually reserved for long-lost friends, nipping around his feet and wheeling in circles of celebration. Slade ruffled Fritzie's ears and conversed with him in dog talk, growling playfully. He cast hopeful glances toward the kitchen.

"No cookies, but I've got some coffee."

At the kitchen table, I gave Slade a list of jobs to do. "I need to be writing at my computer today."

He looked somewhat disappointed that I wouldn't be out there, hauling and cutting wood with him. "I've never before worked with a woman who handled wood like a man."

It was meant to be a compliment. I didn't know whether to be flattered or dismayed.

"Can you come every Friday?" I asked.

"Sure," he grinned. Coffee finished, he headed outside to work.

I congratulated myself that morning on getting some professional work accomplished. It felt good to hear the sound of the log splitter outside and Fritzie's occasional barking, designed to let Slade know about any immigrant squirrels. My inner world burst forth with creative inspiration; my fin-

170

gers tapped furiously on the computer keyboard. As I grew increasingly focused in my thoughts, Fritzie's barking became increasingly distant.

Fate always intrudes on such moments, as if to dispel the idyllic notion that, indeed, life could flow smoothly. It began with a remote howling of pain, at the edge of my awareness. My fingers stopped, my stillness questioning the last sound. Once again, nearer now, the baying of an animal who had been hurt and was running homeward. Instantly, I knew Fritzie was in trouble. My terrier had encountered the large male porcupine who resided in the old oak tree down in the woods.

Pain humbled Fritzie quickly. He arrived in a bloody mess. His nose looked like a pin cushion. Quills protruded way back in his throat and on his tongue; he couldn't close his mouth. Saliva drooled from his chastened jaws. He clacked his teeth together in a futile attempt to get rid of the pain. Clusters of quills embedded themselves in his front paws, as he clawed frantically at his mouth.

Throwing a rug over his writhing body, I muttered, "Oh boy, you really did it this time! When are you ever going to learn?"

Of course, any terrier owner could tell you the answer is "never."

I yelled for Slade who came running. He gathered up his keys and led the way to his pick-up with me following, carrying the slobbering lump of dog. I deposited Fritzie on the front seat, and while Slade held him down, I ran back for my pocketbook. There were too many quills for us to pull. Luckily, Suttons Bay had a veterinarian, Sam Waters; it wasn't more than ten minutes before we walked into the animal hospital, carrying the terrier.

Fritzie looked at me with accusative, woeful eyes, as if to ask how could I have let this happen to him? He seemed to settle down more in Slade's arms. I was angry and upset, and the dog knew it.

Sam injected Fritzie with a tranquilizer. His short legs buckled under him, and Slade gently laid him out on the table. The veterinarian placed a protractor on Fritzie's incisors, thus forcing his cavernous jaw to remain open. It took an hour to extract all the quills. Some had slivered into the tongue; others were caught, like toothpicks, between the teeth. Over the dog's unconscious form, while Sam plucked the quills, Slade and I debated about Fritzie's heroic spirit and bullish stupidity.

"He's just doing what a dog is meant to do." Slade was being philosophical.

"He doesn't have a lick of sense." I adopted the realistic position. "If he did, he'd learn to stop biting porcupines. You'd think one time was enough, but this has to be at least my fifth trip here to have him dequilled!"

Sam interceded, "Well, a terrier is what he is." The voice of experience.

Slade continued, "That old porcupine is what Fritzie would call a worthy enemy. It's not like he's an ordinary enemy, like a squirrel. Squirrels don't come up and chew on the side of the house — unless you trap them in your attic. That porcupine," the philosopher persisted, "has lived a long time, and the back-porch pillar shows tooth marks to prove it. He entered Fritzie's place and tried to chew it up. When anyone hurts your home, you've got to stand up and fight. Even if that means you're going to get the stuffing knocked out of you. It's matter of doing what you got to do. And this here dog knew it." He looked appreciatively at the inert form of the white terrier. Sam nodded in agreement.

I was outnumbered. "Well, if I grant you the fact that Fritzie is a terrier, and terriers fight and defend their property, and you find that to be the noble thing to do, then tell me why he didn't finish off the porcupine? Why does he beat a hasty retreat each time he gets

173

skewered with those nasty little needles there?" I pointed to the flotilla of quills, some not so little, amassing in the vet's metal tray of blood-tinged water.

"Well now," Slade was thoughtful here, "you don't necessarily want to kill a worthy enemy, because then that would be the end of it, wouldn't it? Sometimes you just want to bruise them up a bit, make them a mite more respectful, let them know they can't just walk into your yard and do as they please."

"Fritzie ran because Fritzie was in pain. Fritzie attacked that porcupine, because Fritzie has a short memory."

Slade disagreed. "He remembered me."

"That proves nothing," I countered.

Slade adopted an exaggerated expression of hurt. "It counts for something. The dog looked at me this morning, and I looked at him, and we both remembered that we have a relationship based on something very important."

"What's that? Being macho males in a hostile world of worthy enemies?" I was going strong now.

"No," Slade replied, "it was something much deeper than that."

"What?" I asked, my curiosity aroused.

"The memory of a fine oatmeal cookie, just out of the oven."

twenty-one

Rifles, Respect,
and One Dead Porcupine

★ ★ ★

. . . And this you can see is the bolt.
The purpose of this
Is to open the breech, as you see.
We can slide it
Rapidly backwards and forwards: we call this
Easing the spring. . . . it is perfectly easy
If you have any strength in your thumb:
like the bolt,
And the breech, and the cocking-piece, and
the point of balance,
Which in our case we have not got. . . .

— Henry Reed,
I. Naming of Parts, Lessons of The War

All that afternoon, Fritzie slept the sleep of
the wounded. His paws twitched in dreams
of the hunt, as his nose, tongue, and throat
began the healing process. By supper time,

he lifted up his head, only to flop back on the rug by the fire. I read a novel and watched and waited for my four-legged companion to come out of his drugged state. By nightfall, he lurched to his feet, needing to go outside. I picked him up, took him outside to a bush, placed him gingerly on all fours. He stood there, bladder full, but was unable to balance himself on three legs. His ears drooped, and his eyes were dull. So what else could I do? Leaning his body against mine for balance I lifted a leg for him. Finally, in that most undignified position, he let himself arch a stream that pitifully missed the bush.

After bringing us back from the veterinarian, Slade had told me that the only solution was to shoot the porcupine. I agreed reluctantly. I preferred to live in peace with the animals of Chrysalis. Yet this porcupine not only had cost me money for vet bills but was chewing on the house foundation. I agreed to go hunting the next morning.

Daylight finally arrived. A hearty breakfast of oat-bran cereal, grapefruit juice, and coffee restored my faith that the companionship of dog and man was truly one that would survive its mismatched ambitions. By the time I was starting my second cup of coffee, I could hear Slade's truck coming up the drive.

I had researched my father's closet, retrieved his twenty-two caliber rifle, found and assembled a clip of bullets. It almost seemed as if I knew what I was doing. Slade brought along his twenty-two, parked it alongside mine, sat down, and waited for me to pour him a cup of coffee.

"Brr, the temperature is dropping." Slade rubbed his hands together.

Frankly, I hadn't noticed, so concerned was I in chilling my heart to the necessity of the hunt. I gave Slade a large mug of hot coffee to warm him up.

"I think we'll find the porcupine in the oak tree, probably sunning itself on a high branch." My voice sounded dead, devoid of emotion.

Slade, on the other hand, seemed cheerful and invigorated. "Let's get the job done," he spoke, finishing up the coffee.

We tied up the hung-over Fritzie, hoisted our rifles under our arms, barrels pointed to the ground, safety catches on, and headed down into the awakening woods. Black-capped chickadees flitted over our heads, and a curious gray squirrel watched us from a high perch.

The oak tree was immense; the top of it was just beginning to emerge into the morning sunlight. The floor of the woods was still shadow-cast and damp from the night moisture. At first, I couldn't see anything, as I quietly peered up toward the tall tree limbs, and instantly concluded that we had come hunting too early. But Slade's right arm lifted, pointing up to the high middle left branch. There, taking his morning snooze, waiting for the warmth of the midday sun to shine down on him, was a large porcupine.

Slade put his finger to his mouth, to warn me not to talk. He signaled to me to take the first shot, then took the safety catch off his rifle. I lifted my father's rifle up shoulder high, squinted through the metal notch at the end of the barrel to sight my aim, and then, to my horror, watched the porcupine shift himself into a more comfortable position as he straddled the limb. It would be so much easier to shoot him if he were still, and I could pretend that he was already dead. Slade waited patiently, sensing my indecision. I took a deep breath, heart in my throat, knowing that I was to become an instrument of death, sighted the animal, closed my eyes, and pulled the trigger. Nothing happened.

"Damn!" I exhaled and looked accusingly at the rifle, realizing that I had not released the safety catch. The porcupine, alerted by my expletive, understood he was in danger and began making a rapid descent toward a large hole in the tree. Slade stood there, infuriatingly signaling me to try again. I fumbled to lift the catch. Time was short, as the porcupine was now almost safely home. I swung the rifle back up to shoulder height in the approximate direction of the fleeing porcupine and without taking time to aim, I let off one shot. *Kaboom!* The rifle shot resounded throughout the woods.

The porcupine stopped in mid-flight, wavered to and fro on its branch, and then toppled out of the tree, slamming into the tree trunk several times as it fell. It thudded to the ground, and all the forest was still in its wake. A line of quills, arrowed into the tree trunk, bore testament to its long descent earthward. I felt sick to my stomach.

Meanwhile, Slade took his rifle over to the fallen animal. I heard him chuckling, as I was putting on the safety catch. "What are you laughing at?" I asked him.

He replied, as he rolled the animal over, "I am going to call you Annie Oakley from now on. This porcupine was cleanly shot one ear through to the other, and you didn't even aim the damn thing." Still laughing and shaking his head in disbelief, I watched him extract a cellophane-wrapped pouch of store-bought pipe tobacco, take a pinch, offer it in a circle, and place it in the dead porcupine's mouth. "That," he said, "is for the spirit of the porcupine."

I recognized the motion of the offering and spoke out, "Why Slade, you must have Indian blood in you!"

To which he replied, "Yup." He wiped his hand on his pants, examined the vertical trail of quills stuck in the tree, and ambled toward me. "Well, Annie, I think I better get the shovel and the wheelbarrow."

I didn't understand any need for the wheelbarrow and said, "Aren't we going to bury the porcupine here at the base of the tree?"

He didn't seem to pay any attention to my remark. He continued, "I've got a good skinning knife you can use, and there is a good pair of needle-nosed pliers in the garage. You need to find yourself a pair of heavy work gloves."

I didn't like the sound of this at all. "What for?" I asked.

He looked surprised at my reaction. "Why, to skin the porcupine, of course. To salt the hide, preserve the quills, extract the meat, and take the claws. What else were you planning to do with him?" He nodded to the large dead body on the ground.

"Slade, I thought we could just bury him.

You know, dispose of him, dig a hole, cover him up with dirt, heck, maybe even do a little reading over the grave site. But what do I want with porcupine meat or quills or . . ." I made an ugly face, "porcupine claws." Looking at Slade's impassive face, I knew I wasn't getting anywhere.

"Listen, if you want the claws, the hide, the meat, you skin him." I smiled. Compromise was always one of my strengths. I backed away from the corpse, gesturing that it was all his.

Slade shook his head, asserting, "No, this was your kill, not mine. His death was a gift to you."

I could almost hear Winona's voice now, joined in chorus with Slade.

Slade added, "You need to honor that gift by accepting what the porcupine has to offer."

The inert quilled body lay there in silent reproach. I felt guilty.

"Or else his death would have been wasted." Slade paced his words in deliberate fashion.

I could not withstand any more of the litany and capitulated. "All right. But I don't know how to skin a porcupine!"

Slade knew he had won. "Oh, I'll stand by you and tell you how to do it. The most important thing you have to know about skinning a porcupine is to do it . . ." he paused, grinning all the while, "very, very carefully."

twenty-two

The Dying of the Light

★ ★ ★

Do not go gentle into that good night,
Old age should burn and rave
at close of day. . . .

And you, my father, there on the sad height,
Curse, bless, me now with your fierce tears,
I pray.
Do not go gentle into that good night.
Rage, rage against the dying of the light.

— Dylan Thomas,
Do Not Go Gentle into That Good Night

Pinprick sores dotted my fingers where the porcupine quills had jabbed me, as I had gingerly separated the thick hide from the body of the porcupine. Slade had graciously accepted my gift of the meat of the porcupine, the claws, the quills, and the hide — once I had tacked it down on a board to be salted and dried. I told him that was his due as my teacher. When I tried to pay him for

183

the morning's outing, Slade laughed and said, "No amount of money was worth the watching of your face around that porcupine. I didn't know a woman could hold her breath so long and skin a porcupine while keeping her hands at such great distance from herself! The porcupine is payment enough."

"I'm glad to be rid of it." I felt like a murderer with blood on my hands.

Sunday, in an act of female purification, I cleaned house. My bedroom was stacked with magazines and books to be read. I didn't like dirt on the floor, dust on the counters and bureau tops, or filthy sinks, but I had a high tolerance for a kind of orderly clutter. My parents, however, were of the old school of cleanliness. That Sunday found me scrubbing spots off the walls, washing the kitchen floor, throwing out old magazines, and hiding stacks of books in obscure corners. I made up my parents' beds.

By nightfall, I was really tired. Housework can be, at one and the same time, boring and satisfying. The house at last was neat enough to pass Mother's inspection. I slept the sleep of the good-enough daughter. Monday promised to be a busy day.

Winona's appointment was the last one; both she and Lucy were going to be present. I geared myself up for an emotional session, smudging the room with the smoke of the sage and cedar stick. When Winona entered into the room, a flare of her nostrils told me she detected the familiar aroma. Her discreet sniffs brought a tiny smile to the corners of her mouth. She sought out her stuffed chair and plopped herself into it. Lucy lagged behind her mother, searching the room for a position opposite the old woman. It was obvious that Lucy was in a confrontational mood. The contrast between mother and daughter was most apparent in the way they presented themselves. Lucy was dressed smartly in a brilliant green, satiny blouse with a dark gray skirt, low heels, gold earrings — the appearance of a fashionable career woman. She looked first where she was going to sit, then seated herself in a poised manner. Her back was straight; her facial expression was serious, brooking no nonsense; her hands were folded precisely in her lap.

Winona, on the other hand, had a wrinkled appearance. Her dress was another house duster, shapeless and comfortable, not restraining her body into any fashionable statement. Her shoes were scuffed, worn out at the back. Whereas Lucy was wearing stockings, Winona had on long blue socks. I had before me the sleekness of youth facing the

185

ease of wisdom. What was different this time about Winona was the absence of any mischief in her face. Her expression was one of no expression. She neither looked at me nor at her daughter. Winona had retreated inside of herself. It was obvious that she wanted no part of this session.

It occurred to me that I had committed a therapeutic blunder in inviting Lucy to join us for this session, thus creating distance with Winona. On the other hand, time was getting short, and I felt the need to bring the issue of the impending death out into the open. Lucy's discovery of her mother's will provided the perfect opportunity. I started the session, providing focus for discussion:

"Winona, as you may already know, Lucy called me. She was very upset when she discovered that Hawk had taken you to the lawyer so that you could get your will written."

Lucy nodded her head in assent.

I continued, "I asked Lucy to join us for this session, as I think it important that she be able to share her feelings about this matter with you."

Lucy studied her mother's face for reaction. Winona's expression remained hooded. I could see that I was going to have to work hard in this session, what with one individual chomping at the bit and the other barely in the same room with us.

I continued, "I'm going to let Lucy talk first. I think it's important, Winona, that you acknowledge that you have heard what she has to say. Ignoring her is not going to make her go away." Winona continued to stare at her feet.

Winona's rudeness toward her daughter grated on me. I wanted to go take her by the shoulders and shake her. My foot began to tap impatiently on the floor. I decided to put it directly to her. "Tell Lucy why you want to die."

Winona said not a word.

Lucy leaned forward, her face struggling to mask her resentment with reasonableness. Her voice, however, carried a prosecutorial tone as she turned to her mother, "I asked Hawk the other day why the two of you took so long in town; that's when he told me about your going to see a lawyer to write up a will. At first I thought he was kidding me, but he wasn't, Mama. I then asked him why you were doing that, because you're not sick or dying or anything like that. He looked at me with pity, Mama, as if I was some kind of young kid who wouldn't understand. So then I knew you'd been talking to him about dying, behind my back. I felt like there was some goddamn conspiracy going on in my house!"

Lucy paused a moment and then shot off into another direction, carried by emotion and lack of comprehension. "You told me that you liked coming in here." With a sweep of her hands, she indicated the office.

"You told me you were feeling better, that talking to Dr. O'Connor helped you. Well, what have you been doing all this time, for which I've been paying? I thought you had given up that idea of dying. Obviously . . ." Lucy threw an accusatory look over in my direction, "I'm the only one in the dark. Everyone else seems to have accepted this idea of yours that you are going to die pretty soon."

Winona didn't stir but seemed to be listening.

I asked Lucy, "What does your husband, Larry, say about all this? What are his feelings?"

Lucy neither welcomed my interruption nor did she appreciate having to give me the answer she did. She spoke with sarcasm. "Larry tells me that my mother has to make her own decisions. Larry is not talking about *his* mother, mind you. He tells me not to get involved. Larry sometimes is full of shit!"

I felt compassion for Lucy. Winona was of

no help here, keeping her silence. "And so, it's like nobody understands how much you love your mother and want her to stay alive?"

That insight immediately dropped Lucy from her defense of anger into a well of long-hidden grief, grief from the times when Winona wasn't there for her, grief from the alcoholic-ridden years, grief for the shortness of the time remaining to get to know her mother. Lucy's face fell with sadness.

I wondered how Winona could remain so silent, so still in the face of Lucy's sorrow. I wondered if Winona gave up being Lucy's mother a long time ago, when Lucy was but a little girl, and that Winona just didn't know how to find her way back.

Grief unheard will soon revert to rage. I wanted Winona to pay attention to the integrity of Lucy's sadness, before Lucy retreated back to accusations. I pushed the issue here, "In her own way, Winona, Lucy is saying that your death means you will be abandoning her." Lucy nodded her head in miserable assent.

Winona moved her feet, as if she was wiggling her toes, trying to get some feeling back into them. She shrugged her shoulders and shifted her position in the chair, all the while trying to gain time. Neither Lucy nor I relieved her of the burden of our silence. All three of us were bound in the intimacy of the moment's stillness.

Winona was evasive, but at last she spoke. "I wanted to make sure that I was doing it right. That's why I went to the lawyer."

Lucy responded before I could, flashing out, "That's not the issue, Mother, and you know it! Why is death so attractive to you? Don't you care about your grandchildren? Don't you care about my feelings?"

Winona looked at her shoes again. Her voice was quiet. Both Lucy and I had to strain to hear it. "It's just time. It's just time."

Then and there, it occurred to me that I was hoping that Lucy might make Winona feel so guilty, she would choose to affirm life. I didn't want her to go away. I pushed at Winona, a little harder this time. "Lucy is telling you that she still needs you, that she still wants you to be around her, to teach the grandchildren, to tell her of the love you have for her, Winona."

Winona sighed. Lucy and I had succeeded in breaking through to her. She looked up at both of us, and there were tears in her eyes. Her hands, always before so expressive and strong, now seemed held in a gesture of futility. She cleared her throat and addressed her daughter, "There is no way in our language to say 'I'm sorry.' There is only the way of knowing, of saying, 'Yes, I did that.' Of saying, 'Yes, I am responsible.' I have loved you, but you and I — we have never been in the same circle. I gave you life, my daughter — maybe not the kind of life you would have wanted. But what you do with that life is what you choose. I have respected that. I ask you to respect that there comes a time when I must go on with my life."

Lucy was having none of that. Her voice raised in anger. "We're not talking about my life or your life, Mother. We're talking about your death. Let's not confuse the issue!"

"Winona," I interrupted, "tell your daughter how you came to this decision about dying in two moons. Otherwise, the only sense she can make of it is that you don't care enough for her to stay around."

My intervention had the effect of quieting Lucy, placing her years of anger and feelings of neglect on momentary hold. Winona rounded her hands into one circle, tapping the fingertips together. She grew thoughtful, as if looking for the words that would make sense to her modern daughter and the white psychologist. "I have had two lives. The one before Davis when I was lost and drunk and not much of a mother to you, Lucy. My second life began with him, meeting him at the courthouse. I had gotten so low; I was no longer a human being, and yet, the Grandfathers knew I wanted to be a human being. They looked at me and said, 'Let's have pity on this two-legged.' They brought me to Davis. The Grandfathers knew he needed a woman, a woman for him to teach the old ways. Because in the teaching ways, you always are learning yourself. It was good, and we gave balance to each other. A man of medicine needs the woman to balance him. A woman needs a man. It was good."

She paused before continuing, still tapping her fingertips into a circle. "I learned the plants. He knew the ceremonies. I learned the woman knowledge and the ways of the Grandfathers. Davis brought me the path of the sun. I gave him the mirror of the moon. He taught me flight, the ways of the winged ones, cutting through this . . ." Winona gestured in a sweep about the room, "this world to the world of the Spirits. He taught me the stillness that lets me listen. And then I knew that the Creator hadn't gone away from this world, was still here, still trying. And Davis gave me the gift of letting me love him, and in that love, I brought him the Creation. We came together and . . ." Winona looked at her hands, "and made a circle of our lives."

Lucy winced, remembering that her

mother's recent words had excluded her from that circle. Winona's face grew softer, sadder, as she moved on with her story. "It was meant to be. We knew the Grandfathers had brought us together. I became a human being. I became a healer. I learned that to give away meant first my pride, my sense that I was bad because I was not good, the shame of my first life. All pride. I learned then that to give away next meant not to hold onto things which others needed more. Things are just things.

"Then I learned — and oh this was hard! — that to give away, to become full of the Spirits, meant I had to let go of my self. I had to die then. I no longer held onto being Winona. I gave up being your mother then. I became of the Grandmother and the Grandfathers. They were now within me, and I was of Them. In that giving away, I cried for the loss of who I was, and for a time there, I went crazy. You were away at college then and didn't know. Davis, he just stood by, knowing it was the old way, knowing how scared I was to die to myself. Do you understand what I am trying to tell you?"

It was a rhetorical question, not requiring any answer. I suspect that, if pressed, both Lucy and I would have replied, "No and yes." We both nodded our heads, wanting Winona to continue.

"But one thing I couldn't give away was . . ." Winona stopped, sighed, and looked ready to cry, pressing her fingertips hard against each other. She sighed again, a heavy sigh, and haltingly with great effort, kept on with her answer, "The one thing I could not give away was my need for Davis. He was my lover, my teacher, my husband. He was my partner in prayer. Most of all, he was my friend. Each morning, I would wake up and see his grisly face, baggy eyes, lizard skin, and I would be grateful for being alive. I would get up and sing the sunrise song, saying, 'Thank you for my life.' And each night when the sun would leave, I would say good-bye to it, saying, 'Thank you for my life.' Each day, Davis, he'd say, 'Today is a good day to die.' " Winona laughed at her remembrance of this.

She turned gently toward her daughter, "It sounds like we were saying something different from each other, but no. It was the same thing. Don't you see that now? Davis knew that to cross over is just that, to go on with the next life. I knew, that when we got married by that sacred pipe, we were making it so that we would always be partners, this life and the next and the next. When he died at the end of last year, I knew it was just going to be time. A time of waiting for me. I still get up and say, 'Thank you for my life.' There is no one there in my bed, no grisly face to touch in the morning. You see, I finally had to do even that — I had to give away him." The long-denied tears began rolling down her face.

Lucy leaned closer to her mother, touched by the tears. She reached out, saying, "Mama, we all miss him. He was a good man. He was the only father I really knew." Tears began to gather in her eyes. Winona found the box of tissues on the couch and wiped the tears, as if ashamed at the show of such emotion.

She drew herself up in her chair and shook like an animal casting off the wetness from an unexpected rain. She had more to say: "Pain of the heart has a way of making us more spiritual. When we're happy, our words of gratitude are short and sweet. When we're sad, our prayers are long. After Davis died, I got to a lot of praying. I was angry at the Grandfathers for taking him away. I was scared, because what had been whole was now only half. I took my sacred pipe and held it out before me and said to them, 'What do you want of me now?' I was crazy with my emptiness, but I hadn't forgotten how to listen. And when you pray with that *Chanunpa*, the pipe . . ." Winona turned and addressed this statement to me, "They will hear your prayer and They will answer you. And so I got quiet, knowing all I had to do was to wait for Them. And They did. They told me that what I had to do then was to give Davis away and not to hold onto him. They scolded me and said that as long as I held onto my sadness, my loss, that I wasn't letting Davis go on with what he needed to do over there. I was keeping him bound to me, to this side. I had to let him go."

Winona briefly looked at Lucy then back to me. I didn't know why it was so important to her that I understand these particular words. Even in her sadness, Winona never forgot that she was a teacher.

"Still with anger, Meggie, I picked up my Chanunpa. I held it out there for all the Grandfathers to see. I said in a loud voice, 'I give away Davis now. I give him back to you. I won't call out for him anymore in the dark of the night. I just ask you for one more thing.' I must have been very crazy to be so demanding of the Spirits! They seem always to take pity on you, if your suffering is real. They asked me what this one thing was that I wanted." Winona hesitated, her voice broke, and she couldn't go on.

I was curious and asked the same question. "What was that one thing?"

Winona looked up at me. "I asked Them to let him know I loved him and to be there waiting for me when I came across."

"Did they agree to do that?" I couldn't help interrupting. Hell, what did I know about the whims of spirits?

"They told me he already knew that. They told me that the Chanunpa bound us forever. They told me that it was time to let go of him."

It was Lucy's turn to ask the questions. "And did you, Mama? Did you let go?"

Winona recovered her composure, sat up straight, and said, "When I gave him away with that pipe, it was done. And these past few months, I've been waiting. I am old and not doing much healing these days." Winona looked at me, as if I might be an exception to that statement.

"But my life is not mine," she said in a voice of resignation. "I gave that away long time ago. I wait. I'm tired. I was praying, end of this summer, a lovely still night. And They came to me. They told me I had given myself to the people, and that now I could choose. I could stay here for awhile longer. Or I could cross over, in the dark of the winter. They told me my body would go back to the Grandmother Earth, but my spirit would go to the other side.

"I've been waiting. I told Them I was tired. That I was ready to go. They said they would come for me soon."

It was done, the telling of it. The room settled into quietness. There were no more gusts of rage. We were all tired, deep in our own reflections. Winona had made her confession. In her long speech, she had allowed me to see into a world that I had never known existed. I had a sense of both awe and wonder.

For Lucy, however, the speech made her understand that she would also have to learn the meaning of the giveaway. She looked lovingly at her mother, reached out and took the old woman's hands into her own. With a voice full of choked emotion, she whispered, "Oh Mama, you will never know how much I will miss you."

twenty-three

Moments

★ ★ ★

Days are made of moments,
All are worth exploring.
Many kinds of moments —
None is worth ignoring.
All we have are moments . . .

— Stephen Sondheim,
Into The Woods

I could hear Bev's exasperation over the telephone. "Meggie, this just doesn't make any sense to me. Your client is not ill, depressed, or suicidal, and yet you do a family session of mourning over her impending death. Do you know how crazy that sounds?"

Of course, I did.

Bev continued, "Maybe, I'm not the right colleague for you to consult with on this case. I don't understand. You usually are so rational, Meggie, too rational at times. But this case of your Indian client has really

199

thrown you for a loop. I find myself doubting your objectivity, your over-involvement. It's like a *folie-a-deux*."

Bev was referring to a condition when two people enhance each other's craziness. I couldn't resist upping the stakes. "No, it's more like a *folie-a-quatre*. Remember, Lucy now believes in her power as much as Hawk and I do."

This reference to Hawk gave Bev a chance to switch to a subject more dear to her heart than my therapeutic conundrums. "How is your love life going?"

"Bev, you sound like my mother, who, in twenty-four hours, will be asking me the same question. With you, I can be honest. It's not going anywhere. Zip. Zilch. A good man is hard to find."

Bev chorused, "And a hard man is good to find!"

Bev's good fortune in meeting Coulter made her reluctant to analyze or rationalize the drought conditions I was experiencing. She didn't want me to think she was bragging, and yet I knew she wanted nothing better than to tell me of all the wonderful adventures and conversations she was currently having with him. I did not begrudge her joy, so long in coming for her. I just wanted to have a little piece of it in my life too. After hanging up the phone, I felt even lonelier.

I had a dream that night, as I lay tossing on my mattress:

I was out in Chesapeake Bay, sailing with Walter Cronkite. The hot summer sun was shining off the sparkling water. The gulls were squawking overhead. His face was grandfatherly, full of strength, humor, wisdom. His skin had that sheen of those who sail a lot. As he held the tiller in his left hand, he turned to me and said, "I am writing my autobiography, Meggie." I looked at him too, in a familiar kinship way, laughed in the salty air, and replied, "So am I! Do you know, Walt, what the title of my autobiography is going to be?" He shook his head, smiling in anticipation of my answer. I replied, "Ravaged by a Savage!" In the sun-warmed sea, our laughter shimmered out across the waves.

I woke back up in Michigan, on a chilly morning. The bed was well moored to the floor, as I slowly anchored myself to time and place. *Ravaged by a Savage* sounded like a spicy title for a romance pulp novel; I didn't really know what it had to do with me. I tucked the unconscious back into the folds of my consciousness, threw myself out of bed, and moved quickly to fire up the woodstove.

The house looked a lot tidier than it had in a long time. I made sure not to let any breakfast dishes linger in the sink. Having aired out my parents' room, I opened it up to the heat in the rest of the house. The quilts and comforters were precisely arranged on the beds. Firewood was stacked neatly in the wood-baskets; an unlit fire was ready in each fireplace. I removed a casserole from the freezer to defrost during the day. Once more, I checked the silverware tray to make sure no mouse had wandered in overnight. My parents' bathroom had been scrubbed spotless, and except for the hard-water stains, the enamel bathtub gleamed. All was in a state of preparedness for their visit.

At the Traverse City Hospital, the staff discussed their Thanksgiving plans. Many of the adolescent inpatients were being allowed a visit home, so there was an air of excitement in the psychiatric ward. Infractions of the ward rules were overlooked. The doctors were busy making sure all their patients had appropriate medications. The nurses were busy making sure the physicians knew what they had to do before the patients could be discharged on home visits.

My day finished early, so that I could drive to the Traverse City airport to pick up my parents arriving on a late afternoon flight.

The Thanksgiving crowd made the solitary airport much busier than usual. The airport gift shop, which sold gum, Cherryland souvenirs, and small bottles of maple syrup, competed with a crowded coffee bar.

A four-year-old girl, with a bundle of brown curls bouncing on her head, tap-danced in front of the rows of waiting-room chairs. Her mother, slouched down in her place, watched her listlessly.

More people drifted into the waiting area, having ridden up the escalator. The energy in the large room began to shift in anticipation of the plane arrival. The four-year-old stopped, looked up and studied the newcomers with curiosity. Her mother began to fuss with the little girl's hair and clothes, straightening here and there. The child tore loose from her mother's hands and ran to the big window over the runway, looking far out into the twilight. I too put my book down and went over to where she was peering into the fading light. "Do you see anything yet?" I inquired.

"My Daddy is coming on the plane. He's been away." She said this in full confidence that I would know her Daddy.

"Oh, you must be happy that he's coming home!" I put all my childlike enthusiasm into the remark.

A slight shift in her body, a moving into the pane of glass, a small inflection of sadness edging her words, she replied, "Oh, Mommy says he can't stay." And then, as if she had said too much, she ran back to her mother's side without looking at me. I now carried the taint of her confession.

From the adolescents in the hospital to Hawk and Slade, to the little girl and her bored mother awaiting the child's father, to others in the mingling crowd gathering near the airport gate — we all contained stories worthy of telling, worthy of hearing. I remembered Winona talking to me of the spider, the old grandmother who every day spins her web with a knowledge of that web deep within her. Winona had said to me, "We two-leggeds have a design. Only, we don't see it till near the end. We stand on the edge of things, waiting, always waiting for that design to unfold out before us. To give us that plan of action. But she knows, Iktomi, the spider, that the web is in the unfolding. And then we think we make the big decision, oh-ho! and that turns out to be just a tiny thread. Iktomi, it is she who has the courage to go beyond the edge of things."

My internal musings were interrupted as the crowd pressed toward the gate, in reaction to the announcement of the plane's arrival. The time of waiting was turning over, like a current of air about to touch down on the ground, a last twisting in the wind as the long journey ends and a new one is begun.

twenty-four

Our Lady of All Wild Things

★ ★ ★

Artemis . . . was Goddess of the Hunt
and Goddess of the Moon. The tall,
lovely daughter of Zeus and Leto
roamed the wilderness of forest,
mountain, meadow, and glade
with her band of nymphs and hunting dogs.
Dressed in a short tunic,
armed with a silver bow,
a quiver of arrows on her back,
she was the archer with unerring aim.

— Jean Shinoda Bolen,
Goddesses in Everywoman

No sooner did we pull out of the airport parking lot, than my mother turned to me and asked, "How is your love life?" She raised her eyebrows in a poor Groucho Marx imitation, while her eyes surveyed my state of dress. No matter what I said, I would be found wanting, somewhere in my presentation. I gave her my best smile.

My father, who had been developing a selective deafness with the wisdom of age, interrupted, "How does the driveway look this time of the year? Are you keeping it open enough for the fire-trucks to get through?" Already he was planning how to escape the female environment of talk into the more comforting world of action and accomplishment. He had projects to keep. I reassured him that I kept the road clear with the clippers.

"Is the new handyman trustworthy?"

"He seems to know what he is doing, and he's no more expensive than Olf. He also works twice as fast as Olf."

Father shook his head in dismay about Olf. "I guess he's just getting too old to do this kind of work." Of course, I refrained from pointing out that my father had a good fifteen years on Olf. Back and forth, we ran through the checklist of my father's concerns. It was a ritual between us, a kind of kin sniffship, in which Father once again took his place as the head of the pack.

Once that was established, Mother then took over the conversation. There was never any doubt in the minds of us girls as to who was really in charge. Early on in our childhood, we had learned the difference between apparent authority and real power. With one wife and two daughters, my father never really had a chance in the matriarchal line.

Mother proceeded to enlighten me about my older sister, her husband, and their three youngsters, all girls — their accomplishments, their worries, the anecdotes that form a family's lifeline. She spoke of the new babies in the family of first and second cousins and their ancestral names, commemorating some great uncle or aunt who lived in the time of her childhood. She filled me into the context of family and rooted me in their network. It was this oral history of our family, constantly in the retelling and in the shifting, which gave me a belonging, the sense that my life had a background of meaning, a story hitched to a whole circle of stories. It was Father who let us know what had to be done. It was Mother who let us know who we were.

Again, my mother queried, "Have you fallen in love with anyone yet?"

I shook my head.

"Maybe coming up here to Chrysalis was not such a good idea, Meggie. I worry about your social isolation."

My life was not really a disappointment to her. It was just unfinished, incomplete. I had no lover to add to my story, and I certainly was not about to tell her about Jalenko. I had no baby, no child to assure her of the continuity of my purposes. There was little she could say about me to others. Except that I worked hard and was living year-round up in the cold country, and that pretty much froze up the conversation.

Yet, on another level of mother-daughter connection, we both knew I was living out an old fantasy of hers in which the woman is strong enough to live alone, close to the natural life. When I was a little girl, my mother used to read me the stories of the Greek goddesses. I was always caught between my admiration for Artemis, Lady of All Wild Things, who knew the ways of the wilderness and needed no man to feed her, and the more cultured Athena, the Goddess of Wisdom. Like mother, like daughter, we both settled into the rational comfort of a masculinized Athena, the professional woman. The virgin huntress lurked in our shadows.

"I killed a porcupine with one shot. Slade called me Annie Oakley. Then I gutted the animal, separated its pelt from the innards, plucked the quills, and dried the hide." I didn't tell her about the sense of disgust I had experienced, the way my face had screwed up as if the dead animal had extruded a bad odor, the reluctance with which I approached the task. I didn't confess to her how sick I had felt in the killing of the beast. I was fully into myth-making.

My father seemed pleased. "One shot, huh?" Long ago, he had come to the realization that, despite my gender, I could be anything he might wish for me.

The weaving of our words back and forth, as I drove the car northward toward Suttons Bay, welcomed me back into the fabric of their lives, the extension of their wishes, the ancient rituals of kinship, old dreams and future vision. By the time we pulled into the familiar driveway winding up the hill, Mother had regressed back into her days of youth, noting the silver maples her mother had planted and how high the cedar trees had grown. Father was alert to work that needed to be done on the driveway, despite my words to the contrary. And I was their conductor back through the years into the magic of Chrysalis, the grounds-keeper who kept the place running smoothly, waiting, always waiting for the sound of family to return.

Upon arriving, Mother greeted Fritzie with an effusiveness generally reserved for a grandchild. Fritzie reciprocated with leaps of unbounded joy. Father tended to the unloading of the suitcases. Mother linked her arm in mine and asked that I walk her around the outside of the house. I thought for a moment, with a twinge of anxiety, that she was going to ask me about my love life again. But no, her eyes were far off in memory, into the times of all the years she had graced this house with her presence. She gave my hand a squeeze and whispered reverently into the night air, "Oh, it is so good to be home again!"

twenty-five

To Yield with a Grace to Reason

★ ★ ★

. . . Ah, when to the heart of man
Was it ever less than a treason
To go with the drift of things,
To yield with a grace to reason,
And bow and accept the end
of a love or a season?

— Robert Frost,
Reluctance

A brisk wind blew about the house the next morning, ooh-ing the sounds of a winter's descending chill. I stoked up the woodstove and lit a secondary fire in the dining-room. My father had been awake several hours, reading his medical journals. An insomniac, he didn't believe in wasting valuable time. My mother was up, making coffee and breakfast to her taste. I was determined not to be overly sensitive to her sense of dominion. Even though I could lay claim to having lived year-long at Chrysalis, it had been hers long before it became mine.

I stirred up a batch of muffins, as she made coddled eggs. Soon, the smell of coffee and fresh muffins lured my father to the kitchen. As we sat around the table, dipping our small spoons in dainty fashion into the ceramic coddlers and dropping muffin crumbs all over our breakfast plates, my father asked, "Are you off to work this morning?"

I shook my head. I wanted to spend the time with them.

He seemed pleased. "This morning, I want to check the work of this new man." I knew he also planned to inventory his tools, to make sure everything was still there and that Slade was no thief.

Mother and I drove into town to pick up Thanksgiving groceries. Bev and Coulter were coming for the holiday feast as well. Getting back into my car, parked outside Morey's market, I saw an old familiar red pick-up truck, with Winona climbing down from the driver's seat. Her gaze briefly lit on me and then quickly shifted to my mother, who was busy putting groceries into the car. I smiled at her, lifted my hands out into a circular motion toward my mother's back-side and said, "All my relations." Winona nodded and entered the store grinning.

I was quiet on the short drive home, until we got back up the driveway and finished unloading the groceries. "Can I ask you a personal question, Mom?"

She was pulling out the vegetables, stacking them in the refrigerator crisper, and replied, "Sure. What do you want to know?"

"You and Dad are almost eighty years old, you know that death is right around the corner. What are your feelings about it? Are you scared of what will happen?"

Mother put down the head of lettuce she was holding. "Wasn't it Woody Allen who once said that he didn't mind the idea of dying. He just didn't want to be there when it happened?"

I persisted, "Seriously though, you have always put your faith in science, in medicine. What does that offer you now that death is a closer reality?"

Her voice took on a pragmatic tone. "Your father and I are both grateful for each day we have together. We know it doesn't go on forever."

She sat down at the kitchen table and leaned her chin into her left hand. "We have each lived a long life and been graced with two fine daughters and three granddaughters. I can't speak for your father, but as for me, no, I'm not really scared of death. It gets lonely when you outlive all your friends, when you look for them in the obituary pages of the newspaper. Your father thinks that when you die, it's just a nothingness. I just don't know. I do know that if your father ever retired from work, well, he'd be done with life. So, of course, whenever he tells me he's going to quit and take it easy, I tell him to hush up, that he wouldn't know what to do with himself if he stayed home. The truth is I wouldn't know what to do with him underfoot all the time."

She ran out of steam, lost her point, went quiet, and then picked up the threads again. "I'm not ready. There are still places I want to go and see — New Zealand, Alaska, Thailand. I'm not done yet!"

I ventured, "I have a client who is getting ready to die."

Mother asked the obvious question, "Is she sick?"

"No. She's just ready to let go and die now."

I expected Mother to discredit this sentiment, as had Bev. But Mother always has a way of surprising family members with her thoughts. Looking around the kitchen, she grew reflective. "My mother loved this room so much, a cozy room. You know, Meggie, she knew when she was going to die. She came out from Chicago to visit me in the East, just to say good-bye. I'm sure of that now. You would have really liked her. She had that touch of vision, that ability to see things before they happened. On the night she had a massive heart attack, she crawled down the stairs to unlock the door for my brother, so that he could enter the house. She was always remembering us. But she knew, she knew."

"Would you want to know about your own death?" I asked.

Mother shook her head. "I don't think so. I would waste too much time feeling sorry for myself, rather than having fun and exploring the world. That's why I prefer to be with young people, those in their sixties. Older folks sometimes get to dying inside, long before their bodies give out. I go to Florida and shudder at those old-people parks." She said this with a sense of repugnance. "The old people there often let their minds go disgracefully. They become like little children playing bridge and games all the time. The brain is a wonderful thing, Meggie, but it needs to be kept active."

"And so you would prefer not to know?"

Mother, however, was always one to see both sides of an issue. "If I knew that I had only six months to live, it would give me the

216

opportunity to do things I might not otherwise do."

This interested me. "Like what?" I asked her.

"I would eat whatever I wanted to eat. I might have a hot fudge sundae every day of the week. I would go to the movies in the middle of the day and not worry whether I was being productive or not. I'd cancel all my dental checkup appointments. And I would throw away all my bras, except for those I'd wear playing tennis!"

"That's quite a list, Mom." Her eyes were alight at the thought of such indulgences. She wasn't finished yet.

"Oh, and one more thing!" she added.

"What's that?" I asked.

"I would come up here to be buried, alongside my mother and my grandmother. I would devise a grand old-fashioned memorial service, in which friend after friend would come and testify to what a marvelous character I had been in their lives! I would make sure that the memorial service happened before I died, so that I could hear every delicious moment of it!" She clapped her hands together with enthusiasm.

I responded to her glee with a long self-pitying face. "When you and Dad die, I will become an orphan, unattached, without a family of my own, and the next in the line of generations waiting to march to the grave."

"Oh posh, Meggie, you're scaring yourself with your images. The only significance of death is to remind you not to waste a precious minute of your life. Without death, there is no intensity or value to life. It helps, however, to have a companion with whom to chronicle the rough passages." She gave me a meaningful, motherly look of concern.

twenty-six

Thanksgiving Dinner

★ ★ ★

I wake to sleep, and take my waking slow.
I feel my fate in what I cannot fear.
I learn by going where I have to go.

— Theodore Roethke,
The Waking

The smell of roasted turkey lingered as my father poured us each another glass of sweet white wine. Our plates looked like miniature graveyards, with turkey bones, scabs of sweet potato skins, a forgotten pea or two, and scattered silverware atop the dinner plates. The conversation, however, had not faltered. Coulter traded stock tips with my father, while Bev entertained my mother and me with a description of a six hour horseback trip she took, not having ridden a horse in three years. The female guide commented, when Bev finally managed to get her feet back on solid ground, that Bev seemed to walk in a very stiff manner. "Or to be more truthful," Bev looked at my mother to make sure she wouldn't be offended, "the guide announced to the rest of the group that I looked like I had just spent the night with a good man!" Mother and I both howled with laughter.

Before tackling the three Thanksgiving pies, we all agreed to take a break to let our stomachs shrink. In a grand gesture meant to impress both Bev and my mother, Coulter offered his services in cleaning up the main meal. Mother whispered into my ear, "Now why can't you find a man like that?"

Bev suggested to me that she and I walk down the driveway for exercise. We bundled up for the brisk air, called Fritzie to accompany us, and headed out the back door. Coulter waved good-bye to us, an apron tied round his waist, a spongy glass cleaner in his right hand like a conductor's baton. In his best Jalenko imitation, he said, "You girls have a good time. I've got more important business to do."

We exited, laughing.

"It takes a confident man to play the fool, Bev."

Bev nodded and pulled up her jacket so that it covered her chin; the air was cool enough that both of us could see the vapor of our own breaths. We took rapid strides for the aerobic benefit, until the house was no longer visible. Up to that point, Bev had been quiet. "Coulter wants to talk to you about something, since you are my best friend."

"What about?" I asked.

"I don't know. He wouldn't tell me. But whatever it is, it is real important. I think, Meggie, that he is planning to ask me to marry him."

I cautioned, "But you two have only just gotten to know each other."

"That's true, yet I feel absolutely no reservations. I will say yes in a minute flat. I've been waiting a long time for a man like this. He's not threatened by my strengths. He knows how to cook. He has a wonderful laugh, a joy in being alive. He's strong, and he's vulnerable to me. As a lover, he's unhurried. He's wonderful and . . ."

"And I think you are planning to make this man your husband, Bev."

She grinned at me, blushing. I think that must have been the first time I had ever seen my friend blush. I couldn't help adding mischievously, "But what about that fish without a bicycle?"

"Oh that!" We were both referring to the bumper sticker on the back of her car.

"Well," Bev added thoughtfully, "maybe a fish ought to try it."

We walked on some more. I felt happy in the glow of her joy, so palpable. "What I like most about Coulter for you, Bev, is that he obviously adores you. I can see it in the little attentions he pays you, like giving you this time to go take a walk. He takes nothing away from who you are. Women's liberation hasn't confused him about what it means to be a man. Unlike so many men who . . ."

Bev filled in the missing sentiments, "Think they have no choice between being macho or wimps. What a bore! It's different with Coulter. In his joy of being a man, he gives me room to be a woman of strength, but I'm also discovering that I like his protectiveness. I guess that beneath my tough independent exterior, there is a dependent side."

"For every extreme, there is always the correction." On we walked in silence, each of us respectful of the evolution we saw in ourselves as women. Refusing the passivity of the stereotyped female, we had identified with our fathers and their activity, to be strong and realize the masculine energy within ourselves. But we paid a price as feminists — frightening away a generation of men who were turned off by the anger and our demands to be understood. We had gathered ourselves into the support of our sisters, while a deep loneliness invaded the singular heart.

Coulter was like the prince who came along and awoke the beauty asleep in my friend, with a kiss and nary an apology.

Bev interrupted my thoughts, "I wonder what he wants to talk to you about?"

"Perhaps he wants to ask me what would be the most romantic way to propose to you? To get a woman's view?"

She shook her head, "That's not it. It's about something that makes him anxious. You must promise to tell me everything he says." She gave me a sharp look.

We arrived at the house. After dessert, Bev joined Mother over an old-fashioned, wooden jigsaw puzzle, while Coulter and I retreated to the kitchen for our private talk. For once, Coulter seemed at a loss for words, awkward in finding his beginnings.

I tried to help him. "Bev said you needed to speak to me."

He picked up a dish towel and began, absent-mindedly, twisting it in his hands. He looked away from me, as if embarrassed. "I'm going to ask her to marry me. I've never done that before. But first, there is something I've got to tell her, and I don't know how. You're her best friend and I thought you could give me some advice."

I knew this was hard for him.

"You may think this funny, Meggie, but I haven't liked most women that I've known. I saw them as scatter-brained, manipulative, and unable to handle power without getting all emotional. Or else, I saw them as kind of like mini-men — aggressive, shrill, and lacking compassion. Frankly, I've enjoyed the company of men a lot more. I still do, only . . ."

"Only what?" My job was to keep the narrative flowing.

"Only Bev is different. You are different. Your mother is different. Maybe, it's just that I'm becoming different. I look into my photographs from several years ago, and I don't like what I see there."

"What do you see?"

"I see a man who was into sheer sensuality. Restless. Not belonging anywhere. I look into the photographs now that Bev and I have taken, and . . ."

"And?"

Coulter shifted in his kitchen chair, "It's like I've finally come home. Bev is an anchor to my life now. But my past needs some explaining to her."

I came over and sat down too. Coulter was

moving into delicate issues.

"Meggie, most of my life, I found myself drawn to the company of men. I was into finding out who I was as a man amongst men. I experimented, and for a while there, I even became sexually involved with men. I enjoyed making love to women as well, but I never took them seriously as partners, as someone with whom to build a life. I felt a lot of guilt about the homosexual part of my life and, like most of my friends, I kept that secret. Few of my straight friends guessed, because I was sleeping with women as well. Well, I'm tired of all that now."

"Tired of the homosexuality?" I was confused.

"No, tired of the promiscuity. I could never find what I was looking for."

"Have you found it now?" The romantic in me expected Coulter to give credit for his life changes to Bev. He didn't.

"Yes and no. Four years ago, I was in a bad automobile accident. I almost didn't make it. I guess you could say I had a near-death experience. Only I like to think of the accident as showing me that my existence up to that time was more like a near-life experience.

"All my life I had been searching outside of myself for confirmation. I thought maybe a teacher, a man better than me, could show me the way to be. Or that if I could be successful in my job, then I could be content with myself. But every time I was disappointed. The teacher would become irrelevant; the man would be flawed; and the job lasted only from nine to five.

"When my head hit the windshield of the car and shattered the glass in all directions, something else broke inside of me. If I could get that close to death, then, I thought, I surely could find the courage to get that close to life. No one was ever going to be able to live my life for me.

"So I became my own teacher. Life with no guarantees. I felt utterly alone with no safety nets. I could have become a hermit."

"Only what?" I had no idea of where Coulter was heading in his story.

"Only, Meggie, I was born with a sense of humor that wouldn't let me retreat. I had to laugh at my own seriousness. Life is too funny to withdraw from it. So, as Popeye once said, 'I yam what I yam.' And I have made some kind of peace with that."

"And, Coulter, you've also made room in that peace for love, and isn't that a contradiction to your notion of solitude?"

Coulter returned to his concerns about Bev. "I am worried," he said, "about how she will respond to knowing that I have made love to men in my life. Whether she will look on me as a freak or a potential carrier of AIDS. I won't lie to her nor do I feel any real guilt or shame about it. But I love this woman, Meggie, and I want her to marry me. I don't want her looking at me with pity, as a psychologist examining a new specimen. She has got to know that I'm not gay. I'm not straight. I am who I am."

The question needed to be asked. "Will you be faithful to her, Coulter, neither glancing left nor right?"

He eyed me. "Now Meggie, I can guarantee you that I will look to the left of me, to the right of me. I will look above me and below me, but . . ." and he gave me a big grin, "I promise you, Boy Scout's honor, I will not touch, fondle, fornicate with man, woman, or beast whose name is not Bev Paterson. Does that satisfy you?"

Of course it did. I also knew the revelation would bother her. Coulter had seemed so perfect, but one doesn't come to his level of maturity without some sacrifice to the pain of experience. In time, she would know it too.

Just before the two of them left, full in the belly with Thanksgiving dinner and ready to go home for a heart-to-heart talk, I told them a Persian story about the great teacher Nasrudin:

Nasrudin is scrabbling in the dirt in front of his house, obviously looking for something of importance. A student comes by and sees his teacher kneeling in the dust, and inquires, "Nasrudin, have you lost something?"

Nasrudin replies, "Yes, I lost my key."

The student asks, "Oh, is this where you lost it?"

Nasrudin points to his house and says, "No, I lost it in there."

The student is confused and asks, "But, Nasrudin, then why are you looking for the key here in the dust and not in the house?"

And Nasrudin replies, "Because it is dark in there and light out here."

Bev looked puzzled and checked out Coulter's expression, then understood that this had to do with the kitchen talk. She would find out soon enough. She whispered to me, "I'll call you later with the news."

Coulter gave me a bear hug, whispering, "I'll tell her first and then propose to her tonight. Thank you for your story, for lending me your ears, for your understanding. I only wish I had a twin brother." He gave me another big squeeze of affection.

I laughingly pushed him away and joshed, "You can look, but you can't touch!"

twenty-seven

Blindness

* * *

All but blind
In his chambered hole
Gropes for worms
The four-clawed Mole.

All but blind
In the evening sky,
The hooded Bat
Twirls softly by.

All but blind
In the burning day
The Barn-Owl blunders
On her way.

And blind as are
These three to me,
So, blind to Someone
I must be.

— Walter De La Mare,
All but Blind

Bev didn't call Thursday night. She didn't call Friday either. I spent the time with my parents, reconnecting. Father and I cut a short trail through the woods to a high spot, from which we could see the choppy Bay. The wind was rising, and my parents feared that a storm front might move in during their visit. As they had grown older, their anxieties became more visible; they felt physically less capable of dealing with emergencies. They talked of leaving a day earlier. I wasn't ready to have them go yet. We decided to let the television weatherman be the one to make the decision Saturday morning.

He did. Snow, snow, and more snow was imminent, sweeping northeast over the plains states. With the grim prediction, my parents called the airport, reserved tickets on the next flight out, had me drive them to the airport, and bade me farewell. I felt sad with their departure, knowing that this time might be the last time I would see one of them. They waved good-bye from the airplane, just before it lifted off and away toward the more temperate south.

Traverse City was bunking down, getting ready for the storm. The grocery stores bustled with activity as people laid in supplies. I loaded my car up with groceries, dog food, and flashlight batteries, then headed toward Suttons Bay. Unfortunately, Katya and Paul Tubbs, my neighbors, had left the area for the holiday, and I needed to find someone else who would plow my driveway if, indeed, it was to be as big a storm as predicted. I felt some urgency to get home.

The wind gathered strength along Traverse Bay as I drove homeward. Gulls swooped and rose in reckless aerobatics in the shifting air currents, rough gusts which pushed against my car. I kept having to fight to hold the automobile steady, to keep it from crossing the center line.

When I got home safely, I unpacked the groceries, freed Fritzie, and headed up the new trail to its high spot to watch Lake Michigan froth in agitation. Wind-tossed, the trees began bowing like Chinese courtesans before the Emperor. I retreated to the empty house. A cup of hot tea and a call to Bev was in order.

Or so I thought. Just when I was about to hang up the phone after the fourth ring, Bev answered.

"Well?" I asked, without identifying myself. She knew who it was, and why I had called.

"I thought it might be you, Meggie." She was stalling.

"Well?" I was not about to let her off the hook.

Bev seemed exasperated with me. She sounded tired with herself. Her voice was one of disillusionment. She sighed, "Well, he acknowledged that he had told you everything. So I guess you want to know what I said to him."

I kept silent, giving her time.

"I told him that it changes things. I told him that I would have to think about it for a long time, before I would commit myself in marriage. I told him I didn't want to see him for awhile."

She waited for my response to this. I didn't dare give it.

Bev pushed, "Do you think I'm a coward, Meggie?"

I sidestepped the question and asked, "What did Coulter say?"

"He looked hurt. He was quiet. He said he understood, that he had been afraid that would be my reaction. He said he loved me, that we didn't have to be physical for him to love me, if that was the issue. He said he wanted me to take the time I needed to make a decision. He said he was willing to be real slow in this relationship with me, only . . ." Bev began to sob, unable to complete her sentence.

"Only what, Bev?"

She barely recomposed her voice, "Only, he would not tolerate being banished from my sight. I mean he said it just like that, using that word 'banished.' I felt like a queen talking to a chastened subject."

"What did you say to that?" I didn't trust my friend's common sense.

"I told him I needed time away from him to gather my thoughts together. He had been so understanding up to that point, Meggie! I thought he understood my feelings, but he got mad at me. We had been sitting on the couch holding hands during much of this talk, but then he got up. He threw my hand to the side. He said something to the effect that when I am ready to have a serious relationship with him, for me to call him. He called me 'cruel' and 'unfeeling,' because I didn't want to see him for awhile. Then, he left, slamming the doors as he went. I haven't heard from him since." She sounded disappointed.

I felt so many things at that moment, few of which would have been helpful or healing to my friend. I was angry at what I saw was her coy woundedness, her insensitivity to Coulter's pain. I missed the strong antagonistic feminist she had been, who wouldn't have stooped to this kind of helplessness. I was totally unsympathetic — not a response that Bev needed to hear from me. It was safer to stick to questions than give her my opinion. "So, what do you want to do now?" I asked.

"Wait."

"Wait for what, Bev?" I tried to keep my voice clear of any judgmental tone.

"Wait for him to call me to apologize for getting so angry. I didn't deserve that, you know!" She sounded defensive. She had picked up the scorn in my silences.

"I think you are going to wait a long, long time, Bev. Maybe forever. He's a man with pride, and he's willing to wait for you, as long as you are willing to explore a relationship with him. When you retreat into yourself and into all that head analysis, then he knows you are no longer loving him. You're just loving the image of who you want him to be. You know that; I know that; he knows that. He's a real person, Bev, and he deserves a real response from you. It's out of my love for you that I tell you that."

There were two clicks on the phone. "I've got to go. Somebody else is calling. Maybe it's Coulter." Bev's voice was full of hope.

I kept my doubts to myself and said, "Talk to you later," and hung up the phone.

Outside by the back door, Fritzie yapped,

demanding entrance. Already the snow had started to fall; dainty white crystals speckled his black nose. I let him into the kitchen. He moved to dead center, then shivered and shook until every piece of possible wetness had flown out onto the kitchen floor. Thus satisfied, he waited expectantly for the imperial rubdown with an old towel. He had me well trained. His leg muscles stretched in sheer delight as I dried and massaged him with the towel. After I finished the rubdown, I got out the mop and proceeded to tend to the besotted linoleum. Fritzie attacked the mop, growling and threatening. Each time, I thrust it in his direction, he skittered back, his claws finding scant purchase on the slippery floor. Finally, declaring him the winner in the battle, I retired the mop to the broom closet, its job done. Fritzie looked disappointed that the battle was so soon over.

Nothing could be seen through the southern windows but a blur of snow, falling fast. It was going to be a bad storm. The house was in good shape and could withstand a blizzard, but the driveway was long and winding. The neighbors, who had agreed to provide snow plowing, weren't home. Unless I could find a substitution, I would be stranded. I called Olf's house, talked to one of his grandchildren, and left a message.

The snow continued to fall furiously all afternoon. Toward night, my parents called to say they had arrived home safely. They wanted to know how serious the storm was. I informed them that they had just missed out on the first real blizzard of the season and that I had laid in supplies of food and flashlights on the way home from the airport.

Fritzie and I retired to bed early. The blizzard blew all night. The wind and weight of snow pulled down the power and phone lines. I slept late that morning, unaware that my electric alarm clock had gone dead, stilled in a frozen world. The baseboard heaters turned quickly cold, but the woodstove faithfully belched heat. When I awoke, there was no driveway in sight.

And the snow kept falling.

twenty-eight

Snowstorm

★ ★ ★

*Heroes take journeys, confront dragons, and
discover the treasure of their true selves.
Although they may feel very alone during the
quest, at its end their reward is a sense of
community: with themselves, with other people,
and with the earth. Every time we confront
death-in-life we confront a dragon, and every
time we choose life over nonlife . . . we
vanquish the dragon; we bring new life to
ourselves and to our culture.*

— Carol Pearson,
The Hero Within

I must have slept to nearly nine. Fritzie, too,
snoozed late, in a world that had gone dead
electrically. The usual outdoor sounds were
muted by the falling snow. Fritzie disappeared when he first launched himself into
the yard to find the boundary marks; his
progress was slow and marked by bouncing

leaps from one place to another. Drifts mounded the wood pile on the porch; it took time to extricate a few logs for the woodstove.

Breakfast was dry, uncooked; the toaster, oven, and coffee pot — dead. I picked up the telephone to call my neighbors. Not even a dial tone. I needed to find someone to plow out the driveway. The nearest phone, beyond the Tubbs' place, was at least two miles away. In the attic hung a pair of snowshoes, older than I; it would be a good day to try them.

Fritzie barked at the back door. Covered from head to toe with snow balls, he looked more like a white poodle than a fox terrier.

Dressed warmly in a sweater and ski parka, I adjusted the snowshoes to my boots, grabbed a flat shovel from the porch and propelled myself out into the storm. It was a futile task, digging out around the doors, especially where the drifts had piled up four feet high. I'd toss the snow out into the yard, and the wind whipped it right back. The gusts of snow from the lake blew a second-story shutter loose; it slapped incessantly against the house.

The banging of the window shutter, the barking of Fritzie, the rapid disappearance of the shoveled paths, the isolation from contact with the outside world agitated and grated on me. Despite the fact that it was impossible to see three feet ahead in the white oblivion, I decided to make my way to the distant neighbors. "This will be an adventure for us!" I told Fritzie.

He must have thought I was crazy.

A thin crust to the snow gave little support to the ill-fitting snowshoes. Immediately, I regretted bringing Fritzie. Our progress down the driveway was slow and labored; Fritzie kept vanishing into the drifts, while stumbling in snowshoe tracks. The limbs of the trees hung heavy with snow. As I bowed my head forward, wind gusts flung ice nettles at my face. Down the first hill and past three bends in the driveway, we stomped and staggered. A snowshoe strap broke loose. I knelt to fix it as Fritzie stood behind me. I couldn't hear anything, beyond the blowing of the wind. I didn't even see it coming.

Way up high, laden with ice and snow, a large birch bough snapped off, a missile hurtling down to where I, unaware, was kneeling, working on the snowshoe strap. It crashed, slamming onto my head, and laid me flat to the ground, missing Fritzie by inches. With all that weight, it might have killed him.

A red explosion about the head, a keeling

over to the white drifts, and then darkness. I don't know how long I lay there, sprawled on the ground, but long enough for the snow to be stained by blood, seeping from the head wound. Fritzie was licking my face, frantically. I do believe, to this day, that it was the fetid odor of his breath that forced consciousness upon me. I wanted to rest in the snow, sleeping, but his mouth smelled of rotten vermin. Intolerable. I pushed myself up onto my knees.

A tidal headache surged over me. My stomach retched air; I knew I was in serious trouble. Fritzie jumped at me, asking for reassurance. My head pounded fiercely, as my parka became increasingly bloody. I had to stop the bleeding. After kicking off the snowshoes, I crawled out from under the tree branch, dizzy the whole time. I staggered five steps to the other side of the driveway and sank back down into the snow. I yanked the woolen scarf from around my neck, placed a chunk of snow in its center, and wrapped it around the head wound. Doing that exhausted me. I threw up my breakfast, forcing the head wound to bleed even more. With my last bit of energy, I gathered the frantic Fritzie in my arms for comfort, curled up around him in the snow drift, and waited for the pain to cool. Fritzie sighed and became, uncharacteristically, quiet.

This was what my city friends had all warned me about — being lost or sick in a snowstorm with nobody knowing that I was all alone. But I was hurting too much to feel terror or recognize the danger I was in. I guess I was just ready to die, my head ached so terribly. Soon the scarf around my forehead was soaked in blood. I don't know if it was the bleeding, the warmth of Fritzie's body, or the pain in my head, but I fell asleep, while the storm swirled about me, covering me with a blanket of snow. It would have been a peaceful way to end one's life, to slip quietly away into unconsciousness. I didn't even hear the noise of a truck motor beginning to make its way up the driveway.

From a distance, Fritzie yapped in a high little bark. I was aware only that he had moved out from under my arms. The external world grew more faint, as a soft blanket of unconsciousness enveloped me. It was Slade who, at my bedside, later told me what happened:

"Meggie, I borrowed the plow attachment from Olf, to dig out his customers during the storm. I was planning to call you in the afternoon and see if you needed me to come plow you out. Around noon, I got this strange feeling in my gut that something was

241

really wrong. So I tried to call you, but your telephone was out. I knew something bad had happened. I came roaring over here. Jeez! You have one helluva long drive to plow! I never thought I'd get up that first hill. But the truck hasn't yet failed me. I was already worrying 'bout how I was going to make it up the last hill, when I saw a moving blob of white. I thought my eyes were playing tricks on me in this storm, but that white blob seemed to be tunneling its way toward me and the plow. It was too big to be a rabbit. So I turned off the ignition, and damn! if I didn't hear that white blob bark, just like Fritzie! It was lucky I stopped, because I'd have run over that dog of yours, sure as shootin'.

"He was acting real weird, running back and forth, as if he wanted me to follow. I couldn't imagine why you had let him come down the driveway in this blizzard. Something wasn't right, so I got out of the truck and followed him on foot. Jeez, Meggie, you were so covered over by the snow, I could have run over you too. I found you there, lying in your own blood, with Fritzie hopping about like a crazed animal.

"I yanked off my shirt and bound your head real tight. Your scarf was soaked through with blood. You were moaning, pitiful like, not of this world. I kept talking to you, telling you to hold on 'til I got you to the hospital. Then I took that old blanket from the front seat and wrapped you up real tight, bundled you into the cab of my truck, backed it up to the turnaround, and ran that truck wide open, like a crazy man, to the hospital.

"I ordered Fritzie to lie down on the cab floor. Do you think he paid attention to that? No. I'd push him down and he'd pop right back up, standing on his hind legs to lick your face. All that time, I was talking to you. I had propped you up on the seat, but you kind of drifted over and put your head on my lap. I kept having to be careful not to hit your head on the steering wheel, each time I shifted the gears. Goddam! That truck tore up the road!

"At the emergency room, the doctors stitched you up and pumped some blood back into you. They said it had been pretty close; you were getting weak. They said you had a concussion and lost a great deal of blood, but that you would be okay now. They wanted you to stay there awhile for observation. You were so drugged up by then, you were hardly making sense, 'cept you kept asking for Fritzie. By the time I got out to the parking lot to check on him, he'd put nose streaks all over my windows and fogged up the windshield.

"I told him you were going to live. There wasn't anything else to do at the hospital, so I drove Fritzie home. I fed him some kibbles, dug the path around the house, and went down and cut up that tree branch lying by the road. That's what hit you, wasn't it? Yeh, I found blood stains there. I was mad at myself for not taking care of that birch tree. It had been leaning over the driveway. That shouldn't have happened, Meggie. I'm sorry 'bout that.

"Then I drove back to the hospital. They told me you were going to be just fine, but that I couldn't see you. You were sound asleep. However," he grinned, "they did want to know all about your insurance policy. I had brought your purse and retrieved that information from your wallet. I hope you don't mind my going into your wallet."

I shook my bandaged head slowly, because it was still very sore.

"Then I spent the night at your place so Fritzie would have company. I hope you don't mind. I did find a chuck steak in the refrigerator which I gave him. I figured he earned it." Slade seemed embarrassed, avoiding my eyes.

I wondered why.

Slade continued, "When I came back to the hospital today, they told me to take you home, feed you hot soup, and keep you in bed. So here you are!" He smiled. It had been a long speech for him.

"Thank you," I reached out my hand to him, from where I was propped up in my own bed. I took ahold of his large hand and looked at him. "You saved my life." Despite my headache, I was curious about the flush in his cheeks. I couldn't help asking what only a woman would notice. "Slade, you even changed the sheets on my bed."

A sheepish look passed over his face. He swallowed hard. Indeed, I was onto something.

He confessed, "I was worried about you last night. I couldn't sleep, until I came upstairs and crawled into this bed. Then I slept real good. I didn't think you'd mind, being at the hospital. That's why I changed the sheets this morning, before coming to get you."

We both looked at each other. I knew then, and he knew then — things would never be the same between us.

twenty-nine

Man Prayer: Woman Prayer

★ ★ ★

God answers sharp and sudden on some prayers,
And thrusts the thing we have prayed for in
our face,
A gauntlet with a gift in 't.

— Elizabeth Barrett Browning,
Aurora Leigh

Slade stayed at my house during my convalescence, without, as he put it, "No invitation." I needed the help, and he was there to supply it. We didn't talk of the difference, that subtle shift that occurs in relationships. It was there in the glances, the assumptions, the caring. From handyman to nurse, he wasn't looking to be paid. Nor was it anything as tangible as a touch, for we still kept a respectful distance from each other. I slept upstairs; he slept downstairs. It was just that the air was growing more electric in his presence, charged with possibility. When I said

I felt well enough to go back to work on Thursday, he returned to his own place on Wednesday. Whatever would develop between us would happen in its own time.

Being a small community, most of my clients had heard of the accident. They asked how I was feeling before launching into their own problems. The physical damage seemed minimal — a couple of large bumps on my head and a great blow to my sense of self-sufficiency. I decided not to share this experience with my friends back East, not even my parents. It was too close and too real. The routine of work helped buffer that thin line between life and mortality. The problems of my clients became a safety net between the past weekend and me.

And then there was Winona.

She hurried into my office with great interest and proceeded to look over the extent of my injury. Her voice was without pity, more curiosity. "Well, did it knock any sense into you?" Before I could answer, she quickly followed up with the observation: "You're going to be just fine real soon. I made sure of that!" She backed off from her examination of my head and sat herself down in her usual place.

"Oh," I asked, "how do you know that?"

Winona replied, "I did a healing ceremony

for you last night." She laughed, "I haven't done one of those for a long time! I'm getting too old for the sweat-lodge, but Hawk wanted to do it, and I thought you were worth it."

She was pulling my leg here — or was she?

Winona continued: "Before the sun went down, we got the rocks ready. We made prayers for you in our sacred pipes and then did a healing sweat. It works better though, when the person is right there. It was good anyway; we had both the male and female energies working on you. And after it was all over, we knew you were going to be okay."

Winona had piqued my curiosity. I asked her, "You said Hawk wanted to do a healing sweat. Why? I really don't know him."

Winona brushed this off. "Oh, he knows a lot about you. I told him a lot. What do you think I've been doing in here all these times with you? I've been studying you. Besides, Hawk needed to learn how to do a healing on someone who doesn't have enough sense to even ask for it. It's not like we're doing magic on you, Meggie. The Spirits say that you almost came marching across this time, but . . ." Winona began to chuckle at an inside joke.

"But what?" I pursued.

"The Spirits said They aren't ready for you

yet. You still have too much more to learn, before They're going to let you come into Their territory!" She smiled at me.

I playfully retorted, "They make me sound like I have some sort of a social disease."

Winona shifted in her chair and moved on with her thoughts. "Spirits say to Hawk to get to know you better, that there is something there for him to know. It's what I've been telling him for a couple of weeks. But I'm just a meddling old Indian woman." Winona bowed her head in fake modesty. It didn't fit her.

"And?" I asked.

Winona played dumb. "And what?" She returned the question.

"What did Hawk say?" Maybe my life was going to start getting interesting.

Winona shrugged her shoulders. "Hawk doesn't tell me nothing, for all my advice. You wait and see, Meggie. There's something there all right."

My own thoughts sped to a memory of the tall, handsome Indian man in the cafe, ejecting Clyde Bassett. The embodiment of a man in his prime and the mystery of another race — I would be dishonest to myself if I didn't admit some interest in encountering him under other circumstances. Winona was into matchmaking, but I wasn't about to let her distract me from the therapy process. It was time to take charge.

"Winona, what do the spirits say about you? Do they really want to have to struggle with you over there? You might give them an awfully hard time!" Through the humor, I was going to shift her back to the primary issue.

"Maybe it's not time to go yet. Things are just getting started over here. I'd like to see my cousin's son with a good woman. Even my little granddaughter is now asking about the old ways. I still got so much to do here." She looked thoughtful.

At last a glimmer in her words that, maybe, she could be persuaded to stay. I followed in the tracks of her words. "It would be a shame to go before you find out what happens. Your granddaughter is not the only one who would miss you." I looked in Winona's direction meaningfully.

"But if I stayed," she replied, "I'm not sure the Spirits will give me a second choice. I've got to think about this. . . ."

Winona pulled out her pipe, attached the bowl to the stem, and circled it once in the air. Holding the bowl in her left hand, she sprinkled tobacco into the bowl and tapped it down with the beaded, deer-bone tamper. Her concentration was total. Once she had filled the bowl, she circled the pipe again in clockwise movement. She looked at me and asked me if I was in my moon cycle. I told her that I wasn't.

"Good then," she said, "you can smoke this with me." She lit the pipe, inhaled four times, then raised and lowered it in ritualistic fashion. She explained, "I am offering it to Grandfather Sky and Grandmother Earth. When you pass it back to me, you do the same. Hold the bowl in your heart hand." As she passed the pipe to me, she added, "Mitakuye oyas'in."

To my puzzled look, she reminded me, "That means 'All My Relations.' " I took the long pipe carefully in my hands. My left arm had to stretch out to cup the bowl with my hand. It was warm to the touch; the air was sweet with the smell of pipe smoke. I puffed and drew in a full breath of smoke. Immediately, I began coughing.

Winona admonished me, "Don't inhale the smoke, child! You're not a smoker, I can see that! Bring it into the mouth and then blow it out. Take at least four puffs, before giving it back to me."

The second puff was easier, and I began to gain in self-confidence. After the fourth puff, I handed it back to her, forgetting to offer it to the sky and earth or say "All My

251

Relations." Winona didn't scold me. Instead, she offered it herself and said "Mitakuye oyas'in" quietly in reminder to me. When she returned the pipe to me a second time, I didn't forget again.

The ritual of smoking Winona's pipe had the effect of quieting and centering me. I felt honored she would share this ritual with me. We both sat in the stillness, with the smoke spiraling between us, our only words being "All My Relations." Occasionally, Winona would shake her head slightly in assent; I didn't know if she was just responding to inner thoughts or whether she was listening to the spirits, as she called her "voices." I remembered an old story, attributed to Joan of Arc. When asked by the priests if the voices she heard mightn't be just of her own imagination, Joan reputedly replied, "But how else would God speak to man, except through the imagination?"

The pipe came my way again. Now the bowl was getting hot. The smoke was making me feel almost heady, although that might have been just a side effect of my weekend experience. As I looked at the beadwork on the fringe around the pipe stem, the lightning design shivered ever so slightly. I refocused my eyes and stared back at the design. And there it was! Again the lightning design shifted, as if in vibration.

I looked up in astonishment at Winona and discovered that she had been watching me. She nodded her head and smiled. I quickly said, "Mitakuye oyas'in," offered the pipe, and returned it back to her.

Winona cradled the pipe bowl in her hand, took several strong puffs, then finished smoking it. She hoisted herself up from the chair, thought better of it and sat down, and ordered me to take the pipe apart and clear the stem and bowl. I went and opened the front door of the offices, blew out the pipe, and returned to the office. She handed me the beaded pipe bag and told me to place the bowl in first, then the tobacco pouch and tamper, and finally the stem. "In that way, if you ever need to get to the pipe in a hurry, it will be ready." I returned the pipe bag to her, wondering what Winona was next going to say or do.

She looked at me as if I had asked her a question. "I might stay a little bit longer, but not much. Spirits are impatient with me. I want to go. I'm curious to stay. There are things for me to learn over there. And besides, Meggie, you get what you pray for."

"What have you prayed for that you are going to get?" A tentative question. We were talking not about staying and going, but about life and death.

Winona shifted back into her role as teacher. "Meggie, you've got to learn how to pray."

How did she know that I couldn't pray?

"If you don't learn how to pray, child, how are you ever going to walk in balance during this earth-walk of yours? If you don't learn how to pray, how are you ever going to learn to hear your teacher?"

"What teacher?" I asked.

Winona looked at me for a second, wondering at my stupidity. "Everyone of us has a teacher, a spirit guide, or as the Catholics say — a guardian angel. You have a teacher, Meggie, and you don't even know it. You don't know how to listen, to open yourself up. If you can't hear your teacher, you will always be dumb, blind, lost in the woods. Your life will never find the balance."

I had always thought myself a good listener, especially in the therapy process. Now here was Winona criticizing me. I knew as a therapist that I shouldn't get defensive. She was being a teacher. I replied, "Well, then, tell me how to pray."

Winona had been waiting for that. She began, "First, when you take that pipe in your hands, know that you've got the whole universe in your hands. Remember, that bowl is woman, that stem is man; together they form the whole Creation. When you pray, you hold that bowl, filled with the tobacco of your prayers, close to your heart. You point the stem to the West, and you cry out. You say, 'Grandfather, listen to me. I am hurting. I am needing things to live. Tell me what to do, so that I can live and be a human being.' You cry out from your heart, not your head or your fancy words. That is man prayer, for without that crying out, how can you make an opening for the Creator's answer?

"Always pray within 'all your relations.' Every prayer ends with that; you are just a two-legged in a world of winged ones, fins, crawling things, and four-leggeds. And then, Meggie, that prayer soars out the stem, carried to the Grandfathers by the spotted eagle.

"Remember that in every direction, there is a Grandfather and a Grandmother. If you just pray the man prayer, you will still be out of balance. What must follow now is woman prayer, the stillness, the silence within you, the vision that goes all around you in a full circle. You watch, hold that pipe, listen, and keep your mind clear. Otherwise you won't see or hear or know what They have to tell you. For even prayer goes round in the form of the giveaway."

From the pipe bag, Winona pulled out the stem of her pipe. "Look at this lightning here," she said, pointing to the now inert beaded design. "It doesn't say anything, when it's not part of the giveaway. Male, female have to come together for there to be the energy. Go into one of them fancy churches up the street there . . ." Her arm waved in the direction of the Catholic and Lutheran congregations. "You'll hear lots of man prayer, but when do they get quiet and listen? You'll hear, 'Father, I need this and I need that,' but they don't stick around to hear what the Grandfathers have to say back! Sometimes, I just don't understand whites! What's the use of praying if you're not interested in the answers?"

Before I could respond, Winona resumed, "So, after man prayer, you've got to carry out woman prayer and go real still within yourself. It takes time to learn how to do it. But if you wait long enough, They'll tell you what you've got to do. You may not get what you want, but you'll get what you need. Sometimes a winged one will bring it, sometimes the lightning. Sometimes, it's the sun dawning inside of you. When you learn how to listen, sometimes it will be your teacher who will come and talk with you."

Then she warned me, "But be careful,

Meggie, about what you say. You get what you pray for."

Inspired, I shot back, "And if I were to pray that you continue to live to be really old, what would happen then?"

Briefly, her eyes swept my face so that she could see that I was serious. "Oh, I might stay longer, but would that really be fair to me? Isn't that a decision I should make for myself?"

I felt ashamed. She was correct, of course. What right did I have, as her therapist, as a fellow human being, to change the date of her departure from this life? But I couldn't help wishing, as I said good-bye to her that hour, that maybe, she would tarry a while.

thirty

No Bears In Paradise

★ ★ ★

Then he saw the bear. It did not emerge, appear: it was just there, immobile, fixed in the green and windless noon's hot dappling, not as big as he had dreamed it but as big as he had expected, bigger, dimensionless against the dappled obscurity, looking at him. Then it moved. It crossed the glade without haste, walking for an instant into the sun's full glare and out of it, and stopped again and looked back at him across one shoulder. Then it was gone.

— William Faulkner,
The Bear

Slade was busy that Friday after the big snowstorm. My head still had its lumps. I decided to give myself the day off. I drove over to Omena to find the wine cellars of Leelanau Limited and buy a couple of bottles from their stock. Peshawbestown, the small

Indian reservation, was just south of the winery. So, I decided to visit the small gift shop on the reservation. Who was I kidding? Women have their own hunting expeditions.

The gift shop was almost empty. A dark-haired young woman was chewing gum and listening to the soft sounds from a radio, while sitting behind the counter. She barely acknowledged my presence. I drifted around the room, admiring the quill boxes, the reed baskets and beaded key chains. Dramatic paintings of warrior figures and dream visions stood guard on the walls. While I scrutinized the paintings of spirit animals, the door opened, and a drift of winter air shivered through. It was Hawk.

The young woman at the counter greeted him with a large smile. They exchanged words about the weekend crowds of people expected to come in for the bingo and casino games at the reservation's gambling hall. The sales girl leaned across the counter toward Hawk, her voice flirtatious, her speech animated. Even in small talk, Hawk exuded the charisma of sexual energy and personal strength. I became uncomfortably aware of my attraction toward him and, like a shy adolescent, turned my back on them. I fought the urge to flee.

He said something humorous to the young

woman, and they both laughed. He then turned in my direction, and to my surprise, asked me in a solicitous voice, "How is your head doing?"

I blithered, "Oh, I'm getting a lot better, thank you." I wanted to thank him for the healing ceremony Winona had described. I wanted to thank him for caring. But as a therapist, I could not reveal anything said in session by a client, so I kept quiet. My eyes avoided his face, not so much out of respect, but to hide my own internal yearnings.

He came over to where I was standing and picked up a totem bear, carved out of red pipestone. He studied the grooves, etched on the bear's side. He said softly, "I need to talk with you." Then, louder, he added, "Some of the work here is pretty good." He placed the bear in my hand.

My heart fluttered with rapid beats at that moment. I kept my voice steady, trying to effect a neutral facial expression. I replied, "Anytime." My voice sounded suspiciously like Mae West. "Idiot!" whispered my internal critic.

Hawk probably mistook my exterior calmness for lack of interest because he moved back toward the shop-girl, saying he had to be going. But as he brushed past me, I heard him murmur, "Soon."

I nodded, revealing nothing, but wondering, just wondering how soon is soon and knowing that soon was probably not going to be soon enough. Having two men begin to express a romantic interest in me was exhilarating.

No sooner did I get home than the telephone rang. Bev was down in the dumps; Coulter had not called. She was beginning to contemplate the end of that relationship. On the other hand, what had been a barren love life for me was assuming possibility.

"Let's ascend to Paradise," I suggested.

"What?" her voice sounded cranky, in no mood for my word play.

"Let's go to the town of Paradise and see the Tahquamenon Falls." I wasn't kidding.

Bev's inflection moved from cranky to incredulous. "Meggie, you're talking about driving north to the Upper Peninsula where it snows four hundred inches a winter. There are bears up there, waiting for fools from the Lower Peninsula to come up and get stranded. You could get eaten alive! I'd think you would have had enough of snowstorms."

Bev was unkindly referring to my recent misadventure, but I let that pass. The idea of going to Paradise seemed the right thing to do. I coaxed her with honey. "Bev, that's why I want someone to go with me. You're

261

my best friend. You could use the company while feeling so blue. So, on a whim and a prayer, let's go."

Bev didn't have the emotional energy to say no. She didn't know what she wanted to do about Coulter, so she didn't know what she wanted to do that day or that weekend.

We arranged to meet right after lunch. I called a motel in Paradise and reserved a cabin with a fireplace on Lake Superior. At first, I thought I might leave Fritzie with Hedda and Olf, but the thought of bears changed my mind. He needed to go to Paradise too.

We took off in my car, the trunk packed with weekend bags, Fritzie ensconced in the back seat planting nose smudges on the windows, Bev sitting in a glum funk in the front, and I caught in the freshness of dreams. The car heater on full blast, I drove north along Grand Traverse Bay. We stopped off at Petoskey, to see if the Indian Hills Trading Company was open, but it wasn't. Bev asked me why had I suddenly gotten so interested in Indian craftwork. My dreams were not yet ripe for the telling.

"It's Winona, isn't it?" she answered.

I nodded. As we headed north, we talked clients. We talked climate. And finally, as we neared the long Mackinac Bridge, connecting the Lower and Upper Peninsulas, we talked Coulter. Initially defensive, her feelings finally gushed out into the open. She rummaged around in my car's glove compartment for tissue to dab at her eyes. The very act of talking calmed the inner storms in which her psyche had been held hostage. I knew I didn't have to do anything to help her; all she needed was active listening.

By the time we veered west, Bev's spirits had lightened. The convolutions of feelings and thoughts were no less tangled than before, but were more loosely knotted. Whether to call Coulter back into her life or to write him out of it was unclear. I reminded her that she didn't have to make the decision this weekend, that visiting Paradise might give her a whole new perspective on life.

We took one last jog north and finally arrived at Paradise. It was not what we expected. There were no streets of gold. Rather, eight-foot snow drifts outlined the road entering the town, consisting of one combined restaurant-and-bar, one motel, two gas stations, one closed gift shop, one closed "Art Studyoo," and one closed ice-cream shop. Even Paradise has its off season.

We never once saw a bear walk into town. "That's because," said an old-timer in the bar that night, "the hunters from the Lower Peninsula come up with their hunting dogs. It ain't hardly sporting to do that. They scent the dogs onto the bear. The dogs will tree the young bears. What kind of skill does that take to shoot a young bear up a tree? Them older bears will fight the dogs, so it's the younger crop of bear that's being taken. We've been telling them politicians downstate that the bears are going to be gone if they don't outlaw the dogs, but who listens to us?" He spat in a spittoon. It was obvious that, in the long winters of Paradise, grousing about the government was one of the favorite ways to pass the time.

"Damn Army Corps of Engineers kept Lake Superior high during the summer, undermining the houses on Tahquamenon Bay and sweeping away our fishing piers," another old-timer complained. "Meanwhile the Midwest suffered from drought and could have used that water. Greed and stupidity — that's what it's all about."

"Yup," all the men agreed.

The first speaker added, "Way things are going, Paradise is getting too crowded, overbuilt. Not like it used to be."

All their heads nodded in agreement.

It was too much. Suppressing a laugh, Bev interjected, "I know what you mean. Why, they may even build a grocery store up here someday!"

Again, they all nodded their heads and scowled into their beers.

Back in the cabin, we cracked up, laughing. "I couldn't contain myself around them, Meggie," she confessed. "As far as I can see, Paradise is alive and well, with lots of room for those who seek its chilly serenity."

thirty-one

Life Stories in Paradise

★ ★ ★

You could not step twice into the same river; for other waters are ever flowing on to you.

— Heraclitus,
On the Universe

The next morning I awoke, not to the comforting blaze of a new fire in the fireplace, but to the huffing and puffing of Bev as she did her stretching exercises before she took off jogging. "Jeez, Bev, it's freezing outside. It's cold here in this cabin. Let's turn up the heat or at least make a fire."

Between leg stretches, no response.

Bev continued to do sit-ups and twists with her elbows locked behind her head. I stumbled out of bed and found the thermostat on the wall, then jumped back under the covers. Fritzie didn't even stir. He knew that on a cold morning, the best sense was to lie

266

asleep until the sun had risen farther in the sky.

Bev finished her exercises, bundled herself into a windbreaker, mittens, and knitted face mask. She looked like a monster from the Black Lagoon. She came up, tweaked my cheeks in an affectionate manner, and took off out the door. I grumbled to Fritzie about "crazy people" and returned to my sleep and an early morning dream:

I was walking at dawn when the light glistened on the edge of the green leaves. Ahead of me, the forest was dark and dappled with points of light, but I wasn't afraid. I seemed to know where I was going. I moved off toward the left, where there was a small cave in the hillside. I heard a rustling sound; out of the cave emerged a red bear.

It didn't seem strange to me that the bear was red, but I was struck by the four rings or claw marks that encircled its belly up over its back. The bear turned its head, looked at me, and wandered off, snuffling among the leaves. From deep within the dark cave, I heard a baby cry.

I moved forward, curious. Holding out my hands, I thrust them into the darkness of the small opening. A baby entered my arms, covered up in a swaddling blanket. The baby's face was away from me, and I wasn't sure that the baby was alive, so still it lay in my arms.

The tiny creature slowly moved its face toward me and, to my surprise, the face was that of an elderly Indian woman. Without question, I knew that my task was to care for this "baby" who bore the face of an old crone. I felt ready to do this and held the baby close to my breast.

I awoke to the noise of a door opening.

Bev stomped the ice and debris off her running shoes. She told me that, due to her fear of bears, she had run back and forth twenty times on Paradise's one street. "I have had enough of Paradise to last me a lifetime!"

Later, at the restaurant, Bev ate an enormous breakfast of pancakes, slathered with butter and Michigan maple syrup, three cups of real coffee, and a side dish of two eggs. I ate raisin bran with skim milk and drank two cups of unleaded coffee. Bev was full of energy, no longer weighted down by depression. "Exercise is an affirmation of life!" she pronounced.

After breakfast, we drove to Whitefish Point, where the treacherous waters had earned the name of "The Graveyard of Lake Superior." The fully mechanized lighthouse sat off the beach, warning the ore boats and tankers of shallows and shipwrecks. Fritzie chased the taunting gulls. A small band of Canadian geese winged overhead, off the point. Like us, they didn't have to fight the crowds, as most of their cousins had already made the trip.

The early December wind was sharp and chilling to the bone. Retrieving Fritzie, we headed toward the Tahquamenon Falls. The snow alongside the road was undisturbed by human feet but bore the crisscross markings of birds, deer, raccoon, and squirrel. The state park was open; all the concession stands were closed. A trail led toward the Falls and a massive set of stairs, by which one could approach the waters cascading over a drop of fifty feet.

The surrounding woods had been left un-cut in their primal state, unlike most of the Upper Peninsula which had been well logged. The woods were quiet, hushed, re-verberating only to the sound of our breath-ing and crunching of boots on packed snow.

We spent hours walking alongside the Falls. For Bev, the endurance of natural beauty, despite the history of human suffer-ing, comforted her. Life would go on, with or without Coulter.

For me, teetering on the platform above the Falls, listening to that powerful roar as the icy water plummeted down onto the rocks, unable to resist the pull toward the snow-rimmed edge, it was scary — and exciting. I was fascinated with the sticks that had floated downstream toward the brink, only to be caught at the last moment on some rock, the water scrambling over the sticks, urging them to release and let go. To give way to the stream of life and tumble into the chasm, not knowing if you would break up into many pieces or whether this was just another experience on the journey downstream — that was my question. I pulled back from the edge, wondering how it would feel to become part of the stream and let the stream become me. Nature is like that, holding up mirrors to each one of us and saying, "Look, there you are!" Only most of us don't pay attention.

Late that afternoon, we returned to our cabin with a bottle of scotch, a bottle of carbonated soda, a bag of pretzels, and a sour cream/onion dip. We were going to warm up our insides and drive winter away. Fritzie returned to his sleeping rug and settled down. We built a fire, pulled up the chairs, and began to share our lives with one another. Eating, breaking bread together, sharing drink, telling our life stories while warmed by the flames of burning logs and surrounded by the dark cold of winter, we wrung meaning from our existence.

I began with Chrysalis and my awkward

adolescence, then recycled through my childhood and conversations I had in the apple orchard with a grandmother who had died before I was conceived, then wove back into history the imagined dreams of my great grandparents who were stuck in their own time. I only had photographs, smudged and cracked with age, of these ancestors, caught stiffly in their frozen poses, now recreated and brought back to life in my warming imagination.

I talked of my parents briefly, with love and humor; their warm-blooded reality and recent visit resisted simple characterization. I talked of the erstwhile Tom and our marriage, surprised at how little I remembered of our time together — the passion of love, then bitterness, now dissipated and replaced by an anemic recall. Again and again, I kept returning to Chrysalis as my reference point, from which I would launch into another chapter of my life.

The fire banked down and sputtered. The soda bottle was emptied and trashed. Night shadows crept in through the windows, and our lives unfolded before our own witness.

Bev's life wove a different pattern, and the current strands reflected her early suffering. Her father had been sweet, alcoholic, and ineffectual. Her mother had been fierce, determined, hard working, and rigid. In her own way, Bev had hated her, while recreating her mother deep inside herself. As she saw it, her whole life had been an attempt to reconcile the opposites of soft and hard, affection and effectiveness, male and female. Truly, her mother had been the man in the house, angrily earning the money for the family to survive while her sweet, melancholy father drank himself into dreams.

As Bev saw it, especially as her relationship to Coulter had advanced, she had come to realize that somewhere she had lost the soul of the Feminine. Everything in her bespoke the spirit of the Masculine. Her way of thinking was always to separate the chaff from the wheat; to analyze data; to manage time; to put forth her own constructions of reality. She wanted her life and goals to be clear and sensible, her emotions restrained and reasonable. She believed if she worked hard enough, everything would fall into place. Above all, Bev devoted her life to keeping chaos at a distance, to control whatever happened to her. Yet always, there had been a terrible yearning, lurking in the background of what she was beginning to perceive had been, thus far, an unlived life.

The strands of her orderly existence — the intricate patterns — were full of dark and blue colors, much pride and little joy, with hints of red and yellow subtly woven as discreet flashes of an energy bursting through. I admired the tough honesty of Bev's stories; she gave herself no slack in her portrayals.

My lines were simpler, the patterns less determined and more animistic, past and present emerging in great circular swirls and full of confusing colors, some bleached, some brilliant. Bev's life seemed to be moving forward with great self-awareness, whilst mine was clouded, uncertain, and full of wandering lines, not yet attached to any design.

In our telling of stories and in our making of meanings, we were both wrong and only momentarily right. As professionals, we realized that the future pulls as well as creates. The past and the present, we knew, were the living tissue of our becoming. The patterns would dissolve and reform in fluid structures, rewoven for the instant of the telling, and then slipping back into that stream which would bring all time into one motion.

Tired and weary, nevertheless satisfied with our constructions, we both fell into a heavy sleep that night. Sunday, we drove home, away from the alien isolation of Paradise. Fritzie's wet nose on the car windows traced the frivolous wanderings of his attention. Bev and I had little to say to each other, not wanting to disturb the security of our life summations. Those moments of putting it all together and saying, "This is my life," were too rare. Deep down, we both knew that, even since the telling, the streams of our lives had already changed direction.

thirty-two

Gaps in the Story

★ ★ ★

For God so loved the world that he gave his only Son, that whoever believes in him should not perish but have eternal life.

— John 3:16,
The Holy Bible

After the visit to Paradise, I was ready for the month of December. The town of Suttons Bay hung Christmas decorations on every storefront. Decals of Rudolf and his red nose greeted hungry folk to the local pub. A pot-bellied Santa in a red sweater stood in the window of Bahle's clothing store. Even the brick exterior of the Martinson Funeral Home, edged with graceful evergreen boughs, exuded a respectfully gay air.

My parents informed me that they would be flying to the West Coast to spend the Christmas holiday with my sister and her family. Bev and I made plans to celebrate a quiet Christmas together at Chrysalis, fixing a gourmet meal and watching old movies.

Monday morning, I heated up the offices and waiting-room and walked through them with my smudge stick, leaving wisps of fragrance to linger in the air. I wasn't yet convinced that the smoke of Indian sage truly cleaned up the offices from the leftover debris of past sessions, but the ritual of purification gathered me into a receptivity for a new day of psychotherapy. In such a stillness, I could then move into the unique world of each client.

Winona was, as usual, my last appointment of the day, and I was tired. Perhaps my head was still recuperating. Winona, on the other hand, was bustling with energy. She talked at great length of all the Christmas gifts she was making for her grandchildren. For her granddaughter, she had beaded hair-ties, earrings, and moccasins which she herself had made out of elk skin. Out of a fox skin, she had fashioned a dancing outfit for her grandson, with the nose and eye holes of the fox to fit right over the top of his head. Winona said, "He'll be the best-looking dancer at the pow-wow next summer." She had also created a staff out of turkey feathers and red trade-cloth for the boy to carry into the dancing arena. She had spent hours positioning the head of a hawk atop the staff to face forward, to help the boy step in the right direction. I could see that Christmas delighted her. I asked her about that.

"Well, of course. It's the one time of the year we Indians can understand your holidays. It's the giveaway time." Winona's face lit up with anticipation.

I was curious. "What did you think of the birth of Jesus and the meaning of Christmas?"

"I love it!" she exclaimed. "I love the whole story of it. Babies and wise men, stars and the animals. Jesus was right there in the center of it all. What I can't understand is why people, good Christians, don't believe in the stars anymore. They forget the animals and act as if the only ones concerned with the birth are the two-leggeds. Jesus was born in a manger; his brothers and sisters shared their food bin with him. It's a wonderful story."

I was taken aback by her enthusiasm. "Do you think it is a true story, Winona?"

"Of course, it's true," she answered with a simple smile — although nothing I have learned was ever really simple with Winona.

"Well, then do you see yourself as a Christian?"

She seemed to expect that question. "I'm a pipe carrier for my people. Ours is the way of this land. The land of Jesus was dry, stony, desert country. His is the story from that place. Ours is the way of the buffalo people. The black robes came to my people and told them the stories of Jesus. We said they were fine stories, now let us tell you our stories. We said let us tell you of how this turtle continent was made, how fire came to the buffalo people, the lessons of the coyote. We said let us tell you of the pipe and the seven ceremonies brought to us by White Buffalo Calf Woman. But they were rude people, these black robes. They wanted us to hear only their stories. They told us to throw our stories away, to tell only their stories. They said their stories were the true stories. And then the elders knew how foolish these black robes were, for no one story could tell it all, and all stories are true."

She paused a moment, but had more to say: "There is wonder in the stories of Jesus. The people in the Bible believed the world was sacred; they looked at the world like a child sees it, fresh and newly made. They knew the Grandfathers listened to their cries for help and would answer their prayers.

They made themselves open to that answer. And it was a child who taught them, because you see, Meggie — children, babies, they can see the Spirits right there. Watch a baby sometime, how its eyes are looking, seeing, and you can't see nothing! A baby is born knowing and spends most of its life forgetting or trying to recall. The wise men, the elders, came because they knew the baby could see what they couldn't."

She sighed, shifting her weight in her chair. "It's too bad that so much of the story was lost."

"What do you mean, lost?" I asked.

At this break in the conversation, Winona began to fiddle with her pipe bag, as if undecided whether to smoke or not. It occurred to me that whenever she and I had a conversation that touched on her spiritual life, she would get to hungering for the feel of her pipe. Sure enough, out came the pipe with the lightning design. Winona took her time carefully filling the bowl, turning the pipe in a clockwise direction, offering it first up toward the sky and then down toward the earth. She lit the pipe and puffed on it steadily until there was a bright red glow in the bowl.

I knew she used this time for thinking. She had not forgotten my question.

"You ever notice how the story of Jesus goes from his being a baby to his being a man of strength in his thirties, and there's nothing in between? There's nothing 'bout what he was like as a child. Did the elders watch him and mark him to be special? Who were his medicine teachers? What happened to him as a young man, when he got to questioning about what the Grandfathers wanted of him? What happened when he first saw a woman and needed her? So much that's interesting just got forgotten. When the story starts again, he is into a long vision quest out in the desert, with nothing about his earlier vision quests and how he learned slowly to listen to the Grandfathers. So much is left out of the story, and that hurts the people. I can see that now."

"How did that hurt the people?"

She looked annoyed at my lack of comprehension. "Because," she said, "we go from a story of a baby who knows to a grown man who is finally remembering what he knew. He has learned how to listen for the answers to his prayers. Most of us are stuck in the in-between with no story there to help us. The people go to the churches and are given answers without ever having asked the questions. Oh, they may ask the questions with the mind," Winona tapped her forehead

280

derisively, "but they don't ask the questions with their heart and with suffering on the hill. And one man's question is never another man's question. The answers have no place to go, 'cept back to the mind."

I protested, "I'm sure there are Christians who still hunger for the experience of the Creator." My defensiveness surprised me, as debate is rarely useful in psychotherapy. Winona, however, was describing my own spiritual plight. For years, I had felt untouched in church services by the recitation of old prayers, old stories and sermons that only occasionally seemed relevant to my questions. I hushed, as soon as I recognized myself.

Winona seemed to pay no heed to the brief interruption. She puffed on the pipe, then resumed, "Pay attention, Meggie. The black robes talk about us being born in sin. I don't know about that. It seems to me we're born into a world that will take care of us if we keep the ways of respect. I like them stories about the flood. When people lose the ways of respect and no longer walk in balance and beauty, then the Grandmother gets fed up. She purifies herself. Someday She just may wipe us two-leggeds right off her skin while leaving our brother and sister nations — the winged ones, the four-leggeds, the crawling things — all those who live under the earth and under the water. They'll still be here. You've got to walk in the ways of respect."

Her pipe was empty now. She stood up stiffly and blew the ash into the empty waste-basket. I sat there quietly, knowing more was to come. After rolling up the tamper and lighter into the tobacco pouch, she stuffed the bowl, the pouch, and then the stem into her pipe bag. She cocked her head inquisitively, "What I don't understand is how this man Jesus is supposed to have died for my sins and your sins, Meggie. If I do wrong, the way I see it, then I got to do it right. I make my own suffering. So, once I asked the Spirits about it, in the sweat-lodge."

"And what did they say?"

"It was during the time of the winter moon, getting on toward Christmas. I waited until the third round, the pipe round, and then asked, 'Who is this man Jesus?' The Spirits answered that Jesus, indeed, was a son of God and that he was sent to the white man, because the white man was afraid to die. And that's the real difference between the white man and the red man."

"How so?" I wanted to know.

"We say every morning when Wi comes rising up out of the East, 'Today is a good day to die.' By that, we're meaning — what is there to be afraid of? We welcome the crossing over." She paused, "Still, I like the stories of Jesus. And I love the giveaway of Christmas!"

I couldn't resist saying, "I'm glad you decided to stay for it, Winona."

She whipped her face sharply toward me, as if jerked by an insight, by a thought that demanded expression but was stopped at her lips. She hesitated and rebuked me, "A healer knows when to keep quiet. You keep getting in your own way, Meggie." She stood up to go. The session was over.

I was stung by her words, left speechless. It was unlike her to be so direct and harsh in her personal comments. In short, Winona was telling me I was incompetent. What had I said to provoke such a reaction?

thirty-three

Shadows

★ ★ ★

Taking it in its deepest sense,
the shadow is the invisible saurian tail
that man still drags behind him.
Carefully amputated, it becomes the serpent
of healing of the mystery. Only monkeys
parade with it.

— C.G. Jung

Tuesday and Wednesday blurred in a flurry of professional activity. The sun had already set before I returned home, late Wednesday. The outdoor spotlight beamed me a welcome in the early night mist. Fritzie stood by the back door, wagging his tail effusively in greeting. But instead of jumping all over me and then heading off to the bushes, he began yapping and backing toward the living room, signaling that I should follow him. What was this all about? Obediently I marched after him, oblivious to the small trail of blood zigzagging across the kitchen floor. In a proud warrior stance, Fritzie stood erect in the middle of the living room surveying the battlefield. The room was a shambles.

What once had been prized family heirlooms, two Tiffany lamps, now lay as shattered, glass fragments upon the frayed rug. Gray white stuffing, the guts of the green couch, dangled from couch cushions. One of the couch's wooden legs had metamorphosed into a facsimile of a well-chewed bone. Ashes from the fireplace trailed off onto the living-room rug in large and tiny paw prints. What else could I say but "Oh shit!" With rage rising in my throat and murder in my heart, I was just about to advance upon the terrier, when I spotted a gray furry tail, protruding from beneath the stuffed green chair. I lifted the chair. There, sprawled in the rigidity of death's final pose, was a young gray squirrel. Blood that had seeped out of its mouth had already dried. Fritzie stood there expectantly during my forensic examination, waiting for his laurels of praise.

With the ash shovel by the fireplace, I scooped up the corpse, took it outside, and tossed it far into the woods. I returned inside, rubbed Fritzie's ears, told him what a fine guardian he was of the family honor, and put him outside. The old broom made quick work of what had taken artisans hours to create; the many colored glass fragments tinkled as they slid into the trash can. The couch was given its death notice; I threw out the cushions and their cotton intestines. Slade would have to help me dispose of the rest of the couch at the dump. Depositing the scattered ashes back into the fireplace, I then mopped up the blood spoor.

Fritzie began hurling his body at the door to be let back in from the cold. He sniffed and inspected the clean-up operation. Satisfied that there was nothing for him to add, he headed on upstairs to his bed, letting me know that it was late and he was tired after a day's work.

Lacing a microwaved cup of decaffeinated coffee with cream and sugar, I sat down by the kitchen table, saddened. The squirrel had been a youngster, not yet fully grown. Somewhere in the house, he had discovered an entry into a place of shelter and food. Despite the danger, he had followed his nose and his hunger. Fritzie must have been asleep, for the squirrel to have enough time to chew on the couch leg. But once aroused, a terrier will not veer from his instinctual mission to destroy all rodents from the face of this earth. Tiffany lamps, obviously, had not provided a safe perch. The choice once made, the squirrel had unknowingly entered into his dance with death, a *pas de deux* driven by the large snapping jaws of a canine warrior.

Winona intruded into my thoughts. It was not simply that I was still struggling with her criticism of my professional competence, but I was aware she was also trying to teach me about death, about life, about choices to make. Perhaps, she would have found nothing sad in the dying of a squirrel, and certainly she would have been unsentimental about the reaction of a terrier to an uninvited four-legged guest.

Fritzie knew what his life's work was about; it was just that he so seldom had the opportunity to express it. Today was one of those rare, purified moments of fulfillment of his destiny. Sometimes, I too can get close to that feeling — when a client is able finally to see through the chains of their old convictions and grasp a new understanding of what could be, a quantum leap forward into a future of potential.

Something that Winona had said, my getting in my own way, kept jerking me around, creating an unsettled backwash in my psyche. I could see myself, like the squirrel, always following my nose into what seemed comfortable, what would provide me with that modicum of warmth and satisfaction, to keep the dark shadows at bay. I had no vision, beyond a day-to-day application of myself to work. The forest, outside the house, beckoned me only in the daylight. Hadn't I left the city to bring myself closer to the natural mysteries? Yet, the night drove me inward to the safety of lit corners. I was afraid of unknown shadows.

That night as I entered into the dream world, the Unconscious rebuked me:

I was in California, talking with a psychoanalyst. He wanted to show me his collection of five water glasses, filled two-thirds with distilled water. Floating in each glass were small shapes of albumen-like material. I asked him, "What are they?"

He said, "They are fertilized human eggs which I am growing, but I don't know why." He looked to me for an answer.

At first I thought he had gotten these eggs as aborted material from his therapy clients, but that was not the question. And I knew the answer. Softly, I replied, "Why these are the un-lived parts of our lives."

thirty-four

At the Edge of the Petal

★ ★ ★

The rose carried weight of love
but love is at an end — of roses
It is at the edge of the
petal that love waits. . . .

— William Carlos Williams,
The Rose

Thursday morning, as I was opening up the offices, the telephone rang. It was Winona, sounding as if a thousand miles away. "It's just a cold, but I'm all stuffed up." A loud "aach-choo!" thundered into the receiver, followed by the blowing of her nose. "I think I better stay home in bed. My throat and chest hurt. . . ."

"Grate ginger root, put it into boiling water, and let it steep for twenty minutes. Then, add fresh lemon juice and lots of honey and drink it. It will ease your congestion."

"Old Native American recipe?" Winona sniffled.

"No, Chinese. It will be good for you." An authoritative response.

"Huh," she harrumphed, her voice skeptical.

Truth to tell, I knew I would miss seeing her.

Bev and I had been so busy with our work and Christmas preparations that even the two of us hadn't seen much of each other. I suggested lunch at The Silver Swan to Bev. Over food, we kidded each other about Christmas presents. "Meggie, I'm going to give you ten Victorian love stories so you can rediscover romance." With a mischievous twinkle in her eye, she commanded, "Tell me more about your handyman."

But I didn't. Instead, I talked to her about Hawk. "He wants to see me soon." I omitted telling her that I hadn't heard or seen anything of him since he made that pronouncement in the gift shop.

"I called Coulter last night," she confessed, "but no one answered. I didn't know what to say to him. I just wanted to hear his voice. Maybe then I would know what I wanted to do about our relationship." She sighed, "He's probably out dating again."

I didn't need to tell her that ambivalence

had strangled more relationships than outright dislike. The tentative responses, the readiness to find fault, the question hidden within the questions fostered distrust. Bev knew that as well as I. In our professional capacities, both of us had witnessed marriages unraveled by uncertainty. The ties that bind become the binds that tie, until the marriage is recognized only by the strings that are attached.

The next morning, a cold winter sunshine brightened the Leelanau peninsula. The snow had come and gone, and frost dappled the ground. Bundled in a warm jacket, I checked outside the house but could discover no squirrel hole. Mid-morning, Slade arrived, his truck grinding up the driveway. I hadn't seen him for over a week and was glad for the company. He whistled when he saw the corpse of the green couch and rubbed Fritzie's ears in admiration. Together, we hauled the couch out of the house and placed it akimbo in the back of his truck. As we returned to the kitchen for his obligatory cup of coffee, I noticed that he was limping.

"Durn leg acts up in the cold," was all he had to offer on that subject. We were back to taciturnity. As Slade sat on the kitchen chair, Fritzie kept thrusting his cold nose into the man's warm hand.

"How's your head?" he inquired, the coffee loosening his lips.

"Still as empty as ever," I replied.

I liked the way he grinned, full and open, without holding back. His teeth shone strong and white. He had a large face, a lived-in face. And he seemed to be really happy when I brought the cinnamon buns to the table.

It felt okay to ask him about his ethnic heritage.

"I'm a Parta," he answered.

"What?" I hadn't heard of any Parta race.

Slade smiled, "You know. A part of this, a part of that. A mixed-up breed." He was having fun with me now.

I persisted and asked, "Well, what part is what?"

Now he had me where he wanted me. Grinning, he sat back thoughtfully, "Well, I've been giving it a lot of thought lately. And this is how I put it together. My left leg is Irish, because at night it jerks a little bit, like it wants to do a jig. My right leg is definitely German, strong in step. My arms are certainly Mexican, because at afternoon siesta time, they start to give out and go to sleep on me when I need them to do more work. My head is Cherokee, don't you think? Proud and civilized." He turned his profile toward me in self mockery. "My chest is all Sioux, scratched up and scarred and a heart full of warrior spirit. Only, the Cherokee in me knows better." And then, as if in hindsight, he added, "Oh, and I got these Apache eyes. They say that looks can kill, and women are always falling around me." He pointed to his eyes, then looked around at an otherwise empty kitchen, as if the bodies of gorgeous mermaids were sunning themselves on the floor. Obviously, Slade was a man of imagination. And a Parta too.

We stacked the coffee cups in the kitchen sink and decided to ferret out where the squirrel had made its entry. Unlike me, Slade didn't start with the outside entrance. Rather, he wanted to start from the inside. I asked him if this was due to any particular rationale.

"By all means," he said. "It's warmer on the inside."

Flashlight in hand, we descended to the cold concrete basement, stepping past the large iron water-tank. Slade was looking for a tell-tale light from the outside. Sure enough, there it was in the far corner. Together, we went outside to find the entrance hole. Once we located it, Slade fashioned a shield of flashing, placed it under the shingles, and nailed it in. "That should hold it for awhile," he said, "until I think of something better."

He invited me to come with him to the dump. I noticed that he had cleaned out the front seat of his truck, covering it with a woolen, striped Chief Joseph blanket. The blanket muted the coldness of the vinyl seat. The truck was of uncertain vintage, cranky but comfortable. The shocks were good, the motor noisy, the heater adequate, and the radio broken. Slade expressed great affection for "the old gal." Grinding up into third gear, we shot down the driveway.

A large doe bounded out in front of us, heading toward the stubble in the cornfield. At this time of year, the bucks stayed hidden, now that hunting was legal. Most of the "No Hunting" signs, tacked onto trees along Chrysalis' winding driveway, were shredded with bullet holes. Hunters had a way of telling you that your land was their land when it came time for hunting season. The first year up here, I had hoped that the place would serve as a wildlife refuge. As deer season opened before Thanksgiving, the surrounding woods had resounded with rifle fire.

It surprised me when Slade turned and asked if I would let him take a deer from our woods. "The deer population here has gotten too big due to the mild winters. They are going to starve if this winter is harsh. That's why the doe was willing to risk a daylight trip to the field."

I considered the notion. Starvation is not a nice way to die.

"I want you to go with me," he added.

"Why?" To let him take a deer was one thing but to accompany him during the act was another.

He grinned. "Because you have proven yourself as a big-game hunter with that porcupine."

I protested, "If I killed a deer and looked into those soft deep eyes, I'd sit down and sob. I had a hard enough time disposing of the baby squirrel."

"So, it's settled then," he said, as if he hadn't heard a word I'd said. "I will pick you up at five A.M. tomorrow. Dress warmly with good mittens and make us a thermos of strong coffee with lots of cream and sugar."

I turned and studied him. He was enjoying himself. He winked, "Don't worry about a weapon. When the buck sees you, why he'll just come a-runnin' and give up his life. Them four-leggeds know it's pure foolishness to run from Annie Oakley."

I felt dubious about this whole business but curious. It was settled then; tomorrow we would go hunting.

By means of the reliable old gal, we dispatched the couch to its graveyard. I had Slade stop off at the town of Lake Leelanau so that I could purchase a new one of pastel design, simpler than the green one. We drove over to the Lake Leelanau bakery, as Slade's sweet tooth was acting up again. Standing there, looking over the sweet-smelling pastries, was a retarded fellow, about seventeen years old. He had a goofy sort of grin, and Slade's face seemed to fascinate him. The boy looked up at Slade and said, "You're Indian, ain't you?"

Slade nodded, "How could you tell?"

The boy glowed with the attention. "Oh, because I'm Indian too." Pointing to his left cheekbone with a finger, the boy replied, "I know you was Indian because of them high eyebrows. I got them high eyebrows too," he boasted, again touching the cheekbone.

Slade didn't correct the boy's missed anatomy. He just said, "Very good."

Driving back home, I turned to Slade and said, "You know, I could tell too. It's them high eyebrows." We both laughed.

Slade launched into an anecdote: "When I was heading toward this part of the country, my hair was longer, and I had it pulled back with a bandanna 'round my forehead.

I stopped the old gal off at a State Park to spend the night. Went to take a shower next morning. There was a four-year-old boy there with his father. The boy watched me shave. He said to his father, 'Daddy, Daddy, that man is a pirate.' I guess he was peering at my blue bandanna. His father seemed embarrassed, knelt down by his son, and whispered, 'Tommy, that's an Indian.' But the boy wasn't having none of that and told his Daddy, 'No, he's a pirate!' I had finished my shaving by then. I turned around, looked at the little boy, and said, 'Son, I'm a bit of both.' "

Pirate and Indian, handyman and friend, Slade chose that very moment to reach over and rest his right hand on top of my left hand, as we laughed at his story. The old gal, however, immediately turned jealous and choked down, requiring Slade to retrieve his hand to shift into lower gear. For a moment there, the warmth of that brief contact lingered on the surface of my hand. It had been a long time.

thirty-five

The Deer Hunt

★ ★ ★

Vague, fragile ware,
And beauteous shape
Of fairy workmanship,
With color delicate and rare
O'erblushed, as when, let slip
Her chargers, young Aurora
Pinks the matin air —

— Francis Brooks,
To Imagination: An Ode

At four A.M. the next morning, my alarm clock jangled. I felt like throwing it across the room but, with foresight, had put it out of my reach. I almost fell out of bed grappling for it. There was no hint of dawn in the darkness of night. I seriously questioned my sanity. I put the coffee-maker on for ten cups of the real stuff and then pulled on some warm clothes. Fritzie stayed snuggled in his bed, convinced that his mistress had gone berserk. Daytime would not arrive for a long time.

At ten minutes to five, the old gal rattled up the driveway. I packed a thermos of coffee, laced with sugar and cream, and poured a fresh mug for Slade. He walked in from the black night to the bright kitchen, perky and full of good cheer. I managed a smile. He drank the coffee deeply and quickly. "Ready?"

Some greeting.

I nodded and threw on my jacket and gloves. Slade's arrival managed to roust Fritzie from his sleep upstairs. After letting him out briefly, I shut him up on the back porch. Slade was impatient to be on the hunt.

From the old gal, he retrieved a large hunting bow and a quiver of arrows, smiling at my surprise. I was relieved that there was no weapon there for me. From the long dashboard of the truck, he pulled out an Indian pipe bag. He handed me the arrows, his folded Chief Joseph blanket, and a sheathed skinning knife. I balanced the quiver of arrows and the thermos in my left hand, the skinning knife in my right hand, and the blanket over my arm, imagining myself an old pack mule. He led the way north toward the woods of Chrysalis.

Try as I might to be quiet, my walking shoes made loud crunching noises on the frozen ground. At the top of the first small hill, he brushed off the top of a fallen log and motioned me to sit down, signaling me with a finger to his lips to be quiet. It was icy cold. My breath trailed out before me in white streamers. I sat down and hugged my knees.

Slade took the blanket and, without unfolding it, knelt down upon it. He pulled out a long pipe stem from the pipe bag, followed by tobacco, a lighter, a tamper, and a sprig of Indian sage. He might be a Parta, but at that moment I knew where his real identity resided. I wondered if he had met Winona.

Slade rolled the sage into a ball and placed it on a rock, lit it, washed his face in the smoke, assembled the pipe, and passed it too through the smoke. He was cleaning up the pipe. Facing West, he then took a bit of tobacco and offered it to Wakan Tanka and asked for help in "this thing we are doing." The next pinch of tobacco, he offered toward the West.

"Grandfather," he said, "look at what we are doing and help us. Give our brother Deer a vision of what we are about. Tell him that we come in respect and will honor his gift of life." He placed that offering of tobacco into the pipe bowl and held up the next one to the North.

"Grandfather, we come to you in this time of the cold. Your time. We ask Your help. We ask You to purify us for this hunt. We ask the deer nation to recognize us." The next bit of tobacco was to the East.

"You, Grandfather, from where the sun rises, we give thanks for our life. We ask that You teach us from the inside, the things we must know from what we do here today. We ask Wi to rise and show the deer people that we have come today in respect." Then next to the South.

"Grandfather, You are the mystery of this life, the coming and the going. We ask that the deer people offer themselves, so that one can return home to You."

As Slade made his offerings to the "Sky Beings," a red-tailed hawk flew circles over us. Dawn was cracking in the East, and light was beginning to flood the sky plain. He asked the Grandmother to help us walk upon Her with balance and the spotted eagle to take his prayers to the Grandfathers.

The hawk answered *kee-yer* and flew West. Slade smiled. In a low voice, he chanted a song of leaping rhythms. As he sang, I envisioned a small herd of does jumping gracefully through the woods. I had to shut my eyes to notice that, except for the birds, the woods were still. When his song trailed off to a slurry finish, Slade offered the pipe to all the directions, lit the tobacco, and began to smoke. After every fourth puff, he raised the pipe to a particular direction. The smoke was sweet, pungent, the moment sacred, and my body ached with the freezing cold.

Finally, all the tobacco burned down. Slade blew out the pipe, saying, "All My Relations," packed up the disassembled pipe, the pouch of tobacco and tamper, placed the blanket under an arm, and then signaled to me that we should track northwest. Light edged above the eastern horizon. What had been shadows took on substance in the pink gold hues of morning. He told me to walk in his footsteps to soften the sound. I was glad to be moving again, to circulate the blood. We headed downwind toward the corner of the cornfield. He gave me his pipe bag in exchange for the quiver of arrows. The bottom of the bag radiated the heat from the pipe bowl. I held it to my cheeks, to inspire sensation back into them. Our breaths lingered behind us in frozen vapor trails.

At last, we reached a vantage spot, where Slade wanted to stay and watch. He climbed an old apple tree and whispered that I should find a lookout spot that would be equally comfortable for me. I found an old fallen pine and sat down upon it, unscrewed the thermos, and poured some coffee for myself. The heat of the liquid tumbled deep into my insides. Meanwhile Slade settled himself in his perch. I whispered to him about the coffee; he shook his head and continued to bend branches and secure his roost.

The warmth of the coffee lasted all of about five minutes, as the chill began to seep back into my bones. I huddled, knees to the chest and blew hot air into my gloves. I could have cared less about hunting. Slade climbed down from his tree perch and pointed to a lower limb on the tree. He wanted me to climb into that apple tree with him. I stashed the thermos by a scraggly sumac bush and, with Slade giving me a hand, I hoisted myself into the lower branch. He grabbed the Chief Joseph blanket, unfolded it, and wrapped it around me. Again, he signaled to me to be still and scrambled past my perch to the higher one where he had left his bow and arrows. We both had an excellent view of the deer path leading to the cornfield. We waited, and we watched, and then we waited and watched some more. I was wide awake with the caffeine, and the blanket kept me cozy. Slade hardly moved a muscle from his perch. He kept his bow ready for action, his eyes steady on the path.

It was hard to tell time in the passage of our stillness. The sky continued to lighten. The morning doves cooed, and red cardinals chirped at our presence. A fat raccoon lumbered by, heading for the cornfield, to see if there were any left-over cobs among the ghostly stalks. The woods were astir with activity. I fell into internal musings. It was then I saw movement behind the sumac bushes near the path. At first, I thought it was a branch swaying, but there was no breeze. My eyes kept focusing, until I could see that the movement was of three girls, ages ten or eleven. I was about to call out to them, when Slade signaled me again to be utterly still.

The children did not talk but moved as if in a slow ballet, dipping arms and heads low to the ground. They were dressed in earth colors, but were not close enough for me to discern their faces and know their identities. Slipping in and out of the shadows and early sunlight, they danced gracefully, slowly — at times standing completely still, listening.

I worried about what they were doing out so early in the morning, unaccompanied by any adult. At the same time I was enchanted by the fantasy of them as earth sprites, living

304

in the depths of my woods. I took off my glasses, rubbed them to remove the fog of my breath, and readjusted them to see the children better. Now, only one child remained. The other two had disappeared, melted back into the shadows with no sound of their passing. The one remaining, half hidden by the bushes, moved closer, bending then lifting her head into a position of expectant flight. I wanted to cry out to her, "Don't be afraid. Come closer. Tell me who you are."

It was as if she had heard my thoughts. She cocked up her head in my direction, put her nose into the air, and vanished. I could hear the sounds of her running through the woods in panic. Again I wanted to cry out but kept still. The deer path was empty.

Overhead, Slade let out a sigh of contentment. He reached down, took my chin in his hand, and lifted my face toward him. He studied it for reaction to what I had just seen, then exclaimed, "Weren't they beautiful?"

I nodded.

We shimmied down the tree to the frozen ground. Slade joked and talked a streak as we headed back to the house. I remained in a puzzled silence, not trusting my own perceptions. He packed the hunting gear into the truck, saying it was time for him to go.

I asked him if he was frustrated that he hadn't bagged a deer.

He shook his head, "I'm looking for a five-point buck. I just couldn't bring myself to shoot one of them young ones. But they were beauties, weren't they?"

I must have given him an odd look, as we stood by the truck, for he added, "You did see them young does, didn't you? They sure saw you."

I stared at Slade. I turned around and peered back at the woods, now punctuated with sunlight. My eyes turned toward his pipe bag, situated on the front seat. Slade was waiting for my answer. As with Winona, I knew he was waiting for something more than just a simple yes or no. I couldn't understand what had happened back there in the woods. They weren't does that I had seen; they were children or wood sprites or whatever, but they weren't does. I glanced back at Slade who was grinning at me. He opened the door and slid into the truck seat.

I said nothing of my confusion but answered, "They sure were beauties, Slade. I'm glad you saw them too."

Slade cut me a big grin from where he sat in the driver's seat, reached over and put his hand on my upper left arm, saying, "When you go into the woods with respect, they know that. They come to you and, for that moment, let you be a part of them. Only, I sure wish the old buck had shown himself." He shook his head in mock frustration, revved up the motor, and gunned the old gal down the driveway. With the sound of the engine fading into background, I turned back toward the house, then around again toward the woods. The forest edge was cast in the bold sunlight of morning; the depths had recessed into shadow.

Into mystery.

thirty-six

Waiting until God is Heard

★ ★ ★

As my prayer became more attentive
and inward
I had less and less to say.
I finally became completely silent.
I started to listen —
which is even further removed from speaking.
I first thought that praying entailed speaking.
I then learnt that praying is hearing,
not merely being silent.
This is how it is.
To pray does not mean to listen to oneself
speaking.
Prayer involves becoming silent,
and being silent,
and waiting until God is heard.

— Soren Kierkegaard

When Winona came marching into my office
that Monday morning, I remembered her
most recent rebuke that I keep getting in my

own way with words. When a client gets truly angry at the therapist, that is often a time of real learning for both individuals. I was determined we would examine her annoyance with me. Winona, however, was going to have the first word.

"You want to know about it, don't you?" she said, stealing my agenda.

I remained at professional distance. "About what?" I asked.

"You know." She waved a hand at me in a gesture of emphasis. "About what I said last time. You want to know what I meant. I know . . ." she said, looking right at me, "that's what you're thinking." She smiled at me, having fun putting me off balance.

What I was thinking was that people can't read each other's minds. At least, that's what I had taught many a paranoid client. How was I to answer her? Perhaps she was just making an astute guess. I decided to turn my thoughts to those children I saw in the woods.

"That too, you are trying to understand. But it doesn't make sense, does it, Meggie?" Winona began to settle down in her chair. "You're beginning to find out about the Spirits now, because you finally are learning how to get quiet enough. And that's what I meant when I told you that you keep getting in your own way."

Winona slipped off her boots and began to massage her feet, covered in long, green socks. "You got to be quiet, not let all them questions mess up your senses. Ooo, these toes are cold today. I wish I was born a Pima, then I'd be warm in winter!" Winona shuddered, as if to make her point. She straightened up and smiled at me. Surprise was written all over my face.

Whether she could read my mind or not, I had a job to do, and that was to follow my client where she was leading me, even if that was back into the crevices of my own mind. "Winona, you're very intuitive," I began, knowing that was an understatement. "I want you to tell me more about being a healer. I want you to tell me how I get in the way of the work I do with you. It's important to me to know this." I had to know where I stood with her.

Her face grew thoughtful, serious. She looked at her pipe bag, then back at me and asked, "Are you in your moon?" I shook my head. She spent the next few moments assembling her pipe, filling it, and announced, "You'll smoke with me." It was not a question, but a statement of fact. I sat back. I was learning to let go of time in Winona's therapy hour.

"I've cut a lot of wood in my life," she

310

resumed. "Often, there's a piece that won't cut down the center. You ever see that?"

I nodded. She lit the pipe and puffed until a good smoke was made. Then she offered it to the Grandfathers and the Grandmother and passed it to me, saying "Mitakuye oyas'in." I held the pipe awkwardly to my mouth. Stillness filtered into the office, as the smoke wafted from the bowl. Imitating Winona, I returned the pipe, raising and lowering it, "Mitakuye oyas'in."

She lectured, "Them tough logs teach you something. They let you understand that, to split them, you need to bring the axe down on the outer rings, and it will come apart, like this." She made an unfolding motion with her right hand, "Piece by piece. The core stands solid and can't be cut. And that's the way it is with healing, Meggie. With teaching, with living, with knowing the sacred mysteries. You can't just cut into the center. It won't yield. You come in by the side, piece by piece, step by step." Winona handed the pipe back to me.

She shifted in her chair. "Like with the stars. You can't really see them straight on. To the side, they are brilliant. Or in the morning, take yourself out on a hill and look at the sun rising. It's beautiful, but so bright you can't look at it long; it blinds you. Then turn around and look at the way the morning colors start kindling up the eastern side of the trees, setting them afire. Goose bumps begin rising on your skin. The world is born again. It's a special time during the crack between the worlds. But if you go for the core, you soon lose sight of it. And then, you can't see nothing." She shook her head side to side. I returned the pipe.

I felt restless. Why couldn't Winona get to the point of what she was communicating? Instead, she kept shuffling around and around. Was she talking about having to respect defenses, before dealing with core issues in therapy? Had I been too direct with her or what? I felt confused. Winona passed me the pipe, chiding, "There you go again, thinking too much. Just listen, Meggie, just listen."

I took a couple of abbreviated puffs and passed it back to her.

Winona concentrated on her smoking. She tamped down the burning tobacco and placed her thumb over the head of the bowl to create a temporary vacuum. Each time she released her thumb, the tobacco smoldered. I waited for her to speak again, twiddling my thumbs. Her voice dropped into a mesmerizing pitch, "There are all kinds of healing, Meggie. In this office, you listen to the sick-

312

nesses of the spirit. You may not know it, but that's what it is. People come in here talking lots of feelings, lots of thoughts. They probably tell you how unhappy they are with this man or that woman. Or how they have lost someone or something, when what they've truly lost is themselves. Their bodies talk too, saying that they hurt here and they hurt there, but what's hurting is that which is inside, cut off. By your listening and by your talking, Meggie, you help them hear the voice of their own aching spirit. They've got to hear that spirit cry to know there is sickness."

Winona shook her head. "Helping them to talk better and listen better, it's not enough. Spirit and its cradle, Body, have got to recognize and learn to love each other."

Winona grinned with sudden insight, "Grandmother Earth and Grandfather Sky have come to love each other in the great giveaway. It's the energy that She gives to Him, out of Her body. It's the energy that He returns to Her, out of the four winds. That Giveaway keeps our world alive and whole. Now that is what healing is all about."

"But how do I keep getting in the way of what I do with you, Winona?" I wasn't going to let her off the hook while she waxed poetic.

Winona looked frustrated with me, perplexed. This white woman wasn't getting the message. As much as she unfolded about the edges, I pushed her to get to the core. I was braced for the cut, my body on alert. I wanted her to tell me what she thought I was doing wrong with her. Then I could analyze her perception in the light of my professional knowledge, to know if she spoke truth about herself — or about me.

She spoke slowly, as if addressing a retarded individual. "It's simple, Meggie. You and me, we sit here, and I tell you things your heart already knows. I show you the sun, and you begin to burn. Your skin peels off. You become more red like me." Winona smiled at that thought. She examined the color of her arm. "The layers of you go into the sacred fire, and it hurts. It hurts, because we all like to feel settled. If you race ahead of yourself, there is no protection for you. You got to let your skin grow to a safe color. Your mind makes up ideas to protect you from all your wondering. That way, you can say you're not lost.

"Meggie, it's only when we are lost in our wondering that we can come into the sacred world. And you've got a good mind, Meggie, but you have to shape it up and teach it to be quiet, to listen, to watch for that door.

And it won't come right in front of you. That I can promise you." Winona shook her head vigorously, "It is through the side door we enter." Winona pointed to a wall on my left side. In the middle of the office wall hung a watercolor painting of violet-hued lilacs.

I stared at the lilacs, but they told me nothing. I kept quiet, because I didn't know how to respond to her words. Finally, I spoke, "One of the problems I've had working with you, Winona, is we never really decided who is healing whom. From what I had heard about you, I thought I was going to be dealing with a depressed, displaced widow. But when I met you, you didn't seem all that depressed to me. Except you were talking a lot about your death." I paused, as she passed the pipe back to me. I took four good drags and handed it back to her.

She got up and moved out to the waiting-room door to blow the ashes out onto the ground. Icy air rushed into the warm office, until she shut the door and returned to her chair. She sat back down, crossed her stocking feet, and looked into her lap. It was a respectful pose of acute listening. My voice was intense in its tone, just above a whisper.

"You kept talking about dying," I reminded her, "and I wanted you to live. I have come to care about you. No, that's not truthful enough, Winona. I have come to both respect and love you." Winona nodded her head in agreement, as if she had already known this.

I continued, "You decided, somehow in all of this, that you wanted me to be your last student. Foolishly, I came to the conclusion that if I could learn from you, that might be reason enough for you to keep on living. Knowing how much both Hawk and I were learning. I think what happened last time was . . ." I was beginning to work this out in my head, "that I moved from what I wanted to have happen to burdening you with that wish."

Winona nodded, encouraging me to continue with this line of reasoning.

"If I am right about that, then you still are planning to take the Spirits up on their offer. And you are going to die. You are going to leave Hawk and Lucy and your grandchildren and just go." Winona barely budged in her chair.

Her silence was confirming. And deadly.

I was aware how feelings of abandonment were coming to the surface of my consciousness. I sighed them out. I shouldn't indulge my own issues here in her time. To leaven the moment, I made fun of myself, "My brand of healing hasn't been all that effective here with you!"

Winona perked up, "Ah, Meggie, that's only true if you think that the core of what's between us has been my death. If you look all around you, we've been talking life to each other. We've been talking about your death and my life. And, in that giveaway between us, Meggie, there has been healing. Step by step, both of us are moving on to what's next." Winona hoisted herself off the chair. The hour was coming to a close.

She fumbled on a frayed winter coat, a kind of mottled gray. She moved stiffly as if her joints were aching from sitting so long. Right before opening the office door, Winona turned around and moved closer to me. Her eyes lightened. She looked happy. With a hand, speckled with age spots, she reached out and touched my cheek, as if I were her child. "Meggie, don't be in such a rush to get there. It's good you have questions. Now sit with them. Take your time with them. Keep your eyes always open when praying, not just to what's there in front of you, but what's all about you. There, at the edges, are the entrances.

"When it's time, you too will be ready." She patted my cheek, opened the door, and marched out into the cold morning air.

thirty-seven

Ancestors

★ ★ ★

Listen more often to things than to beings.
Listen more often to things than to beings.
'Tis the ancestors' breath,
When the fire's voice is heard.
'Tis the ancestors' breath,
In the voice of the waters.

Those who have died have never never left.
The dead are not under the earth.
They are in the rustling trees;
They are in the groaning woods;
They are in the crying grass;
They are in the moaning rocks.
The dead are not under the earth.

— Birago Diop,
Breaths

A cold, rough storm blew in from Wisconsin
— snow, sleet, and ice. Going home at night
from the office was treacherous; broken

318

sticks and tree limbs littered the road. When I entered the house, kicking snow from my boots, the wind stirred up Fritzie. He scurried around the house perimeter, checking the scents. I kept a watch on him.

The night was saturated with loneliness. The house was full of spaces. By now, I had become accustomed to the sound of chairs moving and steps ascending the stairway, traces of my grandmother, I assumed. Even those sounds were muted in the gusts of wind. I built a birch-log fire, whose flames cackled and crackled. But even Fritzie's company was not enough to drive away my solitude.

I telephoned my parents; the phone rang seven times. No answer. I called Coulter. The voice of an automaton told me that his line was no longer in service. No forwarding telephone number had been given. The dialing disk of the old rotary phone grew arthritic and sluggish. I gave up trying to foist my loneliness onto the world and returned to the living room. Up on the mantel, above the fireplace, hung the portraits of my great great grandparents. Cracked, brown-stained photographs of my great grandparents, my grandparents, and my parents stood arranged on the walls to both sides of the fireplace. My sister and I had yet to achieve the distinction of getting hung in the family gallery.

In my most respectful voice, I addressed the ancestors on the wall. "You're probably wondering why I have gathered you all here for a family meeting?"

I examined the photograph of my maternal great grandmother, a single frame coupling her with a photograph of my great grandfather. She looked back at me, a sweet expression on her face, while sitting stiffly on a chair ill-suited for her ample frame. She didn't seem the least surprised at my invitation. Her husband, conjoined and separated from her within one conjugal framework, seemed bothered. I spoke to him in particular: "I bet you never would have approved of women's liberation." He looked down over his glasses at me. Behind him was a fake bookcase. Already I had sized him up as a pseudo-intellectual. I harrumphed at him and turned away. I had better things to do than spend my time with stuffed-up men, swollen with their own importance. I blew a kiss at his wife and addressed myself to the other side of the fireplace.

Looking right at me was the exquisitely delicate face of my paternal great grandmother. "Rachel or Rebecca, is it?" I asked. Clear-sighted, of proud bearing, she smiled at my impertinence. Her husband looked away, a rakish fellow with a trimmed beard.

It must be hard to be trapped next to such a beauty, when the body is cut off at chest level. I felt a surge of sympathy.

"I bet you loved her well, didn't you?" He kept his eyes averted. She was a stunner.

Looming over all of them were the portraits of my great great grandparents, or so the rumor goes. Once, Mother had confessed that a wandering artist had painted the portraits from old photographs, now long lost. Mother wasn't sure whether the pair over the fireplace were even married to each other. Maybe they were just two distant relatives, consummated by the artist's brush. It didn't matter. I still owned them as my great great grandparents, even if their love affair was illicit or feigned, kept forever warm by the fireplace. Her name was Jane and plain at that. Reputedly, she was a Todd, an aunt of Mary Todd Lincoln. Her hair was tightly pulled back into an old maid's bun; she looked over and past me in a severe gaze, never blinking.

"It doesn't look like life was much fun for you," I empathized. No response.

Her portrayed husband and lover, on the other hand, was devilishly handsome, and displayed a proud chest; he looked ready to take on any woman. His face and strong chin inspired adoration. "Now you are a man worth loving." I winked at him. He dared not turn in my direction; plain Jane's stern gaze could freeze a wandering soul. He behaved himself and sat quite still.

I got up and went to the kitchen to pour myself a glass of brandy, before returning to the family circle. The wind continued to rattle the windows, while the fire burned hot and cast dancing shadows on the far wall. Fritzie, unaware of the ancestral gathering, napped on the rag rug in front of the fire.

I toasted Jane and her lover, my great grandmother and her stuffy husband, my other great grandmother, the beauty, and her genteel husband. I lifted my glass a second time to the portraits of my maternal grandparents, who, I was sure, had haunted this house ever since their deaths. And to the photographs of my paternal grandparents, frozen forever in the attire of another age. Finally, I raised the glass in salute to my living parents. To my mother who had given me my heart. To my father who had given me my backbone. To both of them who had given me life.

And now the glass was empty.

It occurred to me that no child of mine would ever look up to see my face there on the wall. Unless, by accident, a wandering artist would come by a century later and couple me with a distant relative and give me fictitious children.

I looked up at them, silent sentinels of time, who passed down their dreams, their ambitions, their accumulated treasures to their children's children. Their failures, wrongs, and defeats were mostly left unrecorded. Childless, I felt as if I had cheated them, led them down a one-way street. I should have let them know that their best hope was in my sister's children. I wanted them to know that tonight, in my own lonely moments, I honored the gift of their lives to me.

Only, now my glass was empty.

thirty-eight

A Visit from the Past

★ ★ ★

Better a tooth out than always aching.

— Thomas Fuller,
Gnomologia

Two nights later, much to my surprise, a voice from my past eerily reemerged. I had gotten home early but had not yet made supper. The telephone rang, and a familiar voice spoke, "How about having dinner with me at The Cove?" I knew right away who it was. You can't live with a man for those many years without his voice imprinting itself on the brain's central switchboard.

"Tom, what in the hell are you doing up here?" My voice registered my shock. Suttons Bay was a long way from the East Coast.

I could hear the Lockheed delight in unbalancing me. "Well, I was sent by the company for a boring tax conference in Traverse City. I got your telephone number from the phone book, and here I am asking my former wife out for a date. Now, do you want to go to The Cove or not?" He was never one to mince words. Either his way or nothing. It was also typical of him that he would pick an out-of-the-way restaurant for its atmosphere. The Cove sits beside a small dam in Leland, with a view to Lake Michigan and gorgeous sunsets.

"Sure, why not?" I was, of course, bursting with curiosity. I hungered for gossip of our city friends back East. I also wanted to know how Tom had managed to fare since our divorce. A part of me hoped it had been difficult for him and that, in painful retrospection, he had been filled with remorse over what a fine wife had been lost to him.

He arrived in a rented Cadillac, wearing a conservative suit with a flashy red tie, hair gray and balding. His body and legs were still lean and taut from compulsive jogging. His arms, however, lacked the musculature of Slade. Tom stood taller in my memory; maybe time had shrunk him down to size. On the other hand, I was probably heavier than he had remembered. It had been a long two years since we had last seen each other.

We made our awkward re-introductions with handshakes. He feigned admiration for my independent life at Chrysalis, while insinuating that I was crazy to have abandoned a lucrative practice in psychology to live where the days are short and winter seems forever. In contrast to his suit and tie, my gypsy skirt and blouse accentuated the appearance of instability. Having established our relative positions in life with our clothes, we proceeded to fence with words. Caution and old hurt muttered in the background. Yet time has a way of dulling even the sharpest wounds, and I found myself feeling almost sentimental toward him.

Very much the gentleman, Tom opened the car door for me. After being seated at The Cove and warmed by a glass of rosé wine, he launched into an account of his job as financial consultant to an "environmentally sensitive" waste management company. I never knew there were so many intricacies to waste disposal, or what Tom called "survival of the feces." It was a job that was a far cry from his student days, when he had envisioned himself tackling the government on behalf of the poor and disenfranchised. His cheeks blushed with the wine, but not once did he loosen his tie. That was a serious sign to me that all was still tight within.

"Well," he said, leaning toward me, "what's the single life been like for you?"

It was not a disinterested question. I felt

rusty in the point-and-counterpoint communications in which our relationship had foundered. I did not have the emotional energy to be coy with him.

I didn't ask him why he wanted to know. I didn't cover up the long and enduring weekends of singleness. I didn't throw the question back to him. I simply smiled and said, "Healing." He waited for me to say more; I didn't. I ran my thumb up and down the now empty wine glass.

Persistent, he tried again: "What I mean is, are you seeing anyone special?" His eyebrows shot up. He knew he was treading where he hadn't been invited, but I guess he thought this might be one of the last times he could ask such questions. He wasn't prepared for my laughter.

"Oh, I've shot porcupines and skinned them. I've hunted deer. I've watched the dawn rise with the cooing of the mourning doves. I've listened to wild poetry in my heart, when the storms whip in over the lake and the night sinks into darkness." The Irish in me was holding forth.

He interrupted, "What you're saying is that you haven't been dating much. You forget, Meggie, how well I know you." He sat back, smug and proud that he had scored a point, waiting for the expected deflation.

God, he must have hated his mother, I thought. Maybe that had been the origin of his bullying rage.

I looked him in the eye. "Tom, you haven't changed one bit. Always to the point and no messing around. And how is your mother?" I salted my voice with sincerity.

He turned toward me with a quizzical expression, "What does my mother have to do with this conversation?" Irritated, he signaled the waitress to come and take our order. Food had always been his final source of comfort whenever I turned slightly witchy.

"I recommend the broiled whitefish," he spoke, forgetting that he was now in my area of the country.

"Whitefish," I repeated. He assumed that I wanted him to order for me. Which he did. Which I then immediately contradicted, telling the waitress to bring me a salad. I could feel myself slowly edging toward an anorexia of the emotions. My body was coiling in on itself, and I was beginning to remember why I had divorced him. His need to dominate and control others.

Still, I wanted to be nice.

No, what I really wanted was to be able to relax, be myself, and have him stop being so judgmental. Why should I continue to care what he thought about me?

While he spoke of his professional accomplishments, I listened to the background music and watched the dark shroud settle over Lake Michigan. I recalled the loneliness of living with a man of ideas, for whom the book was always preferable to the experience of the mountain. I remembered the city lights and the closed walls of our existence together, being trapped in apartment buildings on tarred soil. As I listened to Tom, his words became like dry, brittle leaves falling to the ground. All that was green once, now spent.

Outside the windows of The Cove, the great lake continued to shift in its basin, bashing waves onto the marina breakwater. Off in the distance, the channel light in the Manitou Passage blinked to the ore boats, heading north to Lake Superior. I could imagine the deep-throated warnings of the boats' horns to each other, in the windy night crossing.

Mistakenly, I thought Tom was oblivious to my wandering thoughts. He stopped talking mid-sentence and scrutinized me, hurt in his eyes. "I am boring you, Meggie. Aren't I?" Before I could lie, he observed, "You used to say to me, Meggie, that you would love me forever. Do you remember that?"

I nodded.

He repeated, "You used to tell me that you would never leave me — unless I bored you. We'd laugh at that. You see, I remember too, Meggie. You used to love to listen to my ideas, what I had been reading. We'd talk and debate the points, and I felt like a prince in your world. Somewhere, Meggie, somehow, you grew bored with me, didn't you? I am still the same person you had married. I haven't changed, Meggie. It was you, somehow — you changed." It wasn't said as an accusation, although everything Tom ever said was tinged with blame. It was stated as a fact, one that he was now coming to face. It made me sad that he hadn't changed. Obviously, he never realized how his violence shredded the love and respect I once had for him.

The waitress chose this time to bring us our food. I carefully cut my salad, passed him the salt and pepper, sipped from my refilled glass, and wondered what to say next. He made small chat about the food, how well prepared it was. But Tom was always one who took the initiative. "I remember," said he, "how absolutely furious I would get when we'd go to a fancy restaurant, and I'd order a gourmet dish and before I had hardly taken a bite of it, your fork would come crawling over for a sample."

"Curiosity," I mumbled between two bites of raw carrot.

"No, it was outright thievery. You always wanted a little bit of everything I had." His voice carried a trace of old resentment.

"Self flattery?" I suggested, munching my leaf greens.

"Another thing that used to bug me about you, Meggie, was that you always put too much food on my plate, like trying to stuff a dead turkey!" Tom was beginning to sound peevish.

I was down to the chopped scallions that gave a kind of twang in the mouth on first bite. Tom was savoring his dinner, although I couldn't help imagining him all hunkered over it, weapons in both hands to protect his meal from being snatched.

Typical of our dinners, I was done with my meal long before Tom had crossed the mid-point of his plate. The salad went down hard. I sat back and gently pulled on the elastic waistband of my skirt to ease the constriction. I was tired of being bound by experience. It was time to move forward. "Are you having a good time, Tom?"

"You mean here? Right now?" Tom was no dummy. He knew I meant more.

I refused to clarify. "Are you having a good time?"

His mouth was full of broiled whitefish, and he chewed it slowly, making sure no little bones slipped down his throat. He chased the mouthful with a sip of wine. "Yes, I guess so."

Two more sips of wine. He pushed his unfinished plate away from him. I had to admire his discipline. In my entire life, I have never pushed an unfinished plate away. I refrained, however, from reaching over and helping him with his meal. Somehow, his food no longer appealed to me.

I could see that Tom, too, was coming to understand why we had ended our marriage. It just hadn't worked anymore. He sighed and confessed, "One of the reasons I wanted to see you tonight, Meggie, was to tell you that I am getting married in a couple of months. I didn't want you to hear that from another person. I guess," he chuckled, "like most condemned men, I wanted to return to the scene of the first . . ." but Tom couldn't finish the sentence. He was embarrassed.

I, on the other hand, felt relieved. A ton of bricks just upped and lifted themselves off my shoulder. Now the past would stay the past and not haunt me on a winter's night. I congratulated him. And in truth, I silently congratulated myself and felt sorry for his intended.

"Tom," I said, lifting my glass of wine in a toast, "may your days be filled with wonder and your nights with passion. May you eat well on a singular plate. May you grow old after your time, and may you grow young in the heart. May your beloved enchant you with her harmonies and . . ."

Again he interrupted my muse, "Meggie, I think we need to go. Time is flying, and my plane leaves early in the morning. I had a good time with you tonight. I had forgotten how much you love words. But it's time we leave." He signaled the waitress to get the check, left a generous tip, and drove me back to Chrysalis.

We didn't kiss good-bye that night. There were no "I'll see you around" statements. We shook hands and spoke farewell. He got into his rented Cadillac and drove off. Perhaps it was just a reflection from the dashboard, but as I watched the car disappear around the corner, I swore I could see myself, a younger self, trapped there in the front seat of his car. She turned around and waved good-bye to me. There was something pitiful about her. I lifted my hand ever so slightly to honor her passing.

thirty-nine

The Dearest Freshness
Deep Down Things

★ ★ ★

The world is charged with the grandeur of God.
It will flame out, like shining from shook foil;
It gathers to a greatness, like the ooze of oil
Crushed.
Why do men then now not reck his rod?
Generations have trod, have trod, have trod;
And all is seared with trade; bleared, smeared
with toil;
And wears man's smudge and shares man's
smell: the soil
Is bare now, nor can foot feel, being shod.

And for all this, nature is never spent;
There lives the dearest freshness deep down
things. . . .

— Gerard Manley Hopkins,
God's Grandeur

The fog of darkness had wrapped itself around the office windows by the time Winona showed up for her evening appointment. Covered by a gray winter coat, unraveling red scarf, and a grape-purple knitted hat, Winona looked as if she had dressed in a thrift shop. The cold chased her all the way into my office. Winona refused to take off her coat until assured that the office baseboard heaters were radiating heat. Only after ten minutes had passed did she finally shiver into warmth. Outside the office windows, Christmas lights twinkled along the darkened storefronts. A banner at Video Depot declared: Ten more days until Christmas!

Seated but as yet unwrapped from her bulky coat, Winona looked old and frail. The raw December weather was hard on her. I was mindful of our last session. Not knowing where to go with her anymore in our work together, I chose to wait for her opening. Winona was not one to sit too long upon her teachings.

"Meggie, always behind you walk the seven generations. Always before you walk the seven generations. Everything you do, you must do in the name of those seven generations. The people who live for the here and now, they are people without parents, without grandparents. They are people without children or grandchildren. They are a sitting pond, when once they were a great river."

I thought of my ancestors up on the wall by the fireplace. I thought of my own barrenness. I wondered about the legacy Winona was going to leave behind her. I asked, "Do you think your grandchildren have had enough of you yet?"

She shook her head and passed over my comment. "I had a dream once, a story I want to give to you," she said. "It is about Iktomi, a black spider, who was told by her mother that since she was a creature of earth and sky, she was never to go near the water. Well, she was curious. She had never seen her own image except in the dew drops on her mother's web. One day, she headed off to find a pond to discover her own reflection. When she looked at her image on the surface of the pond, she was horrified. Staring back at her was a black, ugly creature with a huge body and twig-like legs. She couldn't believe her eyes!

"Just then, a fish of brilliant colors swam by, rippling the image. A frog, sitting on a lily pad, began to sing in a powerful bass voice. And a duck gracefully slid out of the air, gliding onto the pond's surface. It was too much for the little spider!"

Winona interrupted the story to take off her coat.

"The little spider cried out, 'Grandfather, why can't I have the song of the frog, the color of the fish, the flight of the duck? Why do I have to be so ugly?' Without waiting for an answer, she tried to sing like a frog, only her voice was too thin and sounded like two leaves rubbing against each other in the wind. She found a chokecherry bush and rubbed her black body in the red, crushed berry, but it only made her back sticky and did not add any color. She ran and jumped in the air, trying to take flight to no avail. Her legs could not be wings. Each jump was followed by a hard return to earth.

"She grew terribly sad. She sat down on a rock and cried and cried, and didn't pay attention that the sun was sinking into the dark. Night was coming soon, and for spiders, that's the time to eat. All day long she had chased her reflection into the ground, and now she was hungry. Her mother, her brothers and sisters, her friends had all long since spun their webs to catch their dinner.

"But the little spider, now very hungry, had forgotten how to spin a web. She watched the other spiders very carefully and, like them, she climbed way up on a branch. What design to make? Where to start? For if you really look hard, you'll see that each spider makes a different web."

Winona unwound and relinquished the scarf from around her neck but kept the purple hat on top of her head. Her concentration on telling this story was total. Her fingers shuttled in the air, like the many legs of a wiggly spider.

"So the little spider decided to ask the other spiders, 'Where do I start the web?' The other spiders thought that was a stupid question and besides, they were very busy fixing up their own webs. In the silence that followed, the fish in the pond spoke up to her and said, 'Far below the surface.' Now, this answer puzzled her, as she had truly forgotten web craft.

" 'Well then, what design shall I weave?' She saw that there were a great variety of webs around her on other branches. A very large and attractive male spider nearby replied in a smooth, deep voice, 'Make mine, make my design.' But the frog on his lily pad croaked up a warning to the little spider, 'And be forever his.' "

It began to dawn on me that Winona was not simply teaching me a general truth but was zeroing in on *my* life. I had to pay attention not just with my head but also with my heart.

Winona pulled off the hat and cradled her hands within the knitted fabric. She didn't let these movements interrupt the flow of her story.

"The little spider just stood there, not knowing what to do next. The duck lifted off the pond, flew by her in passing, and whispered, 'Reach down into the Grandmother. She is right there inside of you.'"

With an editorial comment, Winona sat back. "You can see, it's a woman's story."

I was not to be denied an ending. "Well, what happened?" I asked.

Winona replied, "What could the little spider say? She could say only the truth."

"And what's that?"

Winona leaned forward, now becoming the little spider looking around in bewilderment. "I have forgotten how." She opened her hands, palms up, in the universal gesture of helplessness.

In the silence that followed, I had many questions. None of which had to do with the psychotherapy of Winona Pathfinder.

I confessed, "I am lost too." I truly didn't know what to say next.

Winona seemed unconcerned about my dilemma. She took off her boots and leaned them neatly against the office wall. The silence punctuated the story. The misbegotten hat she placed on top of her boots.

I waited. Winona had trained me well.

She began again: "This world you see now, Meggie; it is the world of the Separated Pipe. Women walk the pipe stem; men hide in the bowl." Winona laughed at the contrary images, then elaborated, "Men have forgotten the hunt. Women, like our little spider, can't remember anymore that the Grandmother dwells also within their wombs. And so you got this 'New Age,' when everybody is looking for what they lost and always had. Remember this, Meggie, you take that bowl, and it is just stone. You take that pipe stem, and it is just wood. And the two-leggeds forget you have to bring them together. For how else does the world become whole?"

"And when they are apart . . . ?" I didn't know how to finish my question.

Her face grew sad. "Why, then the world is dead for them, and the sacred is gone out of things. Then they no longer believe in the Spirits. Their religion becomes like a dead fish that can no longer feed the people. They eat and they eat and their soul starves. A tree is pretty to their eye, or something to be chopped to keep them warm against the winter, but is not a tree to them. The stone is to be crushed and reshaped; scars of stone road cover the back of the Grandmother.

Everything is dead to these two-leggeds."

"I don't understand, Winona. Your people, my people have always used wood for heating and stone for building." Her words were poetic, but I didn't follow her logic.

She cupped her left hand, as if she were holding the pipe, "The bowl, Meggie, contains . . ." I could see Winona was struggling to find the right word in English. "It gives the sacred herb, tobacco, a place to be. The Grandfathers provide the spark and the wind, and the Grandmother, she cradles the fire. They come together in the making, in the creating. The round stone bowl, it breathes, Meggie. Hold it in your hand long enough, and you will feel the heartbeat of the people. The pipe stem also lives; the tree has veins, like us two-leggeds, and roots way down deep in the Grandmother. Both the tree and the stone have voices, and sometimes, if you are lucky enough, you can also see their spirits."

I immediately thought of the children I had seen in the woods. Winona smiled at me. Damn! I wondered if that old woman was reading my thoughts again. She nodded ever so slightly. I forced myself away from my own internal transparencies to rephrase what she had been saying: "By the world of the Separated Pipe, you mean we live in a world of objects, don't you?"

She now clearly nodded her head in agreement. "Everything is separated from the source. There is no sacred fire. We have forgotten who we are."

"For you, Winona, what does this all mean to you? To your grandchildren?" I wanted to pull her back to what I considered the reality at hand.

It was a happy smile she gave me. "Why, Meggie, I am simply going home." And up she rose, shrugging on her old coat, stuffing her feet into the boots, and pulling the mismatched colors of red and purple about her head and neck. She had said enough. It was now up to me whether I wanted to stay on the surface of things.

forty

Men, Fishes, and Bicycles

★ ★ ★

. . . she opened her eyes.
he was the first thing she saw
and she blamed him.

— Lucille Clifton,
Sleeping Beauty

Bev came into my office, as I was straightening the room. In her hands was a bottle of Chablis and two wine glasses. She was snorting fire, "If you ask me, they can all go to hell."

"Who?" I hadn't the slightest idea what had riled her.

"Men. I'm through with them." She sat down at my desk and started pouring us each a glass of wine. I stopped the shuffling of papers and turned around to listen. Obviously, it was going to be some time before I would go home.

"Well," I said, "if you are going to give up

men, the least you could have done was to get some cheese and crackers to go along with the wine." Bev looked at me sharply. It was hardly the sympathetic voice she had been expecting.

"Oh bosh, Meggie! Don't you feel tired of them too? I mean, with Tom coming around to let you know he's getting married and to see if you could get him to change his mind."

I laughed. It was true. Bev drank to the midpoint of her glass. "Then you have Jalenko who can't see beyond his own mirror. So what do you, a fine Ph.D. in Psychology, end up with? Why, you end up with the hired man, hunting in the early morning hours, while entertaining sexual fantasies about a guy you met in an Indian gift shop. Jeez, Meggie, we're just going downhill fast." She slumped back down on the couch with determination, her wine glass tipping perilously.

It occurred to me what was bothering her. She too had tried to reach Coulter and couldn't. I asked her point blank, "Has Coulter left town?"

Bev burst into tears. She grabbed my box of tissues, "God, I hate to cry like this!"

I came over to the couch, sat down next to her, put my arms around her, and held her while she sobbed. She muttered "Why?"

several times, yielding to the tears. Mother and child, despair has a way of leveling us all. I stroked her hair and gave her the comfort of touch without the intrusion of advice.

Just as abruptly as the tears started, they stopped. Bev sat up and away from me, dabbing at her eyes. "To hell with them! They're not worth the tears, Meggie." She drained her glass of wine and stood up, preparing to leave the room. I remembered her bumper sticker about women needing men like a fish needs a bicycle.

"Well," I said, "I didn't want to tell you until Christmas, but I am planning to give you a ten-speed underwater bicycle." Bev proffered me a defeated smile.

"Thanks," she answered, "it should come in handy. And thanks, Meggie . . ."

"For what?" I thought she was about to express appreciation for the tissues.

"For not telling me what a fool I've been." Her eyes looked down at my floor. She was embarrassed.

I too felt awkward, unable to retrieve the right words to comfort her and acknowledge her pain. She certainly didn't need my professional opinion or psychological insights.

Bev nodded toward my untouched glass of wine, lifted it toward me in a toast.

"Cheers," she mocked her own despair. She left my room, both glasses in hand.

"Bev!" I called out to her.

"What?" She reappeared at my door.

"Come, sit down." I motioned her over to the couch. "I have a story to tell you."

She settled down into the couch to listen.

"It's a story," I began, "about a little black spider. . . ."

forty-one

Falling

★ ★ ★

A ball will bounce, but less and less. It's not
A light-hearted thing, resents it own resilience.
Falling is what it loves, and the earth falls
So in our hearts from brilliance,
Settles and is forgot.
It takes a sky-blue juggler with five red balls

To shake our gravity up. . . .

— Richard Wilbur,
Juggler

Someone famous once said, "When in doubt (about anything), there is always food." All night long, I dreamt about cooking and the smells of Christmas. I woke early that Friday with determination simmering in the stomach area. After stoking the woodstove, I brewed up a pot of strong coffee. After breakfast, Fritzie ambled into the kitchen to investigate the noise of cookie sheets being hauled out from under pie plates and bread pans. His leisurely stretch was interrupted by my triumphant "Aha!" at discovering old tin molds for Christmas cookies. Fritzie sniffed at the brown paper bag containing the molds, and finding nothing fresh to the nose, strolled to the outside door. He didn't bark. He didn't jump. He just stood there, patiently waiting for me to get the picture. "Okay, okay. So you want to go out, do you?" I chattered.

Only then, with the inflection of a question in my voice, did he vault straight into the air, up and down, up and down, a bouncing ball of fur. It made me wonder if wire-haired fox terriers have a voice-activated spring deep within their solar plexus. I opened the door, and out he charged.

Shifting to the spice cabinet, I discovered an array of colored sugar sprinkles, silver buttons, and red cinnamon dots, left over from the last visit Mother had with the grandchildren at Chrysalis. My grandmother's cookbook had recipes for sugar cookies and gingerbread men, instructing the reader to use butter "the size of an egg." I checked the shelf containing basic cooking supplies, and again I was in luck; there, unopened, was a new box of raisins I could use for the eyes of the gingerbread men. On second thought, given Bev's current state of being, I decided that I might be better off making gingerbread women.

The tin molds looked to be about fifty years old. I laid them out on the table to see what I had: a large Christmas tree, an angel blowing a trumpet, a corpulent Santa Claus with full beard, a sled, a reindeer running, a circle, a five-pointed star, and a large person, gender undistinguished. Out came the flour bin, the sugar canister, eggs, milk, butter, brown sugar, dark molasses, cinnamon, cloves, ginger spice, and vanilla. Hidden beneath a stack of unused pans, I discovered a heavy wooden rolling pin with faded red handles. The cookie production line was ready for action.

Upon his return, Fritzie appeared unimpressed by the bustle of activity in the kitchen. First I pressed the dough onto a large wooden board and then covered it with a jigsaw pattern. Next, I lined up the dough figurines on the cookie sheet, ready for the oven. The first batch I made plain, imagining that adults and toothless babies would prefer them that way. I became quite reckless with the second lot, showing a definite preference for red: red Santa outfits, red-nosed reindeer, red stars, red balls, and even a red angel.

I lost track of time. A knock and a face at

the door reminded me that Slade was due to arrive at ten o'clock. Once inside the kitchen, Slade lifted his nose to the air, inhaling the fragrance and looking hopefully toward me. I retrieved a coffee mug for him and filled it as he peeled himself out from under his winter jacket. On his plate, I placed two misshapen reindeer. In four bites, he devoured them and looked at me in an asking kind of way. It occurred to me that Slade did a lot of talking with his eyebrows. I told him he would have to earn his keep that morning, but that I was willing to pay him in cookies.

The back-porch gutter had come loose; a piece of barbed wire fencing was down by the driveway; wood, cut in the summer, stood ready to be stacked in the woodshed; and the house bin for kindling was low. I enumerated all these tasks, trying to get Slade organized and out of the kitchen. Finally, he rose from his chair and put on his gear, grumbling about the way "field hands" are treated. His eyes were alight with unexpressed mirth. I think he too was getting caught up in the Christmas spirit. He called to Fritzie, and the two of them headed on out to the garage. While I was still alpha dog to Fritzie, Slade was fast becoming beta dog.

Inserting a tape of Christmas carols in my

tape player, I lost myself again into the cookie production. I was shaping my gingerbread women, when Slade came stomping back in, his nose red from the cold. When I wasn't looking, I saw him sneak a red star and munch it down quickly. "Hey!" I barked.

"Well, are you going to ask me for lunch? Or do I have to ask myself?" He sat down after offering himself a seat in the breakfast alcove.

I was in the middle of extracting hot cookies from the oven. "If you look in the 'fridge, you'll find a quiche mix. In the freezer there's a frozen pie crust." I didn't finish the directions, as I thought he'd know enough to pour the liquid quiche mix into the pie crust. He ambled over to the refrigerator, as I began carefully sliding the hot cookies onto a wax sheet. I turned around to see Slade clutching the carton of mix in front of him and shaking his body in great big shivers.

"What are you doing?" I asked, hands on my hips.

He pointed to the instructions on the carton, "Well, it says right here to 'Shake Well Before Using,' and that's just what I'm doing."

"Yeh, right," I said. "Go sit down, and I'll take care of it." Slade ignored my suggestion and proceeded to pour the mix into the crust. I indicated to him that the oven was free, and he placed the pie pan on the center rack.

He lowered his tall frame back down onto a kitchen chair. I finished with the cookie sheets, while he watched. Then I retrieved my pocketbook and extracted the money to pay him. Despite our friendship, Slade needed the money, and I had to have someone willing to do the heavy work around the place. He pocketed the bills. There was a moment of awkwardness as our roles shifted from friend to employer to friend again. I put the cookie sheets in the sink to soak.

Slade came up behind me. I could smell the natural scent of him and could sense the warmth of his body. I felt inexplicably shy. I didn't turn around or give him any indication that I knew he was right there behind me. Instead, my hands busied themselves with the dish-washing soap and scouring pad. He just stood there, neither touching me nor moving off, our fields of energy occupying one space. I waited to feel his hand on me or his breath against my ear. The moment I anticipated some gesture of invitation, he backed away and gave me breathing room. Until then, I didn't realize that I had been holding my breath.

His voice came gentle, "Meggie, while we

are waiting lunch, I want you to go out to my truck and tell me if you like my new seat cover. It was sent to me by a Navaho friend. I'll make some more coffee." Slade began to busy himself at the coffee pot.

It was clear enough that his request was a lame excuse for something else. But, I felt thrown off-kilter by what had not passed between us. I threw on my winter jacket and headed out to the pick-up. Sure enough, a white, fluffy sheepskin covered the bench seat. Positioned on the middle of the seat was a small package, wrapped up in the plain brown paper. On top of the wrapping, Slade's handwriting stood out: *"Meggie O'Connor. Merry Christmas. From your field hand, Slade."*

Ah, so that was what he had intended for me to see! I picked up the package and shook it. It slid from one side to the other.

I returned to the house, my nose turning red from the cold. "Look what I found!" I announced, holding up the package in my right hand. Slade broke into a grin, pleased that I had not overlooked it. I placed it carefully down on the table.

"Well, aren't you going to open it?"

"Slade, it's not Christmas yet," I replied. His face fell, and I took pity. I picked it up and peeled off the paper, revealing a white box. Inside was a set of dark blue-and-white earrings, intricately beaded, with two long quill loops.

"I knew I wouldn't see you at Christmas, and I won't be here next week, and I wanted you to have them. Besides, Annie Oakley, the quills are from that porcupine you shot. It's only right that you should wear his gift to you." This was definitely one of the longer speeches coming from Slade.

The beadwork was bright and colorful. "Did you make them, Slade?"

He nodded.

I felt really touched by his gift. I got up from where I was leaning on the table and went to where he was sitting. I don't know what came into me, but before I could think about it, I placed my hands on his cheeks, lifted his face, and kissed him on the lips. Slade reached up and pulled me gently down into a sitting position, astraddle his lap, and kissed me back, a long and lingering kiss. His hands touched my shoulder blades, and he closed his eyes during the kiss. I forgot to breathe. He released me and, flustered, I got up and walked back over to the sink, to dry the wet cookie sheets.

His chair scraped against the floor, as he pushed himself away from the table and rose. Once again, I could feel his breath behind me at the sink. It was hot and shallow. This time, his hands reached out to play with my hair. His voice was soft, "You have yourself a good Christmas."

"Are you running off now?" Things were just getting interesting.

He fingered three hot cookies and looked toward the outside door. "Yup."

I persisted, "Do you have to go now?" I was shameless.

Slade bent over the table and picked up the quill earrings. He brought them over to where I was standing and painstakingly attached them to my ears. He stood back, admiring his handiwork? Or me? He moved closer. "I've got only one thing to say to you, Meggie O'Connor."

"What do you have to tell me?" I arched my eyebrows. At the very least, I expected him to kiss me again.

Instead, he picked up the three sugar cookies and exclaimed, "Mmm, Mmm good!" With that, he exited the kitchen and drove away, cookies still in his hand.

Bev was right after all. The downhill gravity of the human heart was pulling me full force.

forty-two

A Flat Tire

★ ★ ★

*There's nothing the world loves more than
a ready-made description which they can
hang on to a man, and so save themselves
all trouble in future.*

— W. Somerset Maugham,
Mrs. Dot

The next morning, I transported some of the
cookies to my neighbor, Katya Tubbs. Her
three children and their friends would devour
them all by Saturday night. We sat and drank
tea in her kitchen nook. Katya, born and
raised in Suttons Bay, had become a good
friend. Bev couldn't understand this and in
her less charitable moments referred to
Katya as "that Polish dumpling." The two
women had little in common; I kept my
friendships with them apart. Katya's house
romped with children. Stacks of drawings,
broken crayons, baseball caps, toy guns, and

empty cereal boxes inhabited every corner of the house. What I liked about Katya was that she never apologized for the mess.

"Miracle of miracles," Katya sighed, "I have the house to myself tonight. The kids are going to be at a Christmas party and Paul has a late meeting. Imagine, time to myself! What am I going to do, Meggie?"

"How about going to the ballet with me?" A sudden inspiration.

"The Nutcracker Suite in Traverse City?" I nodded.

Katya's eyes glistened. Not only a night away from the children but the ballet too! Before I could reconsider, Katya ran to the phone and reserved tickets for the night's performance. "A done deal," she exclaimed.

Both of us dressed to the hilt that night. Katya wore black, offset with a red scarf and earrings. My dress accentuated just the right curves and managed to cover up the rest. The quill earrings caught her attention.

"Those are beautiful, Meggie. Where did you get them?"

"A friend made them for me."

Katya oohed and aahed, "Well, you must be sure to remember and give me her name. I would love a pair like them."

We dined in Traverse City and then headed for the Opera House. The ballet company was well received, especially as many of the children and dancers in the production came from the area. At the end we all rose to give them a standing ovation.

Drifting out of the magic of the theater, we discovered that the temperature had dropped. The cold night air stung our faces. We hurried to the car and revved up the engine and heater. It was late. Katya wondered aloud if her husband, Paul, had managed to get the children home and into bed. Driving back toward Suttons Bay, the road seemed dark and deserted. There was no traffic.

The car bumped over a rough section. Katya was the first one to understand the problem. "Meggie, the wheel."

"For God's sake, what's the matter with the car?" I complained. The steering wheel became sluggish. The car was pulling toward the right.

"Flat tire. You've got a front flat tire." Katya remained calm.

I braked gently and pulled the car over to the side. There wasn't much of a shoulder. "Stay here," I commanded. Only one of us should have to suffer in the bitter cold. I jumped out of the car to inspect the damage. The tire was deflating rapidly. "Damn!" I muttered. I retreated back to the warmth of the car.

Katya retrieved a flashlight and instructions on changing a tire from the glove compartment. "Would you like a dramatic reading of the instructions?" Katya cheerfully inquired. The tone of her voice suggested that everything would work out just fine. My mood, however, was black and foul. As I was not about to let Katya ruin her one fancy outfit, I knew that I had to sacrifice both dress and dignity to put a new tire on the car.

Katya intoned, " 'It is wise to have the car in a braking position, so that it will not roll while you are changing the tire.' Are you ready for the next step?" Katya grinned.

"Sure," I answered, resigned to the task.

"'Next, remove the hubcap and loosen the lug nuts with the specially constructed hollow end of the jack handle.' Meggie, let me help you. It's icy out there." Katya undid her seat belt and got ready to open her door.

"No, it's a matter of pride with me. Someone has got to stay warm and clean. It's my car." I thrust myself out onto the cold road again, opened the trunk, uttered some more choice words, found the spare tire, and lifted it out. A greasy grime began to settle on my winter coat. Before long, my stockings began to unravel with the exercise. Over on the side of the trunk, I discovered the jack, placed it by the flat tire, and then retreated back into the car. "It's freezing out there!" I exclaimed.

Katya looked askance. She reached into her pocketbook and pulled out a handi-wipe cloth and washed my hands for me. "Would you like a piece of gum?"

I could see that, to Katya, I was like an angry child in need of soothing or distraction. I shook my head. "What I really want is a garage mechanic to drive by this very moment." But the only sign of life on the road were the emergency lights blinking off and on, reflecting flashing red snowbanks.

To avoid becoming complacent in the warmth, I forced myself back out into the cold. Katya's glove wiped streaks on the side window, as she strained to watch my doings. First, I had to pry the hubcap off. The jack handle, however, was too blunt. The damn hubcap wouldn't budge. There were no other tools.

As frustration began to freeze into despair, six car lights blinked onto the dark road behind us. I stood up, straightened my smudged coat and tried to look appropriately helpless. The first two lights, on high beam, illuminated an old man and woman, driving in slow motion. They took no notice of the flashing emergency lights of my car but passed on by, nodding toward me graciously.

360

Tailgating them was a jeep full of teenage boys who, upon seeing my frozen form, waved vigorously as they too sped past us. I began to nurture disparaging thoughts about humankind. The third and last vehicle, an old pick-up truck, slowed down. The driver pulled over just ahead of my car.

It was Winona's truck, and who should emerge out of the driver's seat but Hawk! Dressed in a light-brown suede jacket lined with lambskin, fancy cowboy boots, his shiny hair neatly braided with a bandanna wrapped around his forehead, Hawk looked as if he had been out on the town.

Katya grew alarmed at the sight of the tall Indian walking back toward us. Hawk nodded at her and gave me a confident smile. He pointed to the flat, "It sure looks to me like you could use some help. Why don't you let me change your tire?"

I could have kissed his feet. Instead, I told him about my problem with the hubcap. He retrieved a screwdriver from his truck and, with one nudge, popped off the recalcitrant hubcap. He asked me to shut off the engine of the car and gave me the keys to the truck. "Go sit in the truck and keep warm. I'll have the tire changed in no time."

I had to pull Katya out into the cold night air to switch vehicles. Her nose wrinkled as we clambered into the front seat of the pick-up. It smelled of stale pipe smoke. An eagle feather dangled from the rear-view mirror. Katya kept silent. I told her, "Don't worry. I know this guy. He's okay. He's not going to rape us or anything." Katya did not look reassured.

Surreptitiously, in the side-view mirror, I studied Hawk. He worked fast in the cold dark. The heater in his truck belched warmth. Finally, he lifted the trunk lid and threw in the flat. Rubbing his hands together, he walked toward his truck. Katya's fingers reached for the door handle to make a quick exit.

Hawk opened the other door. "All done," he announced. "Get that spare checked tomorrow, so that the tires have equal pressure." He noticed Katya leaning away from him, his eyes missing nothing. He said, "You can go back to the car now, if you want." Katya didn't need a second invitation. Out she fled, back to the security of the automobile.

I had been sitting in the middle of the front seat and moved over toward the door to make room for him. He slung his frame up into the seat, massaging his hands in front of the heater. "It's colder than a well digger's ass in Alaska out there."

I felt awkward sitting next to him. Some men have that animal magnetism, and some don't. Well, Hawk possessed an abundance of it. I stammered, "I appreciate your fixing that tire. Can I pay you for your time or . . . ?" Or what — an invitation to come back to my house? My unconscious was doing overtime, while my mouth knew enough to keep shut.

Hawk smiled and shook his head. "I'm glad I came along." His eyes shifted to the rear-view mirror. He nodded, "I think your friend back there is getting worried about you. Tell you what. I'll follow behind, to make sure you don't have any more trouble on the way home. It's not a good night to get stuck."

Keeping the truck at a distance so that his headlights wouldn't blind me, Hawk followed behind us. Katya was relieved when we started back on the road, eager to get home.

Once we arrived at the Tubbs' home, Katya begged, "Meggie, let Paul escort you home." She exited the car, eying the truck idling at the end of her driveway.

"Ridiculous. I don't need anyone to accompany me homeward." It was the simple truth.

She glanced nervously back toward the

363

truck, then toward me. "Promise to call me when you get . . ."

"Tomorrow will be soon enough," I interrupted, rolled up my window, and drove off, waving good-bye to her.

She needn't have worried. Hawk trailed me to my driveway, honked and waved, and sped off down the road toward Peshawbestown. I made a note that night to send him a tin of my Christmas cookies.

It was the least I could do.

forty-three

It is as You Wish

★ ★ ★

Once upon a time, a wise old hermit lived in a cave at the top of a mountain. He was known far and wide among the people as a sage who could answer the most difficult questions about life. He was a truth-teller. But, as always in the ways of youth, there were those who doubted his ability.

One such young man boasted to his friends that he would go play a trick on the old hermit and confuse him with his questions. The youth held a defenseless little chickadee in his hand and announced to his friends, "I'll go find that old man and when I do, I'll hide my hands behind my back. I will ask the old man if this bird is alive or dead. If he says the bird is dead, I will bring out my hands and show him that the bird is alive. If he answers that the bird is alive, I will crush this bird and show him that the bird is quite dead."

With that plan in mind, the youth climbed the mountain in search of the hermit's cave. When he discovered the cave, he called out, "Old man! Old man!"

A voice answered from within and said, "What is that you want, my son?"

"I want to ask you a question," replied the youth, hiding the bird and his hands behind his back.

The voice answered, "Then ask, my son."

The youth grinned and said, "Behind my back, I have a little bird in my hands. I want to know if that bird is alive or dead."

There was a moment's brief silence, and the voice that answered was a weary voice, "It is as you wish, my son."

— Traditional Folktale

That Monday, when Winona walked into my office, I handed her the tin of Christmas cookies and told her it was for Hawk.

"Why, what's that boy done?"

"Didn't he tell you? The other night on the way home from Traverse City, I had a flat tire, and he fixed it for me. So, I thought he certainly deserved a tin of my Christmas cookies."

Winona gave me a puzzled look. I shrugged my shoulders. Maybe Hawk hadn't mentioned it to her. She unbuttoned her coat and sat down onto her favorite chair, holding the tin of cookies on her lap. Next, she kicked off her shoes and flexed her feet, snug in grey socks. The tin of cookies swayed on her lap. It was inevitable. She looked up at me and I at her. Shamelessly, she popped open the tin and extracted one of the cookies, then closed the lid. Into her mouth, the cookie disappeared. She nodded her head in approval, "Yup, Hawk will really like these." Only then did she relinquish the tin to the couch.

I couldn't help commenting, "Maybe he'll share some of them with you — that is, if there are any left by the time he gets them."

Winona didn't pay the slightest bit of attention to that remark. She had other things on her mind. Abruptly, she announced, "I wasn't planning on being here this morning."

"Oh?" I was curious.

She sighed. "It's just time to go home now."

"You mean to Pine Ridge?" I was being obtuse.

"Lucy says it's not a good time to travel, right before Christmas. I tell her it's the only time. I'm just ready, that's all."

I heard a wistful undercurrent to her voice, something that had not been there before. Winona wasn't really talking about going back to South Dakota. My voice choked and came out scratchy, "So, it's time then?"

It may have been the foggy morning light or the clarity of imagination, but it seemed to me that Winona was dissipating at the edges, ever so slightly, right there before me. Already partially gone. Strings to this life were being cut, even as she focused her attention outside my window. She was here, in this office with me, and, somehow, out there too. She began talking, her voice low and intimate.

"I took my pipe out yesterday at dusk. I told Them I was ready now. They could come and take me. I waited. I prayed some more. I sang the old songs. It was getting cold outside. I was getting cold. I looked up toward Wakan Tanka and saw a fierce woman on horseback riding toward me. Her face kept shifting, and at times I'd lose sight of her. Then, she'd reappear from within the clouds, and I'd offer up my pipe to her. I knew she was coming for me, and I began to dance on the Grandmother. Our heartbeats grew together. I started walking toward her. Right in front of me, two large black columns formed a gate, and since I didn't know what else to do, I passed through it. Ahead of me, two more black gates, swaying back and forth, like tiny tornadoes rising way up into the sky. I pulled my glasses out of my pocket, and I could see that these columns, these gates, were swarms of tiny flies, circling round and round. I looked up to search for the woman on horseback, but she had gone on. Perhaps, I didn't move fast enough." Winona grew still, as if defeated.

I had nothing to add, so I sat into the silence with her. Her eyes kept peering out the window, as if looking for some clue. Inside, I began shifting, wondering if Winona had gotten her cues all wrong. Tiny flies don't swarm in cold December weather but had long since died off, to make way for the new generations.

To my thinking, Winona answered, "It was insects They sent. I wanted a warrior woman to come claim me, and They sent fruit flies!" She snorted in disgust.

"Why do you think they did that, Winona?"

She turned her gaze back into my room and onto me. "They're always teaching, Meggie. It don't matter how old you get or how little you know. They're always showing you just a bit more. I guess They're just letting me know who I am and not to get too big with myself. The trickster Spirits play with us a lot, which is why we are always getting into trouble. But They're always teaching, and in that teaching, They are loving us pitiful two-leggeds."

"What are they teaching us?" I wanted to know.

"How to be human beings." Winona shifted in her chair. She shook her head, with admiration in her voice, "That warrior woman was something else."

"Maybe, it's just not your time."

"No," Winona disagreed. "The gate is there and opening. And I'm real tired. I just don't know exactly when. I never was much good on predicting those things." She turned to me: "I've given you a push, Meggie. You're going to have to be doing this yourself. Others will come. And when They come from your left side, pay attention. You think I've been working with you, because I had nothing else to do. Or that I had some strange liking of you."

I nodded yes to both of those thoughts.

"What you don't know is that, maybe, I was suppose to have gone over earlier, but then They saw you. And took pity on you. And kept this old body going for just a little bit longer. Lot of maybes in this world." She started looking at the tin of cookies again.

"Maybe . . . maybe you want one of them right now?" I asked, glancing at the tin.

Winona didn't wait for a second invitation.

She leaned over to the couch, pried open the lid, and extracted a gingerbread woman. She examined it with a great curiosity. "There's still so much for you to learn, Meggie. But you have a good heart and a searching spirit."

With enthusiasm, she bit around the head of the gingerbread woman. "Don't keep putting everything into that brain of yours. Learn to dance some, Meggie." She nibbled on the gingerbread feet.

Winona plucked the raisin eyes off the gingerbread woman, holding the figure up for inspection. "Now, that's how most of us are most of the time. We have forgotten how to see. This world of ours is so much more alive, more full of . . ."

"Enchantment?" I added.

Winona appeared confused at that word so I tried to explain as best I could. "It's a word that implies magic, little people under the mushrooms, spells. A world that is hidden and slowly revealed."

I'm not sure Winona fully understood what I was saying, but she nodded yes. All the while, she circled and reduced the gingerbread woman with small nibbles. She noticed my watching her and replied, "I'm moving to the core of things." Soon only the heart would be left.

Finally, even that disappeared into her mouth, and only a small crumb lingered at the corner of her mouth. Like a snake, her tongue emerged, trapped the crumb, and whipped it back in behind a satisfied smile.

With curiosity, I watched her every movement. In the space of two months, Winona had introduced me to a world I never had suspected. I was afraid that if she left, that world would disappear back into the mists.

"No, it won't," Winona intruded into my thoughts. She fastened down the lid over the cookies. "You lived in a world of edges and corners; I took you to where the world is round. You will have to walk round and round, Meggie, and each time around, the way will grow clearer. You will have other guides who will come and open your ears and eyes. You will come to understand that inside and outside are no difference. And perhaps, eventually," she hesitated, "you will learn to give away yourself."

"I don't understand, Winona."

She grew pensive, searching for the words to lead me closer to the core. She sighed, "It is a painful thing to learn, and your head is useless in the learning. There comes a time, as you walk this red road, a time when to fully live, you first have to let your *self* die. And that kind of dying is so hard to do."

372

She paused. I waited.

Then with a flash of inspiration, she said, "My grandson came home from school last week. He told me that there was a time when the people across the ocean thought the sun circled the earth. One of the elders finally said no, that it was the other way around. The people put the man in prison, until he said he was wrong. The people weren't ready for what he had tried to tell them. It was too painful. There comes a time for all of us when the world shifts, like that, and we have to choose."

"And what is the choice for you, for me?" I asked.

"We have to decide where we belong. Whether we live within the medicine circle along with the other beings or whether we continue to live in the center of our own existence. All alone."

"What if I make that choice — to live within the medicine circle?" I wasn't sure where to go with this.

She led me on: "You will be no better than the little spider, and she will become your sister. You will honor the elders before you, and protect the generations after you. You will be nothing, Meggie, and yet you will be everything. You will join the river and no longer be the person with the boat, skimming over the water. You will never forget that behind this world is the sacred mystery. And you, what you now know as you, will become less and less, as the circle grows. Until one day, you will even make the gift of your body back to the Grandmother, to feed the great great grandchildren of those who had given their lives to feed you."

"Why is it so difficult to make that choice, Winona?"

Her face filled with compassion at my ignorance. She knew that only experience would teach me to understand the paradox of dying to live. She answered my question, carefully choosing her words, "Meggie, listen to me. I'm an old woman. I'm about to cross over. I know these things in my heart. I know them to be true. Still, I get scared. For to give up yourself is to accept being lost. To give up yourself is to stand there within the Creation, to call out, and trust that They will come for you. It may be your sister, the spider. It may even be the little fly, when your heart was really set on the warrior woman. It's a yielding, which we have to do over and over and over again, for always our pride rises. And we get in our own way then."

Her eyes misted over. "Believe me, I'm full of joy now. I'll be going home soon. I'm curious about what is to happen next. I'm sad to leave my family behind. In certain moments, I still get scared. All my life, They have been trying to teach me how to be a human being. All my life, I keep falling back into the center. You see, Meggie, I'm no different than you. Only older and with more living to my wrinkles."

She extended her hands, sculpting two interconnecting circles in the air. "As I have taught you, so too it comes back to me full circle. I hear my words; they return as gifts to me as well. It is the way of the teacher."

The hands on the clock had moved one full revolution; our time was done. Winona lifted herself off the chair, adjusted her winter coat, slipped on her shoes, and picked up the cookie tin. Against my better judgment, I found myself asking her, "Will you be here for our Thursday session?"

She shrugged her shoulders, to let me know that it wasn't up to her anymore. Before walking out the door, she turned and gave me one last mischievous grin, while shaking the tin of cookies. "I hope to stay around long enough," she laughed, "to finish up these cookies!"

forty-four

Harry Truman

★ ★ ★

It is my land, my home, my father's land, to which I now ask to be allowed to return. I want to spend my last days there, and be buried among those mountains. If this could be I might die in peace. . . .

— Geronimo,
*Letter to President Grant
after surrender, 1877*

On Tuesday and Wednesday, the temperature dropped even further, the outside air tightened and froze, and still the atmosphere refused to release into snow. Even the trees seemed hunched over into themselves. My clients came to session anxious about the weather, about their relatives coming for Christmas, about memories of past, forlorn celebrations.

My parents telephoned from the Northwest, where they had arrived to spend the holiday with my sister's family. Mother described, in great detail, her sightseeing trip to Mt. St. Helens. "An old man, Harry Truman, lived on the south side of Spirit Lake, in the shadow of the mountain. When the earthquake rumblings began, the Forest Service blocked off the area, but Harry refused to leave his home. He declared that he and the mountain were one. When it blew in May 1980, the lateral blast of the mountain sent a huge mud-slide tumbling down toward Spirit Lake. Harry had two minutes warning before the mud entombed both him and his dog under a couple hundred feet of debris. There is no doubt now that Harry Truman did, indeed, become part of the mountain."

With awe in her voice, Mother exclaimed, "Here it is, years later, Meggie, and still the forest lies in an eerie quiet. The logs are all bleached, half covered with snow; everything is down, except for tree stumps standing four feet high. Miles and miles of devastation, as if an atomic bomb had exploded. It's a National Park; the biologists are watching to see what happens, how the land will regenerate itself. But all I can observe is the sheer emptiness of a once lively forest, now leveled to nothing."

She continued, "Your father says that the treeless mountains around St. Helens remind him of his once luxurious hair; that even Nature has to grow bald over time!" We both laughed. "So," she asked, "how is your love life?" It could have been worse; she could have asked me how was my weight.

"It's okay." I didn't want to fuel her hopes or her questions. I wasn't quite sure how my parents would take to the idea of my being attracted to an old rodeo rider or to a handyman, both Indians. Intellectually, my parents espoused a prejudice-free philosophy. Emotionally, they would have had a very hard time if I had fallen in love with a black man, but what about a red man? Better to keep quiet.

Mother tried to persuade me, in vain, to come out to my sister's place for Christmas. "It's not too late to get tickets. It's just not right, your celebrating Christmas without family!"

"Bev is family to me." I distracted her, "Tell me more about Harry Truman and Mt. St. Helens."

It worked. She answered, "I don't know much more about him, except that he was afraid of earthquakes. He was old. When the mountain blew, it sent forth a blast of heat that was four hundred degrees hot and three hundred and fifty miles per hour fast. He probably died from the heat and lack of oxygen. What a way to go! I bet, in the future, they'll erect a memorial to him on the mudflats by Spirit Lake, with the words 'Here Sleeps Harry.' But the mountain — and Harry is part of that mountain now — keeps on fuming and sending up smoke signals that all is not well underneath. There is an old Indian legend around Spirit Lake, about how the mountain would blow when the spirits of the Lake got angry. But you know, that's just myth."

Although I no longer knew what "myth" was anymore, I wasn't going to challenge her. I had another question: "Why do you think Harry stayed there, when everybody knew it was going to blow?" An adolescent might choose to stay out of curiosity or conviction in his or her own immortality, but what would have been the motive of an old man?

Mother replied, "When you get older, Meggie, you have the sense of living on borrowed time. You're grateful for each day. But when you get to the age of your father and me, well, you notice that most of your old school chums have long since died. Your friends get younger and of a different generation. When you can see that your children are going to do all right and survive without you . . . then life becomes both a gift and a burden. The inner clock runs down. It seems to me that every time I get something fixed, like my teeth or my toes, something else breaks down. I can understand a man coming to love his home, the mountain — and saying that the mountain's destiny will be his destiny. He accepted his time on this earth."

I could feel many "buts" rising in my throat. I choked them down while saying good-bye. There I stood, between the younger generation, who see forever stretching way out before them, and the older generation, standing on the edge with grace. It was up to my generation to be the caretakers of these two other generations. Yet both the old and the young seemed to be the ones who take the greater risks. It was my generation, caught in the middle, that appeared most haunted by death's shadow.

My clients in their teens and twenties spoke fearlessly of bungee jumping, wind surfing, bridge diving, roller coastering, and rock climbing. But clients in their thirties and forties came to my office speaking of their fear of ordinary plane trips, especially take-offs and landings. Suspicious lumps and moles, coughs that lingered too long, high cholesterol levels occupied their attention.

Most of us in our late thirties and forties found it hard to pass up free medical testing booths at county fairs. We recognized, for the first time, our mortality.

Death placed limits on my life; I could either hunker down in fear or make choices about the second half of my life. The move to rural Michigan was a big step. I could accept the demise of a marriage, as long as that loss held the promise of new life. The fear of death hadn't gone away, but it had changed locale and context. I had the questions, and Mother, Winona, and Harry Truman were all trying, in their own ways, to serve as guides.

If I could have gathered them all together and asked them to tell me the answers: Mother would say that the way through life is singular. Winona would tell me that the road is circular. And Harry would remind me that the mountain and I are essentially one.

forty-five

The Pipe

★ ★ ★

The Pipe is being brought to you.
With respect you must hold it!
Maybe you will doubt me
but I speak of that which is sacred.
Maybe you will doubt me.

— Traditional Lakota Pipe Song

I did not spend my time over the next two days worrying about Winona. I was preoccupied with the rest of my clients and making preparations for Sunday's Christmas dinner. Right before leaving home Thursday morning, however, I remembered the appointment with Winona that night. I quickly packed a small tin of Christmas cookies for her. If cookies could keep her alive long enough to reconsider, then so be it. I had faith in her belief that she was going to die soon, but I had doubt that it would actually happen. I assumed she would be on time for the appointment, despite her date with destiny. Sure enough, Winona showed up that evening.

I was encouraged by the vitality of her presence. She seemed less faded, more colorful. She came in, full of energy and wanting to get right down to work. She threw her winter coat carelessly onto my couch, took off her boots, rubbed her chilled hands into warmth and finally settled down, leaning her pipe bag against her chair. Scarcely had we exchanged greetings, when she began:

"There was a time, when I would not have told you all these things, Meggie. We had good reason not to trust you white people. Your genius is for wanting to change things, improve on them. We knew you'd take our ceremonies and have better ideas about them, and soon they would no longer be the old ceremonies. Even now, there are whites who build sweat-lodges and use them as saunas, go into them naked and without modesty, smoke dope in them, call themselves instant shamans, and go around giving weekend workshops on finding medicine power. The white people don't want to take the time to learn what can only be learned over a long slow time."

I asked, "What happened that you are willing to share these things with me?"

Winona leaned over and straightened her coat, jumbled up on the couch. "There was a prophecy among the Hopi that when strangely dressed, long-haired people would come by with a name like Hopi, then the young people would return to the old ways."

"You mean the hippies, don't you?" I interrupted.

Winona nodded, "The elders of the different tribes across the country began to see that the bones of the white people had been on this continent now for over seven generations. That there were whites and blacks and yellow people who have been on this land longer than on the lands across the waters. It was decided that the knowledge was to be shared with those of good heart who wanted to follow the way of the red road."

Winona shook her head in consternation, saying, "You can imagine how that made some of our younger people feel, because they hated the whites for what the whites had done — and are still doing to my people — with the breaking of all those treaties."

"Do you hate the whites, Winona?" I was curious.

"Well, I wouldn't want to be one, that's for sure! I don't like the way whites live, so out of touch with the Grandmother and the medicine circle. It's a stiff people you belong to, Meggie. You're afraid of dirt, you forget where you came from, and you don't know where you are going. Your people don't know how to walk in balance." Winona screwed up her face, as if the very mention of white life was distasteful.

She paused and added, "I don't hate them. I feel sorry for them." She nodded, satisfied that she was saying what she meant.

"Does my being white bother you?" I pushed her.

Winona smiled and laughed. "Oh no!" she said with emphasis. "It just means that there was more I had to teach you. Like a little child." She held her hand about two feet off the floor, to show me just how little I was in my ignorance. She was teasing.

I changed the conversation back to her. "Winona, you are here today. What do you think that means?"

She quickly replied, "That I'm not yet dead." Then, with a sly smile on her face, she asked, "Or am I?"

I answered, "You look quite alive to me."

Winona pulled out her pipe. Again, she checked with me to make sure I wasn't in my moon. She pointed to the lightning design, saying, "Davis beaded that for me. That's why this social pipe is so important to me, because he gave it to me, after he carved the bowl and shaped the stem. Many years, I've used this pipe for teaching. The other one, my sacred pipe — the Chanunpa Wakan — I keep in my medicine bundle for ceremony."

She assembled the lightning-streaked pipe. "It's time to teach you how to pray with the pipe. First, you've got to smudge yourself with the sage or cedar, to clean yourself up and to purify the pipe." She passed the pipe over the smoke of the burning sage several times. "Then you take the pipe and hold it out. The stem should be pointing to the West, the bowl in your left hand."

With effort, Winona stiffly knelt down on the large oriental rug. She placed the bowl of sage on her right side, while holding the pipe bowl with her left hand. I knelt beside her. She continued with her instruction: "I take this pinch of tobacco, smudge it, and then offer it to Wakan Tanka, the Great Mystery, while circling it in all the directions, sun-wise. I ask Him to pay attention to my prayers and to recognize the pipe. Then I offer a pinch of tobacco to the Grandfather of the West, the one with His face painted black. I pray about the visions I have been given or that I am needing. Next, I offer a pinch of tobacco to the Grandfather of the North with the face painted red, asking for purification and healing." While giving instruction, Winona offered pinches of tobacco in circles, after smudging them and then gently placing them into the bowl of her pipe, tamping them down ever so lightly.

She then took a pinch of tobacco and offered it above and behind her to the Grandfather of the East, the one whose face is painted yellow. "I pray to Him for the knowledge that comes from within, that moves slowly into knowing." She offered tobacco to the Grandfather of the South, whose face is painted white, "I pray for the wonder of a child and to understand the mystery of birth, death, and the circle of our life here." She then lifted a pinch to Wakan Tanka — the Sky Beings, giving thanks for the light in the darkness and the power of the Thunder Beings. Finally, she leaned over and touched a pinch of tobacco to the Grandmother, giving thanks to Her for food and clothing. She asked the Grandmother to give her strength, as she walked upon Her. Finally, she added a pinch for the spotted eagle and her medicine helpers. Again, she drew the pipe lovingly through the smoke of the now smoldering sage.

Winona held the pipe out, away from her body, and began chanting a spirit-calling song in Lakota. I wondered whether Bev and her client could hear it through the office walls. I felt strangely moved by the music. After she had finished, Winona started to pray in earnest. She asked the Grandfathers to watch over the young ones in her family, so that they could one day find the road they needed to walk. She prayed for Hawk, that he would learn to temper what he already knew with wisdom and not to be drawn off the pipe road by power or pride. She asked that the Spirits help Lucy come to understand what she was doing and why. She mentioned a host of other people on the reservation, and finally to my surprise she prayed for me. "Grandfather, look at this woman beside me and have pity on her. Teach her gently and give her no more than she can handle. She has much to learn. Help her to open her eyes, to empty her mind, to know how to walk on you, Grandmother. She reminds me of me in the old days, Grandfather, when I knew nothing. Have pity on her." She then prayed for herself, to have courage to face what was ahead. She ended with "Mitakuye oyas'in." At which point, she then turned and handed me the pipe, saying, "Pray with it. Ask the Grandfathers for what you need."

I moved into a kneeling position, took the pipe, and then promptly squeezed my eyes shut to pray. Winona nudged me in the ribs with her elbow. "Always keep your eyes open, to see what happens." I raised the pipe up toward the West.

Part of me was giving myself a hard time. What in the hell are you doing, Meggie O'Connor, on the floor praying with a client? My supervisors had never trained me for such an occasion.

Several minutes passed before I stammered, "Grandfather, I ask your help in knowing what to do with my client here, Winona. She tells me she is going to die soon. I ask you to help me to help her." I started to hand the pipe back to her, then remembered, and said, "All My Relations."

Winona nodded in approval of my prayer. She lit the pipe and offered it to all the directions and passed it back to me. We knelt there in the quiet, smoking and offering the pipe. When the pipe had finally smoked down, Winona again said, "Mitakuye oyas'in," left the office, and blew the ashes outside. She returned to her chair and seemed satisfied. I pushed myself off my knees and moved back into my chair. She stowed away the parts of the pipe, the tamper, the sage holder, the lighter, and the tobacco into the pipe bag. She started to put on her coat and boots.

I pointed to the clock. "We still have ten minutes left to our session."

Winona shook her head and said, "It was good to pray with you, Meggie. You must understand that the pipe is at the center. The more you work with the pipe, the more it becomes you and you become the pipe. There is nothing that I have to share with you that is more than that. It's time for me to leave now."

"Oh!" I remembered, "I have a little Christmas gift for you!"

"What's that?" she asked.

I handed her the tin of cookies. She smiled at me and touched her hand to my cheek. "It's good for you to remember your elders, Meggie." She picked up the tin and her pipe bag and headed out the door.

I called out, "Winona!"

She looked back at me; frigid air wafted into the waiting room from the open outside door. I reminded her, "Don't forget our appointment next Monday."

She replied, "You'll be all right. You know how to pray now." Gently, firmly, she closed the door behind her.

forty-six

Christmas Eve

★ ★ ★

. . . were we led all that way for
Birth or Death? There was a Birth, certainly,
We had evidence and no doubt. I had seen
birth and death,
But had thought they were different. . . .

— T.S. Eliot,
Journey of the Magi

Friday, the snow let loose. All day Saturday, amidst the swirling whiteness, children celebrated their time off from school shaping snow men, erecting snow forts, and instigating snowball fights. Despite the storm, Morey's Food Market was packed with parents gathering their final ingredients for the Sunday Christmas dinner. The music of carols jingled throughout the stores. I bought shrimp cocktail, made a quick stop at the Video Depot for movies, and then retreated homeward in gusts of snow-filled wind.

Saturday afternoon, I took an axe and headed out toward the white-shrouded woods, Fritzie snapping at the snowflakes falling onto his nose. I found a blue balsam tree, which he promptly marked before I chopped it down. "This tree is now off limits to you, old boy!" I warned him. He cocked his head, as if indifferent to my implicit threats.

I sang "Oh Come All Ye Faithful" all the way back to the house, Fritzie bounding in the snow before me, the tree dragging a trail behind me. We deposited the tree out on the back porch to wait for Bev's help to set it up and decorate it with mementos from Christmases of years' past.

As the daylight shaded into twilight, Bev finally arrived, her car slithering up the driveway around slick corners. The car was laden with unopened Christmas gifts, groceries, and her suitcase. Parking near the house, Bev emerged, swearing, "Jesus H. Christ! I never thought I was going to make it up that last hill! You know, Meggie, one could get stranded up here!" I knew that all too well. The thought of being trapped and unable to get to work caught her fancy, and a smile broke out on her face. "Well, one thing's for sure." She pointed to the bags of groceries. "We aren't going to starve!"

I helped her unpack the car, while Fritzie

kept trying to interest her in a frozen tennis ball he had found. Clenching the ball in his teeth, he'd push it right into her hand, but could not surrender the ball without a tug. Finally, Bev could stand it no longer and gave in to his invitation. She wrenched the ball from his jaws (no mean feat when you are wearing mittens) and tossed it into a drift of the new snow. Despite its bright yellow color, the ball sank into oblivion. Fritzie leapt into the air after it, puzzled by its disappearance. He vanished into the snow after it, making stiff-legged jumps from the ground. Bev took pity on him and went to look for a hole's imprint in the snow. With an expression of triumph, she found the ball and handed it over to Fritzie. He, in turn, tried to revive the game, but she shook her head. Enough was enough between friends.

We celebrated Christmas Eve, snug by the fire, telling tales of friends and family. The tree was hung with decorations, and the house smelled of homemade soup and bread. We mulled cider and drank toasts to the old year. Coming to the year's end, there was a certain amount of reckoning to be done. Bev ruminated over what went wrong in her relationship with Coulter, and each time she found herself deepening into rationalizations. "Once gay, always gay. It was just a recipe for future disaster. I'm better off this way. If he couldn't wait through my ambivalence and give me the time and separate space I needed, well then . . ." Each rationalization sputtered into a silence.

Finally she turned and said, "I guess I just botched it, didn't I?"

I shook my head, not willing to be the judge. "There are those, Bev, who would say it was a good thing the relationship ended. All I know is that when a man falls in love and confesses his deepest wound, he is looking for the healing that only a woman can offer him. For at that time, she becomes the Great Mother, and she gives him life and she gives him absolution. In that moment, he is made whole again. But when that is withheld, even for the shortest of times, he knows himself to be forever guilty. And then he closes off the wound and tucks it way back down again."

Bev rebutted: "Yet I would have probably come around and let him know that it was okay between us. I just needed time, that's all."

"What you would have done, Bev, and Coulter knew this — you would have forgiven him and forgiven him and forgiven him his past, and all his life you would be forgiving him for what he had renounced in the name of love. That's not absolution.

That's power in the name of Christian forgiveness."

The ability to tolerate blunt truths was what characterized the relationship between Bev and myself. I would never have dared to be so straight-forward with someone like Katya.

"Well," she lifted her glass of cider, "maybe he'll come back. Then again," she sighed, "maybe he won't."

Bev reached into her pocketbook and pulled out a button. It read: *I've given up looking for the meaning of life. All I want is a hot fudge sundae!* She pinned it onto her sweater. "I've been saving this button a long time for an occasion just like this."

I didn't know it then, but the past two months had marked a turning point for me in my life. I sat there before the fire on Christmas Eve, warm in the friendship with Bev, recounting the year's passing — the successes, the failures, the not-so-sures, as if life could be scored with a school grade. I shared with her both the perplexity and fascination I had experienced with Winona. As the flames curled around the birch logs, I briefly mentioned Slade and spun fantasies about Hawk. Falling snowflakes landed on the windows, forming strings of crystalline pearls. We piled the wood onto the fire to prolong the conversation.

At two to midnight, we rose from the couch and walked to the door, flinging it open to the freezing air. The snowstorm had passed and the midnight sky was clearing. Blue stars darted in and out behind fast moving clouds; the moon struggled to make itself seen. Linking arms, Bev and I peered into the night as if expecting to see Santa's sleigh and eight reindeer in harness. The cold made us shiver, as we waited for midnight to arrive and pass on into Christ-mas morning. Just as the indoor clock began to chime the first of twelve times, a flash of light zig-zagged across the western sky. Before we could puzzle its origin, it was followed by the booming drums of the Thunder Beings.

And my heart knew then.

"Good grief, what was that?" Bev asked.

My knowing heart shivered, clutching at the cold night air. My hand tightly grasped her arm, as if to steady myself.

Bev turned to study my face.

And then a brutal gasp of frigid air wrenched me loose unto myself. A long sigh slipped out of me, white tendrils of breath rising and dissipating into the dark night sky.

"It was the lightning passing on through," I answered.

forty-seven

Christmas Merriment

★ ★ ★

*"I don't know what to do!" cried Scrooge,
laughing and crying in the same breath. . . .
"I am as light as a feather, I am as
happy as an angel. I am as merry as a
school-boy. I am as giddy as a drunken
man. A merry Christmas to everybody!"*

— Charles Dickens,
A Christmas Carol

A prettier Christmas morning would have
been hard to imagine. During the night, the
wind had chased away the clouds. The late-
rising sun sprinkled gold on the snow's surface. The driveway was not to be seen; there
was none. The white surface of the outside
world was smooth and unbroken. Not even
the animals had started tracking trails across
the wind-whipped drifts. It was as if, just for
this moment, God had given each one of us
a blank slate on which we could retrace and

recreate our journeys. Or to make entirely new beginnings.

Up before Bev, I put on the kettle of water to make oatmeal. A winter morning such as this required the tradition of an old fashioned breakfast. The coffee smells and my walking about in the kitchen stirred Bev from her winter sleep. Hair akimbo, old slippers on her feet, and a faded bathroom robe tied loosely around her waist, she shuffled into the kitchen, resembling a she-bear roused from hibernation. "Is that real coffee?" she whispered, so as not to jar herself awake.

I nodded, pulled out the cereal bowls, spooned out the oatmeal, sprinkled it with brown sugar, placed before her a pitcher of milk, poured us both some coffee, and sat down to eat. With each spoonful, consciousness began to dawn within her. "Soul food," I commented, pointing to the oatmeal.

Hoisting her coffee cup and gulping, she countered, "The stuff of life."

Being a good friend means knowing when to keep the conversation short and sweet. I had cranked up the woodstove; it was belching heat. We sat there like that, warming our insides and outsides, digesting the change from night to day.

After breakfast, Bev and I assembled our

ingredients and started cooking the Christmas dinner. With pots simmering on the stove, Bev proposed that we move into the living room and open all our presents. I had other ideas in my head. I shook my head, "I want to go outside and play in the snow. Look at it, Bev. It's beautiful out there; the whole world is sparkling with the sun's reflection, gold on white. In the garage is an ancient wooden toboggan, with a stuffed leather cushion and rope handle. I want to get it, fly down the unplowed driveway, and feel the wind in my hair and the cold on my cheeks."

"You what?" Bev was incredulous. She amended her question: "You know, Meggie, sometimes I doubt your sanity. We have all these beautiful Christmas gifts waiting to be unwrapped, and you want to go out and freeze your rear end."

I nodded yes.

She continued, "You want to go out there, where it is very cold, to get on a sled, and careen down the hill where a tree could rise up and hit us? A stump might break our tail bones. We will surely end up in a ditch." Bev shook her head in mock dismay, "Well, why the hell not. I mean, what are friends for but to accompany each other into their insanities?"

And so that Christmas morning was spent, slipping and sliding down the hill in the old toboggan, while the presents languished, unopened, under the tree. I insisted that I be at the head of the toboggan, to give pretense to steerage. Bev pushed, braked, and fell off the back end repeatedly. Frequently, I found myself way down at the bottom of the hill having crashed into a bush, companionless. Turning around, Bev's body was usually splayed midway down the slope, as she collapsed into laughter. We collected bruises for future anecdotes. The rapture of flying, unconstrained, barely in control, urged us again and again to trudge up the driveway for yet another wild plunge.

Finally our bottoms began to chafe with the damp cold, and we quit. But not before Bev pelted me with three well-aimed snowballs: "This one is for getting me up early. This one is for making my rear end suffer frostbite. And this one is for forcing me to delay opening my presents!" Bev entered the house first, as only a victor should.

The house glowed with the warmth of the woodstove and the delicious smells of food. It wasn't long before we doffed our winter wraps and dove into the presents. My favorite gifts were the books, so I opened them first. Bev looked at me strangely as I put my nose down into the middle of a book and inhaled deeply. I explained, "I've always loved to open up a new book and smell the pages, to get a whiff of the adventure before I read the first page. I've never understood those people who read the last page first; they fool themselves that life is always headed for a clear resolution. I like the suspense of living it through."

"I'll take clothing over books any day," she sniffed. Carefully she unwrapped her gifts of clothing and, like a little girl, insisted on trying on each new piece. She snuggled into a soft flannel nightgown, then sashayed about in a low-cut blouse.

We didn't neglect Fritzie. I had wrapped six brand new tennis balls in separate packages, and he delighted in rolling them about the floor.

The opened presents lay sprawled about the living-room floor, when we adjourned to the dining room for our international feast. Shrimp cocktail preceded an African peanut soup, accompanied by sparkling grape juice. Then a salad of hearts of romaine, decorated with artichoke hearts, spiced croutons, minced purple onion, and topped with Parmesan cheese and a light garlic dressing. Bev served buffalo strips, grilled for a brief moment after having been marinated overnight in a tomato sauce. She accompanied the meat with a dish of buttery taboule. After such a meal, we forswore dessert and believed ourselves virtuous.

Day sank into night, as we cleaned up the meal and the sprawl of Christmas presents, called our families, talked to each other, supervised the snow plowing of the driveway by my neighbor, and watched movie classics. Both of us were satisfied that one more Christmas had been celebrated in style. It had been a good time, full of fun and nostalgia, bruises, round bellies, old memories and truthful mirrors. Apart from our families, Bev and I made a family unto ourselves. Apart from a spiritual tradition, we wove a psychological tapestry of meaning. We were aware of the loneliness of our "aparts" but not devastated by them.

Christmas evening came, and Bev packed up her clothes and said her fond farewell, driving down the freshly plowed road. The silence in the house wrapped around me, as if I were a gift still waiting to be opened.

A surprise even unto myself.

forty-eight

The Circle Gathers

★ ★ ★

If I should die,
And you should live,
And time should gurgle on,
And morn should beam,
And noon should burn,
As it has usual done:
If birds should build as early,
And bees as bustling go, —
One might depart at option
From enterprise below! . . .

— Emily Dickinson,
If I Should Die

Monday morning, I checked my answering machine to listen to the messages: two cancellations and one newly referred client asking for an appointment. Then the machine played back this brief message: "This is Lucy Arbre. Mother died Saturday night." After a moment of silence, as Lucy choked back her grief, "Wednesday night, we're holding a prayer ceremony in our home. Mother would like you to be there." The hollow sound of the phone's disconnection punctuated the terse message.

I dropped down into Winona's office chair, doubting the announcement, yet knowing it was true. Time stretched and suspended itself, as I sat there. Sadness crept in on the edges of my disbelief. I sank inward, hearing myself say to her, "I'll see you on Monday," and her reply: "You'll be all right now; you know how to pray."

"It's not all right for you to go now. I don't know how to pray. I'm not ready for you to go yet." I protested, my voice angry and no one to hear me. I was beginning to sound like Lucy in the family therapy session.

I hoisted myself from Winona's chair, my body gone heavy on me. I had other clients to treat. I turned back toward the chair, as if she were still sitting there, boots off, in a rumpled house dress. Out loud I said, "Oh Winona, I will miss you!"

All day long, during the sessions with my clients, my eyes leaked tears. I was not aware of crying, only that I had to keep dabbing my eyes with tissues. "It must be an allergy," I lied. Fortunately, most of my clients were suffering post-holiday blues and took my tears as a sign of empathy. It was as if my body had its own agenda, despite my determination to get about the business of the day. It was clear to me that I had to go to the memorial prayer service for Winona.

Bev's reaction to Winona's death was incredulity. "How did she die? Did she kill herself or what?"

I could only shake my head. I didn't know. "I doubt that she would kill herself, Bev. It just wasn't her style." Still, I didn't know. It was partly out of respect and partly out of curiosity that I was planning to go to the prayer service. Bev made me promise I would tell her all the details. She reminded me, glint in her eye, "Hawk will be there."

I called up the Arbre household and one of Winona's grandchildren gave me the directions. It was dark outside Wednesday evening, when I pulled my car up into the driveway. There were barely any places to park, as pick-up trucks crowded around the house. Light was streaming from every window, illuminating the crowd of people in the house. I felt conspicuously Caucasian. I reminded myself that Winona wanted me there, so in I went.

The front door opened up into a small entryway between the living room and dining room. Set off in one corner in the dining room was a large coffeepot surrounded by paper cups, sugar, and creamer. Cigarette smoke permeated the house. Over in another corner by the dining room, old heavyset women with long dark hair were sitting watching everyone, commenting on what they saw, occasionally breaking out into giggles. The younger women moved about, offering coffee and cookies to newcomers. Children raced back and forth, while the men congregated toward the living room. Lucy came over to greet me and show me where to put my coat. She thanked me for coming.

"Is Hawk here?" I asked.

"He's in the back room, getting everything ready for the prayer meeting." She nodded to a set of closed doors and then hurried to the front door to greet arriving guests.

I looked over toward a bookcase and, to my surprise, saw Hawk standing there, leaning against the bookshelves, talking with another Indian man. He smiled at me and tipped his head. I smiled back. Lucy walked up to him and whispered in his ear, indicating with a nod of her head where I stood. He excused himself to the friend and ambled over toward me. "I'm so glad you came," he said and took my hand in a brief shake. He offered me coffee, and I said, "Yes."

The mood of the house began to quiet down. The women summoned their children. Hawk returned with my coffee, and I thanked him, noticing how deep set were his eyes. He turned, looking toward a back bedroom, and said, "We will start now. All is ready for the ceremony. He told me to be sure that you were made comfortable."

"Who?" I asked. Who was it that wanted me to be comfortable?

He looked straight at me, "Why, Hawk, of course. And there he is with the medicine bundle." He nodded toward the opening door of the back bedroom. I was confused!

Out stepped Slade, carrying a blue-and-yellow blanket wrapped with leather strips. He wore a black shirt bedecked with four ribbons, jeans, and beaded moccasins. His face was serious, studied. He spoke to Lucy, and she went around asking if any of the women were in their moon cycle. No one was, and so the ceremony could continue. Lucy came up to us and said, "Larry, Hawk wants everyone to sit down in a large circle and take off their shoes. Would you ask those in the dining room to move into the living room?" She then turned to me and said, "Dr. O'Connor, if you would tell the women the same thing, I would appreciate it." Off she went, organizing others.

Larry took his leave of me. I began to put two and two together. Larry, whom I always thought was Hawk, was Lucy's husband, the one who worked at the casino. And Hawk apparently had always been Slade. I shook my head in confusion and headed toward the circle, now gathered in the living room. Only then did I remember that Winona had told me that Indians often have two names, one for the white world, one for ceremonies. I wondered if Winona had known about my mix-up? If not, it would have been the kind of joke on me that she would have thoroughly enjoyed.

It didn't look as if I had to tell anyone to gather around, as everyone was already bunching into the small space. Slade/Hawk had Winona's little granddaughter come up, and he gave her a bowl in which he placed the sacred sage. He lit the sage and showed her how he wanted her to smudge the people with the smoke. Alert and proud, she carried out the task with great attention.

He unwrapped his bundle and extracted his sacred pipe, bowl and stem. He assembled the pipe and placed tobacco in it, praying to the Grandfathers and to the Grandmother. Everyone was quiet, even the youngest child.

I watched him, reassessing the past two months that I had known Slade. He was sure in his motions, and the people obviously respected him. He held the pipe aloft, pointing the stem first toward the West, then around in a large circle.

"We come here, Grandfathers, to say good-bye to Winona who has crossed over." For a brief moment, he talked in Lakota, a language foreign to those in the room. He returned to English. "She is over there now, Grandfather, lost and confused. We ask You to help her. Send her someone who will point the way to her, so she can make that journey South. Let her know, that though we love her, we will not keep her. We give her back to You. We release her from the need to hold onto our mother, our aunt, our sister, our teacher, and our friend. There are things for her to do there, Grandfather. She has done this earth-walk in a good way. She has worked hard for her people. I ask You now, Grandfathers, to listen to the prayers of my aunts and uncles, my sisters and brothers, my nephews and nieces here, for they, too, miss her and want to say good-bye. All My Relations." He raised the unlit pipe, offered it, and passed it to the person on his left.

Everyone, in turn, offered a prayer about Winona. Some remembered her humor.

Some, like Lucy, wept as they prayed. Others appeared not to have known her at all well, but were there to give support to Lucy and Larry and the grandchildren. Winona's eight-year-old grandson took the pipe on his turn and stood up. He sang a song, beginning with the word "Kola" that pulled at the heart. When he finished, he said, "Grandmother, I sang that White Buffalo Calf Woman song for you, the way you taught me. Ah hau!" He sat down. All the men and old women nodded in appreciation of the young boy's song.

The pipe moved around to where I was sitting and finally came to me. An unusual pipe, it had a round stem and a bowl carved in the shape of a flying hawk. Hanging from the stem were six feathers: four hawk feathers bounded by two eagle feathers. Strips of red cloth lashed long sage pieces around the stem, so that the unlit pipe gave off a strong fragrance of sweet sage. I held the pipe for a moment in silence, totally unaware of what I would pray. I began:

"Grandfather, I give thanks for this woman who walked into my life." The older women nodded to these words. I continued, "It is hard for me to say good-bye." In the periphery of my vision, I could see Lucy bend down with her head in her hands, crying. "I ask you to help me understand all the things she taught me." Now the tears leaked out of my eyes too.

"She knew, Grandfather, she was going to die, and I didn't want to know that, Grandfather. Help me, help all of us here, to know what she knew — that death is just a beginning. Mitakuye oyas'in."

The circle of people responded "Hau!" to these words. I offered the pipe and released it to the next person in the circle. Hawk/Slade looked at me and smiled. He knew how hard this had been for me. My tears had stained the sage on his pipe.

Finally, the pipe returned to him. He took firm hold of it, stem to the West, and said, "And now, Grandfathers and Grandmother, we will tell of Winona's passing over."

He turned back toward the circle, still holding the pipe before him. He began to recite the story of her last days. "She told me on Friday to come spend the afternoon with her. There were things she had to teach me. She told me she would be crossing over on Saturday night and that she needed to tell me more of the pipe. I had to know how she wanted to be buried and what to do with her sacred pipe. She told me of my responsibilities as a medicine teacher to the people. She talked to me of the things that pull a person off the red road and how to be always knowing of what I did and why I did it.

"She talked to me for hours about these matters, and I listened and paid attention. Still I did not believe she would leave us, as her health was good. She told me she was tired, and it was time. Then she said for me to gather the family together on Christmas Eve. She asked that the grandchildren be allowed to open their Christmas presents from her, as she wanted to see the joy on their faces. After we ate on Saturday and the kids had opened their presents, she asked everyone to gather around her, where she sat on the recliner here in the living room. I think I'll have Lucy tell you the rest of it."

Hawk rose from where he was sitting and took the pipe over to Lucy and put it into her hands.

Lucy looked momentarily startled. The pipe didn't come naturally to her. She composed herself, struggling for the words at first. "Mom told us that last week — the Spirits came to her and said They were ready for her now, that she could go with Them." The tears began to drip down her face. She looked to Hawk to take over, but he just nodded supportively.

She continued, "It was late Saturday night, almost midnight. She told me she was sorry about not always having been a good mother to me, but that she loved me. She talked to the kids about always honoring their elders and their being Indian, that they had brought her much pleasure these past few months. She told us where her will was and that she wanted to be buried in as flimsy a coffin as we could find." Lucy began crying softly, "So she could return to the Grandmother as quick as possible."

Everybody waited as Lucy again tried to pull herself back from sobbing. "I thought Mom was crazy, because she wasn't sick. I took her wrist in my hand and could feel a very strong pulse. That reassured me. Mom smiled at me. I guess she knew I wasn't believing any of this stuff about her passing on. She said that a warrior woman had come for her and was standing there in the corner." Lucy pointed over to the television area.

"Mom seemed real pleased. Said that the warrior woman was just waiting for her to get ready. Well, I kept my hand around her wrist. Maybe I thought that by touch I could keep her here. I don't know. Mom closed her eyes. She got real peaceful. There was this grin on her face. Her heart kept pumping *ka-thump, ka-thump, ka-thump*. Real steady and strong, for about fifteen or twenty minutes. We were all quiet, waiting for her to open her eyes. I never took my hand from her wrist, and finally, her heartbeat went from *ka-thump, ka-thump, ka-thump* and . . . It just stopped. There was no beat. Then, I knew she had gone away from us." Tears flowed from Lucy's eyes, and Hawk gently went up to her and retrieved the pipe.

He returned to his place in the circle to say, "So, even in her death, she remained a teacher to us all. All My Relations!"

Everyone responded, "Ah-hau!" Hawk raised the pipe, circled it, lit it and offered it to all the directions. He then raised it higher, offered it to the Grandfathers and then the Grandmother, and passed it to the person on his left, saying, "All My Relations. We say this, because we pray in the name of all our relations." The lit pipe then passed around the circle with everyone, even the little children, taking a puff, the grown-ups helping them hold the pipe steady. When the pipe returned to Hawk, he smoked the tobacco to the embers. "Mitakuye oyas'in," he exclaimed as he disassembled the pipe, going to the front door to blow out the hot ash.

Afterward, the people mingled; though friendly to me, I still felt like the stranger. I decided to leave early and thanked Lucy for inviting me to the ceremony. She told me that they had buried her mother, placing her sacred pipe over her chest, according to her mother's instructions. Lucy managed a laugh when describing how the undertaker thought they were a bunch of cheapskate Indians asking for the flimsiest box. I muttered some words of support, inadequate to the occasion. Larry too came up and said good-bye, after telling me that with Winona's passing, he no longer needed to meet with me over his concerns about his mother-in-law. Knowing who he was now, I suppressed my fantasies about him. He had become taboo for me.

Just before I slipped out the door, the real Hawk (the real Slade) came up to me, saying, "She would have been happy to know that you came." He held a long skinny cardboard box in his hands, which he placed into my arms. He said, "Here. She asked me to give you this, said you would know what to do with it."

With that, he gave me a mysterious smile and walked back to join the others in the living room. I drove on home, the gift in the seat beside me, all the time wondering what it was that Winona had left me as her legacy.

forty-nine

The Gift of Old Ecstasies

★ ★ ★

*perhaps we shouldn't plan to arrive at the end
of love, but should move inside its mystery
like chickadees, those acrobats darting in and
out of branches, paled by frost.*

— Roberta Hill Whiteman,
A Song For What Never Arrives

The telephone was ringing when I arrived at
Chrysalis. I put down the package and
headed for the phone to answer, then
stopped and turned away. The package took
precedence. I was not going to be distracted
from Winona's last message. I retrieved a
knife from the kitchen and slit open the taped
cardboard edges of the box. Whatever it was,
Winona had intended it to be well-protected.
The telephone stopped ringing. It was probably Bev wanting to know about my encounter with Hawk. I suspected she was going to
have a good laugh on my account.

416

The box opened easily, full of dried sage and aromatic. There, in a cradle of dried sage, rested Winona's social pipe, the lightning design clearly standing out in the beaded pattern on the stem. In the corner of the box was her pipe bag, four zip-locked bags of a tobacco mix which she had labeled "Sacred Tobacco," and one small catlinite smudge bowl in the shape of a red totem bear, the four paws serving to ground the bowl. In the pipe bag were two lighters and a well-worn, familiar tamper, beaded at the top.

I sat down, stunned, the box and its contents securely on my lap. So, that was what Winona left me. Even then, I didn't really know what she had left me. I remembered that she had said that if one cleans up a social pipe with sage, it could be used for prayer. She knew I wasn't a smoker. It was clear that she meant this pipe for prayer.

I looked about the living room, my ancestors peering down from their portraits and photographs on the walls. If I chose to pick up this pipe and use it for prayer, my ancestors would come alive to me. If I left the pipe unused, just another Native American artifact, they would remain comfortably ensconced within their gilded frames, long since dead.

If I prayed in the way of the pipe, I knew the lightning design might shift on me, tilting the axis of my familiar twentieth-century world. The doe and the porcupine would become my sisters and brothers, and I could no longer rise above them in my human pretensions. If I chose to follow the red road, I might even travel so far as to encounter the little people from my own remote Celtic tradition.

Reason within me balked and argued against imagination, vision, and superstition. Despite my fear, I felt the most human of emotions — curiosity. I wanted to know what would happen next.

It was no simple gift this wise old woman had left me. It was a path and a journey that didn't end even at the border crossing of death. Winona meant for me to make a decision, to be comfortable in the illusions of the twentieth-century — or to choose to learn the old teachings that the Earth is our Grandmother and we are Her children. To know about Spirits and other realities that coexist with our own apparent reality.

I felt bereft of a teacher now, alone, without a guide. I suppose like all good teachers, she knew there comes a time when the student would leave, but I didn't feel ready. Perhaps that was why she had encouraged

Hawk to take interest in me, to assume a position as my next teacher. I wondered about all this, sitting there in the living room, my ancestors looking down at me. I knew enough not to underestimate Winona's schemes.

The pipe lay inert on its bed of sage. It didn't rise up and force itself into my hands. It waited for me to make the choice.

Perhaps the choice had already been made for me, long ago, when I used to climb the old apple tree in my grandmother's orchard, reading my summer adventure stories. I knew that my grandmother's spirit hovered about, though I never could see her. Chrysalis was a place of transformation. I wondered if the caterpillar was ever afraid to die to the new life. Was it painful to melt away the secure earth-bound connections and grow the bulky wings? Did the caterpillar have any choice?

Looking about me, at the ancestors inside and the land stretching before me outside, I knew I would honor the spirit of my grandmother, the vision of my teacher, and follow the red path.

I took off my shoes, reached into the box, and pulled out the pipe bowl and stem. Breaking off a piece of the sage, I crumpled it and placed it in the bowl on the back of the totem bear. I lit the sage and washed myself in the pungent smoke. Joining the stem to the bowl, I cleansed the pipe in the smoke. I turned, kneeling toward the West, pipe held out before me, bowl lovingly cradled in my left hand and began the ancient ritual as Winona had so carefully taught me — placing the sacred tobacco in the bowl, praying to each Grandfather in turn and finally to Grandmother Earth. In the bowl, I offered a pinch of tobacco for the spirit of Winona, asking the Grandfathers to help her find her way in her life over there. I gave thanks to my ancestors.

When I had finished my words of prayer, I sat there in the silence, eyes opened, attentive to the circle around me. The air was thick and moving, and in the dark, pin-point lights flashed about, what would have been called in the old Celtic days "faerie lights." Winona had spoken of these lights, saying they were the Spirits letting the two-leggeds know that They were pleased.

It must have been five or twenty minutes into the stillness, when I heard a voice, a woman's voice, calling from the West. I didn't recognize the voice, only that it was outside of me. Startled but not scared, I felt surrounded and protected.

The voice spoke a simple message, loving

and accepting of my ignorance. It would be a long time before I would hear another stated as clearly:

"It will be all right now. You know how to pray."

MITAKUYE OYAS'IN.

Bibliography

* * *

Black Elk, Wallace & Lyon, William S. 1990. *Black Elk, The Sacred Ways of a Lakota.* San Francisco: Harper & Row.

Bolen, Jean Shinoda. 1985. *Goddesses in Everywoman.* New York: Harper & Row.

Brooks, Francis. 1896. "To Imagination: An Ode," in *The Poems of Francis Brooks*, ed. by Wallace Rice, p. 56. Chicago: R.R. Donnelley & Sons Co.

Browning, Elizabeth Barrett. 1857. "Aurora Leigh," in *Bartlett's Familiar Quotations*, ed. Emily Morrison Beck, 1980, p. 507. Boston: Little, Brown & Co.

Campbell, Joseph. 1988. *The Power of Myth.* New York: Doubleday.

Chesterfield, Lord Philip Dormer Stanhope (1742–1752). *Letters to His Son*, 1940. New York: T.Y. Crowell.

Clifton, Lucille. 1991. "Sleeping Beauty," in *Quilting: Poems, 1987–1990*, p. 33. Brockport, N.Y.: BOA Additions Limited.

De La Mare, Walter. 1955. "All But Blind,"

in *Modern American and British Poetry*, ed.
Louis Untermeyer, p. 512. New York:
Harcourt, Brace & World.

Dickens, Charles. 1843. *A Christmas Carol*,
1983 edition, p. 108. New York: Holiday
House.

Dickinson, Emily. 1858. "If I Should Die,"
in *The Complete Poems of Emily Dickinson*,
ed. Thomas H. Johnson, 1960, p. 29.
Boston: Little, Brown and Co.

Dickinson, Emily. 1862. "The Spider Holds
a Silver Ball," in *The Complete Poems of
Emily Dickinson*, ed. Thomas H. Johnson,
1960, p. 297. Boston: Little, Brown and
Co.

Diop, Birago & Barnwell, Ysaye M. 1980.
"Breaths," in *Good News/Sweet Honey In
the Rock* (audio recording). Chicago: Flying Fish Records.

Eberhart, Richard. 1955. "If I Could Only
Live At the Pitch That Is Near Madness,"
in *Modern American and British Poetry*, ed.
Louis Untermeyer, p. 338. New York:
Harcourt, Brace & World.

Eliot, T.S. 1927. "Journey of the Magi," in
Modern American and British Poetry, ed.
Louis Untermeyer, p. 221. New York:
Harcourt, Brace & World.

Faulkner, William. 1961. *The Bear*, in *Three
Famous Short Novels*, pp. 202. New York:

Vintage Books.

Frost, Robert. 1913. "Reluctance," in *The Poetry of Robert Frost*, ed. Edward Connery Lathem, 1969, p. 30. New York: Holt, Rinehart & Winston.

Frost, Robert. 1934. "Desert Places," in *The Poetry of Robert Frost*, ed. Edward Connery Lathem, 1969, p. 296. New York: Holt, Rinehart & Winston.

Fuller, Thomas (compiler). 1732. *Gnomologia*, p. 869. London: B. Barker.

Geronimo. 1877. Letter to President Grant, in *Bartlett's Familiar Quotations*, ed. Emily Morrison Beck, 1980, p. 603. Boston: Little, Brown & Co.

Heraclitus (540–480 B.C.). On The Universe, in *Bartlett's Familiar Quotations*, ed. Emily Morrison Beck, 1980, p. 70. Boston: Little, Brown & Co.

Hopkins, Gerard Manley. 1876. "God's Grandeur," in *Gerard Manley Hopkins*, ed. W.H. Gardner, 1963, p. 27. Baltimore: Penguin Books.

John III, Verse 16. *The New Testament*, in *The Holy Bible, Revised Standard Version*, 1952 edition. New York: Thomas Nelson & Sons.

Jung, C.G. 1953. *Psychological Reflections*, ed. Jolande Jacobi, pp. 121, 217. New York: Harper & Brothers.

Kierkegaard, Soren. Quoted by Joachim Berendt in *The Third Ear*, transl. Tim Nevill, 1988. Shaftsbury, England: Element Books.

Lamartine, Alphonse de. 1850. From Count d'Orsay, Letter to John Foster, in *Bartlett's Familiar Quotations*, ed. Emily Morrison Beck, 1980, p. 464. Boston: Little, Brown & Co.

Lawrence, D.H. 1955. "Ship of Death," in *Modern American and British Poetry*, ed. Louis Untermeyer, p. 553. New York: Harcourt, Brace & World.

Lawrence, D.H. 1955. "Kisses in the Train," in *Modern American and British Poetry*, ed. Louis Untermeyer, p. 547. New York: Harcourt, Brace & World.

Maugham, W. Somerset. 1912. "Mrs. Dot," in *The International Thesaurus of Quotations*, p. 613, 1970. New York: Harper & Row.

Pearson, Carol. 1986. *The Hero Within*. San Francisco: Harper & Row.

Reed, Henry. 1955. "Lessons of the War. I. Naming of the Parts," in *Modern American and British Poetry*, ed. Louis Untermeyer, pp. 679–680. New York: Harcourt, Brace & World.

Rilke, Rainer Maria. 1904. *Letters To A Young Poet*, transl. Stephen Mitchell, 1986. New York: Vintage Books.

Roethke, Theodore. 1953. "The Waking," in the *Collected Poems of Theodore Roethke*, 1966, p. 104. New York: Doubleday.

Shakespeare, William. 1622. *Othello*, in *The Complete Plays and Poems of William Shakespeare*, ed. William Allan Neilson and Charles Jarvis Hill, 1942, p. 1102. New York: Houghton Mifflin Company.

Sondheim, Stephen. 1988. "Moments In The Wood," in *Into The Woods*. New York: RCA Corporation.

Thomas, Dylan. 1955. "Do Not Go Gently Into That Good Night," in *Modern American and British Poetry*, ed. Louis Untermeyer, pp. 678–679. New York: Harcourt, Brace & World.

Tolkien, J.R.R. 1938. "On Fairy Stories," in *Tree and Leaf*, 1965, p. 31. Boston: Houghton Mifflin Co.

Traditional folktale, "It Is as You Wish," origin unknown, from oral sources.

Traditional folktale, "The Nature of Truth," origin unknown. First heard told by storyteller, Carol Burch at NAPPS festival. Another version can be found in Yolen, Jane, *Favorite Folktales from Around the World*, 1986, pp. 3–4. New York: Pantheon Books.

Von Franz, Marie Louise. 1970. *Interpretation of Fairy Tales*. Zurich: Spring Publications.

White Hat, Albert Sr. 1983. *Lakota Ceremonial Songs*, pp. 10, 11, 14. Rosebud, S. Dakota: Sinte Gleska College Inc. (Translations used in *Winona's Web* are by Priscilla Cogan, from the original Lakota.)

Whiteman, Roberta Hill. 1984. "A Song For What Never Arrives," in *Star Quilt*, p. 64. Minneapolis: Holy Cow! Press.

Wilbur, Richard. 1955. "Juggler," in *Modern American and British Poetry*, ed. Louis Untermeyer, p. 397. New York: Harcourt, Brace & World.

Williams, William Carlos. 1949. "The Descent of Winter 10/28," in *Collected Poems of William Carlos Williams: 1909–1939*, *Vol. I*. New York: New Directions Publishing Corp.

Williams, William Carlos. 1949. "The Rose," in *The Selected Poems of William Carlos Williams*, p. 27. New York: New Directions Publishing Corp.

Woodman, Marion. 1985. *The Pregnant Virgin*. Toronto: Inner City Books.

Wyman, Leland C. & Haile, Berard. 1970. *Blessingway*, p. 164. Tucson, Arizona: University of Arizona Press.

Yeats, W.B. 1928. "The Death of The Hare," in *The Collected Poems of W.B. Yeats*, 1985, p. 250. London: MacMillan.

Glossary of Lakota Words

★ ★ ★

Chanunpa Wakan — sacred pipe

Heyoka — person with vision of the thunder beings, contrary one, clown

Iktomi — spider spirit, trickster

Inipi — sweat lodge, ceremony

Mitakuye oyas'in — all my relations

Mni — water

Wakan Tanka — Grandfather, Great Spirit

Wazi — Grandfather of the north

Wi — sun

Yuwipi — healing ceremony in which the medicine man is bound in a star quilt

The employees of Thorndike Press hope you have enjoyed this Large Print book. All our Large Print titles are designed for easy reading, and all our books are made to last. Other Thorndike Press Large Print books are available at your library, through selected bookstores, or directly from us.

For information about titles, please call:

(800) 257-5157

To share your comments, please write:

Publisher
Thorndike Press
P.O. Box 159
Thorndike, Maine 04986